NOVAC'S WAY

by

Mike Downs

ISBN 978-0-578-42948-9
MKD Publishing

Books by Mike Downs

The Artimus Box

Novac's Race

Novac's Run

Bobo's Raid

Sounds of Deception

Agent Keys Steps Out

Novac's Way

Author's Note

Please keep in mind that this is a work of fiction. The names, characters, organizations, dates, and events in this novel are a product of the author's imagination or are used fictitiously. Any resemblance to actual events or persons living or dead is purely coincidental.

This book is available in print and digital formats at most online retailers.

Dedication

Dedicated to the memory of Peggy Kastner, a great friend and supporter, who will be missed by her many friends.

Novac's Way

1937 Los Angeles CA

Jack Novac rolls gently out of bed, stepping lightly to the bathroom so as not to wake his wife. He runs a cold razor over his lathered face noting that his left eye seems less cloudy. His left hand resting on the basin still aches, the fingers gnarled from hammer blows, the eye damaged from a vicious kick to his face delivered by a fanatical Nazi.

As a professional racing driver Jack went to Europe after winning the Indianapolis 500 to capitalize on his fame. Smashing international speed records, Jack traveled the continent where he met Maddy Rosen, a sports journalist. The Nazi, Count Von Steuben, hated the brash American, Jack Novac, and everything he stood for from the time they first met. The Nazi arrested Jack on a trumped-up espionage charge, torturing him to try and make him sign a false confession.

Wiping away the lather, Jack winks at the mirror; all that is behind him and life is good now; he is happy to be alive and home in California. At thirty-four he is back in good physical shape. He has jet-black hair smoothed straight back with a Clark Gable like mustache that complements his square jawed face.

Before the Nazi closed in, Jack won a huge amount of money racing his Miller front drive racing car against the might of Ferrari. He and Maddy then survived a harrowing escape across Europe, Nazis at their heels. They married shortly after arriving back in Novac's native California.

With America still in the throes of the Great Depression, Jack's winnings from the Monza Italy race afforded him the opportunity to buy the house of his dreams in Santa Monica, undeveloped land in Orange County and an electronics plant in Culver City. He knows he's a very lucky man even if the injuries he received ended his auto racing days.

Dressed and ready for work, he stops at a little diner off Lincoln Boulevard to grab some coffee and toast on his way to the plant on Jefferson Boulevard in Culver City. Usually in fairly good cheer, today he is feeling he'd like to be back racing. His business is going well: when he first started it took all of his time and dedication to make it work. Now with the business established, his mind turns to how racing fulfilled his need for speed and competition.

It seems almost like another life-time to him. Jack and his front-drive Miller up on the high-banked Monza, Italy, race track. The kid Ferrari put in the Alfa is blocking Jack off every corner. Jack takes a higher line up the banking each lap, then counting down the laps. Last lap and Jack has the kid at the very top of the banking, blocking him. Last corner and Jack dives low, his car slewing sideways as he slides up in front of the kid's Alfa. It's an angry crowd. Working people bet their hard-earned cash on the Ferrari Alfa to win. Jack and Carl, his mechanic, beat it out of town with bags full of Lira. They were never more alive.

That's what Jack thinks about driving south on Lincoln Boulevard. Then he thinks about watching daredevils flying at air shows that fascinated him from childhood, even before he started racing. With his left hand not strong enough for auto racing, he needs something to spark his blood. Jack had recently put his mind to getting a pilot's license. Math and navigation were a struggle, but he enjoyed flying. The sense of freedom in the sky and mastering the control of the aircraft, were very satisfying. Having endured multitudes of operations on his hand and eye, he feels fit enough to try racing airplanes.

Jack savors the salt-tinged smell of the sea. His memories of Europe under the control of dictators give him an even greater appreciation of America's freedoms. He takes great pleasure in the beauty of California: while in the hands of the Gestapo he once thought he would never see it again. Turning inland onto Jefferson Boulevard he pulls the car's visor down against the new day's blinding sun. As he enters the parking lot, he still feels a nudge of pride when he looks up at the lettering on his new two-story brick building that spells out 'NOVAC ENGINEERING'.

***

Jack, as usual, is first in this morning. He unlocks the front door, then goes upstairs to his office. The pile of paperwork on his desk gives him pause before he sits down. He huffs out a breath then lifts the top paper. A few minutes before 8 a.m. Jack looks up from the paper he is reading, hearing his employees filtering in.

Mori Able, a man whose features only needed a green-shaded visor to peg him as an accountant, is Jack's number one man at the plant. Mori taps on the door frame, then enters with two paper cups of coffee. He offers a cup to his boss. "Morning Jack, what's up for today?"

Jack takes the top off, blows to cool the piping hot brew, then sips the coffee. "Thanks for the java, Mori. I'm havin' trouble tryin' to keep my head in the game today. We've got things goin' good here an' I'm gettin' itchy."

A worry wrinkle crosses Mori's brow. "Itchy as in you want to sell the business and do something else?"

"No, that's not what I'm sayin', Mori. You're such a darn good manager that I'm not doin' much anymore other than this damn paperwork. The doctors have got me in pretty good shape an' I'm thinkin' about doin' some air racin'."

Mori's eyes go big. "Jeez Jack, that's dangerous. Those guys get killed all the time."

Shaking his head, Jack looks up at Mori. "Racin' Indy cars was dangerous and I lived through that. I believe when your time comes it doesn't matter who or where you are. I've seen guys that've crawled outta wrecks that no one shoulda survived.

"I saw a guy back East spin and back it into the wall, it looked pretty harmless. The car coasted down to the infield and everyone waited for the guy to pop outta the car. The light hit he took to the back of the car broke his neck.

"My philosophy is live it while you can, devil take the hindmost. If I buy the farm the business will be headed by Maddy with you as manager. She's a lot smarter than me so you'll probably be doin' twice the business."

"That's not what I meant, Jack. I don't want to see you get hurt."

"I know that, Mori. And I know I'm lucky to have you here. The business wouldn't be this successful without you. But don't worry, Maddy would murder me if I got killed." Jack sees Mori roll his eyes. "Aw, come on, Mori, that was funny."

"If you say so boss. I think I'll go find something to work on."

Jack looks down at the papers on his desk then picks up the phone to call the man who taught him to fly.

"Hi Ross, Jack Novac here. Look, we talked about air racing and I'd like to try it. I know you don't want me practicing in your Staggerwing so, do you know where I could rent a plane?"

Ross Elmore grins on the other end of the phone call. "I kinda knew it wouldn't be too long before you got the urge, Jack. Bring me some lunch and we'll talk about it."

Jack digs into the paperwork with a renewed vigor. He looks forward to lunch with Ross who flew war planes against the Huns in the Great War. Elmore has plenty of stories about the dogfights he survived during the war. Jack enjoyed Ross's animated descriptions of the aerial combat maneuvers in the frail ships of the day.

Novac fidgets, watching the clock, then stacks the paperwork in a neat pile, pops out of his chair and goes to tell Mori he's off to lunch. Anxious to get to Ross's airport hangar, he stops to buy tacos at a somewhat greasy little roadside stand and is quickly on his way.

He zips into the Clover Field airport, grabs the bag of tacos and enters the front of Ross's office. Jack puts the bag down and raps on the counter, bringing Ross from the back of the place. He spots the bag on the counter and makes a bee line for it. Ross tears open the bag to pull a foil-wrapped taco out.

"How'd you know about Esse's place? She make these special for me?"

Jack watches Ross take a huge bite out of the taco. "Ah, I don't think so. I just stopped at a joint on Centinela and ordered tacos. You gonna save one for me?"

"I might, I'm mighty hungry," Ross says, a little juice running down his chin. "Could be the price you gotta pay for me takin' you up in the Stag."

"I'd gladly pay if you'd show me some tricks," Jack says.

Ross wraps the bag of tacos up and puts it on a window sill to stay warm under the sunlight. "I'll eat the rest when we get back. You'll have to help me clean up the plane after we get back, I've got a student comin' later this afternoon."

Outside, next to a runway, is Ross's pride and joy. A brilliant yellow Beechcraft Staggerwing. The plane is Ross's bread and butter. He gives flying lessons and does charters with the plane. It is always immaculate inside and out; the brown leather interior almost glows.

"Buckle up, Jack. If you're gonna rent a plane for air shows or racin', the renter's gotta know you can handle a plane. I'll show you a coupla tricks and you can try 'em. Just be real careful. If I don't like what you're doin' I'll grab the yoke an' you let go, hear?"

"Okay, Ross."

In the air Ross takes them out near Apple Valley where there is no air traffic. He does a slow roll, then a barrel roll. Ross takes his hands away from the yoke. "You try it."

Jack mimics Ross's moves, levels the ship, then takes his hand away. Ross takes the yoke, shoots Jack a look, then pulls the plane up to gain more altitude. He shuts the power off allowing the plane to side-slip. Just as the ship starts to spin, he adds rudder to counter the spin. He lets the ship side-slip in the opposite direction before countering with just enough rudder to right the ship. He is showing his skill with controlling the ship. He doesn't over-control or under-control; he uses just enough rudder to stop a spin.

"Your turn," he calls to Jack. Jack mimics Ross's moves to the letter, then takes his hand away from the yoke.

Ross takes the yoke and pulls back to gain more altitude. He looks over at Jack to study him for a moment. "Okay, smart guy, let's see what you've got."

Jack takes the yoke, pulls the ship up hard enough to stall it, then lets the nose drop into a spin. The ship spirals downward gaining speed, the cork screw motion coming faster and faster. Jack lets the spin intensify. Ross watches the airspeed indicator climb as the altitude drops. As the spin rate increases Ross watches Jack, wanting to make sure he's in control. Finally, with the altitude falling too much for Ross's liking, he slaps Jack's leg hard.

Jack pours on the power, pulling back hard on the yoke while calmly working the rudder and stick to recover the plane. Both men experience the force of gravity compressing their bodies, then, at less than a thousand feet above the desert floor, Jack levels out. With a big grin on his face he looks over at Ross. Ross, however, does not look happy.

Without a word Ross takes control and heads west back to Clover Field. After landing they taxi up outside of Ross's hangar. Ross climbs out and begins to inspect the plane, paying close attention to the wings. Jack walks behind, watching. He feels awkward, not understanding the man's mood; he doesn't want to lose Ross's friendship. As Ross finishes his inspection his mood seems to lighten. "Come, Jack, let's go finish those tacos."

Ross motions Jack to follow him to the office. Inside, he takes the bag of tacos, grabs a few paper napkins and shakes the tacos out on the counter. Jack hesitates, then moves to the counter.

"I'm sorry if I pissed you off, Ross. If I hurt the Stag, I'll pay for any damages. It may not seem like it to you, but I really was in control. I don't want this to ruin our friendship."

Leaning over the counter, Ross puts his taco down, then rubs his forehead, his eyes narrowed as he looks up. Jack grows even more apprehensive.

"I'm not mad, Jack. I am concerned, and I don't know how to really say what I'm thinkin'. You're a damn good pilot, you know it and I know it...mostly you know it. You're a natural. You don't even have to think about what to do or how to react. I don't need to swell your head anymore than it is, but there are very few guys with your talent. But, you fly by instinct...I'm worried that's gonna bite you.

"Now if I send you off to one a the guys in the valley to rent a plane, am I gonna get you killed? I don't know if their planes can take the loads you're capable of putting on a plane. You see what I gettin' at or am I talkin' to myself?"

"Aw, you don't have to worry about me, Ross. I've been takin' care of myself since I was a pup."

"Don't be stupid, Jack, I'm offerin' to help. You can fly 'em all right, but I know what makes 'em tick. I'm gonna call ol' Charley and see what he's got. You hold your britches till the weekend and we'll go up to the valley and I'll give his crate a goin' over before you fly it. The one thing you lack is a more technical background. You would serve yourself well to study up on aeronautics. You have the basics of how a plane flies, but the more information you have the better you'll be. You need to be able to look over a plane and know if it's gonna be structurally sound enough for the punishment you want to give it.

"Instinct is fine, but if you ever have to fly blind in heavy overcast and can't see the ground, your instinct will kill you. You can't judge level flight in those conditions. If you study instrument flying and obey what the instruments indicate, you can fly in any weather."

"Thanks, Ross, I do appreciate you lookin' after me. Maybe I outta get my own plane."

Ross slowly shakes his head. "What kinda plane, Jack? You want a stunt plane or a racin' plane? You can't have both. A stunt plane has lots a drag but can do all the tricks. A racer is purely built for speed. Low drag, low weight, short wings. See what I mean? Most of the guys that have good race planes have 'em built. Guys like Roscoe Turner spend a hundred grand and more on racing planes."

Jack nods, rubbing his chin. "You've given me plenty to think on. You know my company makes flight instruments, and I should know more about them. I'll work on it and see you this weekend. Thanks, Ross."

Chapter 2

Jack looks forward to the weekend. With Ross in his corner he's excited to try out a real high-powered stunt plane. After what seemed a very long day at the plant, Jack drives to his house in Santa Monica. Heading up the hill Novac turns into his cement driveway facing the Pacific Ocean. He sits for a moment looking out of the windshield at the ocean sparkling brilliantly in the sunshine. Encouraged by his renewed health, feeling energized, he bounds out of the car anxious to see Maddy.

"Hello, Maddy, I'm home." Jack cups his hands to his mouth, calling from the living room. Not hearing a response, he goes through the house before going out of a rear door to the backyard.

Maddy is sitting in a deck chair by the pool staring out at the ocean.

"Hi, Maddy. You enjoying the weather, the view, or just being Mrs. Novac?"

Maddy starts, then turns toward her husband rubbing her eyes. She leaves the chair, coming quickly to Jack. Clinching her arms around him, she presses her head against his chest. "What's the matter, Maddy? Is your mother all right?"

Maddy looks up at Jack, her eyes teary. "Bill Robbins called for you, Jack. He said things are even worse in Germany. I was thinking of all my friends there. I feel bad for them Jack, I just wish I could do something."

"When you feel bad I do too, Maddy. I hate to see you upset. Maybe the best thing for you to do is to get your emotions into the book you're writing. One of the guys at work said he read that article in the paper about your book. I think that could wake people up. I know there are some people out there that care about what's goin' on in Germany today."

Jack tenderly brushes the long, dark hair away from her face to kiss her forehead.

Maddy brings her head back to look up at Jack. "I have been making notes, but it does not seem enough. I can't seem to get my heart into it. America is turning Jews away too, Jack. That seems awful to me. These people need sanctuary or they will be killed."

Jack's face clouds with anger. "Did Robbins say what he wanted, or did he just want to make you upset?"

"He said he had to talk to you; he wouldn't say anymore about it to me. I think he wants you to do something we both don't want you to do. I wrote down the number he gave me on the note pad by the phone."

"I owe him, Maddy. We both knew there would be payback after he got your mother out of Germany and saved me from that Nazi prison. Both times he risked his life and his men's. I have to hear him out, but before I do let's walk down to the beach and get some dinner. I was just thinking how beautiful the ocean looks."

Maddy, still troubled, is not moved much by Jack's suggestion.

Jack spins her around several times holding on by her waist. He stops when she is facing him and kisses her cheeks, then her lips. Maddy resists the spins but soon responds to his kiss.

"I am so lucky to have you, Jack. I love you more than I ever dreamed could be possible."

Jack kisses her again. "I'm the lucky one; you're the best thing on this earth. Nothing in my life will ever be as good as you. Come on, pal, we haven't been to the beach since the big flood. Let's go get some sand between our toes. We'll talk more about how you feel and come up with a plan to do something about it."

Jack and Maddy walk hand in hand on the beach, their shoes swinging from their free hands. Maddy's long dark hair dances about on the ocean's salty breeze.

Jack sneaks glances at Maddy to see if he has lifted her mood. He drops back, then reaches out to tickle her ribs. Maddy slaps at his hand, then turns to him with a smile. Brushing her hair back from her eyes, she slowly shakes her head.

"You are still the school boy, Jack Novac."

"I just can't stand to see you upset, Maddy. You've got the prettiest face of any woman alive; your smile makes me happy. Let's go to that seafood place off the pier. We can have some fresh salmon, a little wine and you'll feel better."

When they cross Ocean Avenue on their way back to the house after dinner Maddy pats her stomach. "Whew, that was too much food; I'm going to take a nap when we get home. Are you going to call Bill Robbins?"

"Yeah, I might just as well get it over with. He's still touchy about the shoot out with that Nazi Von Stupid."

Maddy takes Jack's hand in hers. "I hate that you had to kill Von Steuben, but no man deserved it more. I hope one day we can forget all of that."

Jack kisses her forehead. "We can forget that now; it's in the past where it belongs. Take a nap sweetheart. If you feel like it when you get up, we'll go to a show."

Jack dials the number on the pad and waits for an answer.

"Robbins here," comes through on Jack's phone.

"Hey, Bill, what's up?"

"Novac? You took your time callin' back."

"I took my time because I came home to find my wife in tears, you heel. I've been tryin' to jolly her up since then. You know you're a changed man since we were in Europe."

"I'm a changed man because I've been bumped up to oversee a division I can't talk about. I see a

15

world war coming that we aren't prepared for. I see senators and congressmen with their heads in the sand; they don't want to know about a war. I hate to say it but the biggest fear they have is not being reelected and fallin' off the gravy train.

"I'm sorry if I upset Maddy, but Germany is much worse than when we left, if you can believe that. I called to see if you could help me out. I hear you're a pilot now. Do you know how to parachute?"

Puzzled, Jack holds out the phone receiver. "Okay, Robbins, get straight to it, man. What is it you want?"

"I need to put you in France to get a document out. I'm sending a plane ticket for you to come to New York and meet with me."

"You're pullin' my leg, Bill. You've got guys trained to do that cloak and dagger stuff. I've got a business to run that involves the government if you don't remember. I can't just flit off."

"Come on, Jack, you do what you want and we both know it. I'll tell you what, I know you wanta start racing airplanes: I could help grease the skids. I've got a budget that'd choke a horse. Some people...let me say some of the more forward-thinking people...are interested in fast planes. You could be a very highly paid consultant. I know you well enough that you're gonna want to go first class."

"Man, oh man, Bill. Now you've got me worried. How the hell do you know about me flying? Oh, I get it, you found that out from Maddy."

"I'm just trying to look out for you, old friend," Robbins says. "Go to your shop tomorrow and tell 'em you have to go to meet with a budget committee back east. You'll be gone about a week or two. You can tell Maddy the same, but nothing else. You have an open ticket at Burbank; I'll meet you at the airport when you get here."

"Just take off, huh? Don't tell Maddy where I'm goin' or what I'm doin'? You think she's gonna buy me goin' off on a lark with my ole buddy? What happens if I get caught? You gonna get me a junior G-man magic signet ring to nail on my coffin?"

"Ha, ha, very funny, Jack. What you'll get is the satisfaction of doing a job your country needs to have done."

"I got it, Bill, don't hard line it, man. I'm very aware of my debts since you got me and Maddy outta Germany. I know first hand what monsters those Nazis are. There's no doubt we live in the greatest democracy in the world, which I am prepared to do my best for. I owe you, Bill, we both know that. But I don't like this, man, so just don't stand on my neck about it, okay?"

"I'll see you in New York day after tomorrow, pal. Don't forget your passport." Robbins hangs up the phone and looks up at the men gathered around his desk.

"Got 'im. You guys make sure this goes right. Goux and Novac ain't exactly buddies. I want that list, but I don't want Novac dead."

Jack makes his excuses to Maddy and Ross, then sets out tasks for Mori before boarding the

Douglas DC 3 in the late afternoon for the coast-to-coast overnight sleeper flight to New York. After three refueling stops and 16 hours, the plane touches down at the airport.

When Jack stops at the top of the mobile stairway to stretch, he sees Robbins, standing by a long black four-door Packard, waving to him. As Jack approaches, Robbins opens a rear door and motions Jack to get in.

"Good to see you, Jack," Robbins says, shaking Jack's hand. "You look good. I'm glad Maddy made you see the doctors."

"Good to see you too, Bill. Are we headed into town? I could use a shower and a good meal."

Robbins shakes his head as Jack climbs into the car. "'Fraid not. We've got about a half hour before you get on a plane to Newfoundland." Robbins climbs in beside Jack and closes the door.

As the big car moves off to another taxiway, Robbins opens a compartment in front of them to pour two glasses of scotch. "Bottoms up, Jack. You'll be there for the night, then on to England. I need this to be quick. I want you in and out as fast as possible. We have one chance to get a list of agents in Europe the French took off a captured German spy.

"The deal is your old friend, Goux, won't give the list to anyone he doesn't know. That's what he told his captain because he doesn't want to give us the list at all. I remembered you tellin' me about your run in with Inspector Goux in France. I told that to his boss and Goux tried to back out saying

18

he didn't remember you. I asked the captain if he had a case report on the murder of the man that was supposed to be your guide to the Montlherey race track."

Jack lowers his glass to give Robbins a hard look. "Police Inspector Goux? I'd forgotten all about that schmuck. Why's he the guy with your list?"

"He's the guy that caught the German spy and found the list. But my people tell me Goux is not a team player. He's a hard-liner that thinks the list is his to do with as he sees fit. I kinda got the idea from his captain that Goux is on a short leash. He wouldn't mind seeing Inspector Goux doing guard duty on Devil's Island."

Jack reaches by Robbins to pour a splash of scotch in his glass. "So how am I to know if this list is the real McCoy?"

Robbins takes the scotch bottle from Jack to refresh his glass.

"He's to give you a photostatic copy that will have the numbers 41680 in the upper right-hand corner and the captain's signature under it."

Robbins takes a notebook from his jacket pocket. He removes a slip of paper from between the pages. "I have a copy of the captain's signature, and the numbers." He hands the paper to Jack.

Jack takes the paper, scans it, then looks at Robbins. "How'd you get this? I mean if you got this, why didn't you get the list, too?"

Jack watches Robbins' jaw muscles tighten. Robbins relaxes, slaps Jack on the knee and says,

"I just told you Goux won't let it go. Even if he would, I don't have a hell of a lotta faith in the diplomatic pouch that gets thrown on a German ship to cross the Atlantic.

"This isn't fun and games, Jack. I need to see if the Germans have discovered any of our people. They're dead if the Nazis get 'em. You know first hand what's in store for 'em. I trained some of them and I don't want 'em caught. I've got two men deep inside getting good stuff, but I'll pull 'em if they're on the list."

Jack finishes his drink, then responds to Robbins. "You coulda started with that Bill; I wouldn't a hesitated to volunteer."

Robbins nods resignedly. "Yeah, you're right, Jack. I'm the new head of this department, and I'm learning I can only make these lousy bureaucrats do something if I hold something over their heads. You're a right guy, I know that; when you get back let's go out and tie one on. I'll walk you to your plane."

As they walk across the tarmac, Jack stops. "I gotta get my bags, Bill."

"I had them put on the plane, Jack." He reaches into his jacket. "Here's your new passport. Use it when you get on this plane and in France. You're Jack Stevens, a new rep for Toy Towne. I don't want the krauts to know you're in France. They'd pick you up if they could; I want you in and out, no problems. You remember Chuck and Paul? Paul Winslow will meet your plane in England and be with you to Paris.

"Chuck Brody is in Paris and will be overseeing this operation. He's there to make sure it goes right. He'll meet with both of you at your hotel in Paris. Stay sharp, Jack. Get the list and get out. Chuck and Paul will look out for you."

Chapter 3

Jack squints coming out of the plane, raising a hand to shield his tired eyes from the sunlight. Crossing the Atlantic in the no-comfort mail plane quickly wore thin. The weariness of not being able to sleep shows on his haggard face. He waits by the plane for the ground crew to bring his bags off the plane. Lighting a cigarette, he draws the smoke in, makes a face, drops it and crushes it under his shoe.

"Hey, Jack, how's it goin'?"

Paul Winslow slaps Jack on the back. "Long time no see, buddy." Winslow shakes cigarettes out of a pack of Luckies, offering Jack one.

"Hi ya, Paul. Another slap like that and I'm liable to fall over. No thanks on the smoke; they taste like crap right now. I hope you've got a good place to stay, I need a shower and some sleep."

Jack ambles over to the baggage being unloaded. Paul takes the bags from Jack. "Here let me get your bags. We'll talk it over in the car; follow me."

Paul opens the passenger door for Jack on the little Austin sedan. He puts the bags in the back and squeezes in behind the steering wheel. As Paul pulls away, Jack rolls the window down to bring a cool breeze to his face. Revived somewhat, he turns his head to look at Paul.

"So, let me guess. We're not headed for a hotel, a shower, or a hot meal, are we?"

"You got it right first try, Jack. We're off to another airfield to catch a flight to France, courtesy of our English cousins."

"Terrific," Jack replies. "Wake me when we get there."

Paul shakes Jack's shoulder; Jack's head rises slowly from his chest. "We're here," Paul says. "Rise and shine."

Out of the little car, Jack pulls his coat closed. It is getting dark with an overcast sky. Looking around, he sees small huts on a grassy field, with some ancient looking bi-planes scattered about.

Paul nudges Jack. "You can take one bag with a toothbrush and a change of underwear. We'll leave your other bag in the car."

Jack points to the bi-planes. "Are we goin' in one a those crates? Whose gonna fly it, you or me?"

Paul grins at Jack's dismay. "The RAF has a real cushy little transport plane for us. Nice comfortable seats and everything. We just have to give them a copy of the list when we get back. The plane should be here any minute."

"Why didn't you just fly me to Paris, Paul? I could be in a bed asleep after a shower and a good meal."

"Robbins wants to make sure the krauts don't get you and we'll need a quick way out of France once you get the list. We're pretty sure Goux is gonna try something cute. Chuck is in Paris putting a plan together. When we get there, you'll get the shower and sleep you need, and we'll go for the plan tomorrow."

"Do I get a good meal, too?"

"Yeah, yeah, a good meal too, Jack." Paul points at a dark shape coming out of the overcast. "Here's the plane now."

The plane is a small 6-seater Airspeed Envoy, a modern monoplane, not what Jack expected. It lands gracefully on the grass field and taxis to the end of the field. Jack picks up his bag to follow Paul. The pilot opens a door behind the wing and hops to the ground. He looks up to see Paul and Jack coming toward him. "You two my French passengers?"

"We are," Paul says.

"Climb aboard, mates. Weather's due to close in and I want to get back home tonight."

Paul moves aside to let Jack climb in, then follows: they both have to hunch down in the low cabin. They sit in the forward seats and stow their bags.

"Parachutes are on the rear seats," the pilot says as he passes them on the way to the cockpit. Jack looks over questioning with his eyes, Paul winks back. The little plane buffets at low altitude but is fast and not uncomfortable. An hour and half later the plane begins to circle. The pilot pulls back the curtain that separates his cockpit to yell to the men.

"Put your parachutes on, gentlemen. If I can't find an opening in this soup you're going to have to jump."

Paul's face loses color as his cockiness fades. "Jump? Are you mad? I've never parachuted. What's down there? Do you know? I mean, are there trees and houses, maybe cars or trucks that'll kill us?"

Paul looks over at Jack, wide-eyed. Jack winks back.

"Don't get your knickers in a twist, mate. I'll make another pass to see if I can find a clear patch. If it's not on, you'll jump or we all go back. I've landed here before: it's a level field, no trees or fences, an easy jump."

Paul stays in his seat arms firmly crossed over his chest. "Says you," he says.

Jack gets up, steadying himself with the seatbacks, to go to the rear and get the parachutes. He goes forward to give one to Paul who holds his hands up wanting no part of it. Jack dumps the parachute on Paul's knees.

"If we go, you'll go first. Just remember to count to ten, then pull the rip cord. When you see the ground coming up, don't go stiff. Bend at the knees or you're liable to break your legs."

Paul looks down at the parachute, then up at Jack. "Are you nuts? If you're so sure we're gonna survive this why, don't you go first?"

Jack smiles down at Paul. "Because I'm the one that'll have to throw you outta this plane."

"Sorry to break up the fun, gents. You better take a seat, sir," the pilot yells to them. "I've got a clearing; I'm going to shut off the cabin lights."

Jack sits down and looks out of the large rectangular window as the cabin goes dark. Far below he can make out a string of lights marking the landing strip. The pilot makes an expert landing, the plane jouncing lightly over the grass. He goes to the end of the runway, turns the plane around, then throttles down. The pilot flicks on the cabin lights, he remains in the cockpit.

"You gents can show yourselves out. I'm off as soon as you're clear. Just leave the parachutes on your seats, if you will please. I'll meet you back here when you give the signal."

"Thanks, mate," Jack says, giving the pilot a thumbs-up.

Chuck Brody, silhouetted by the landing lights, waves to the men as they come out of the plane. As soon as the pilot sees them clear of his plane, he throttles up and makes his take off.

All business, Chuck shakes hands with Jack, nods to Paul, then says, "Follow me, the car's over here."

Chuck holds the lid up while Paul and Jack put their bags in the trunk of the Citroën Rosalie. "Jack, you take the back seat; you can stretch out a little back there. We're about 30 or 40 minutes out of Paris."

The car bumps out of the field on to a paved road. Chuck shifts through the gears, then shakes out a cigarette. "I've got a coupla places picked out for the meet tomorrow. If Goux doesn't like 'em, we'll just have to make do. I want the meet to be in a public place where he can't easily foul it up. We can go over the plans in the morning when everyone's rested."

"Are you asleep back there, Novac?" Paul asks.

"Not yet. Something eatin' you, Paul?"

"Yeah, I don't see any reason to jump out of a perfectly good airplane. We coulda just come back tomorrow."

"Scared, Paul?" Jack asks.

"Damn right. You'd a had a hell of a time tryin' to get me outta that plane."

Jack chuckles. "I don't doubt it, but I think the pilot was just tryin' to liven up the trip. I could see some lights on the ground, so I knew it couldn't be all that closed in. I'm pretty sure that pilot could a landed on that field with his eyes closed. He was havin' us on, old duck."

"Very funny, Novac. I'll bet your first jump wasn't over a strange place in the dead a night." Paul flops back in his seat, arms folded tightly against his chest.

Chuck glances up to see Jack's face in the rear-view mirror grinning back at him. He concentrates on the dark road ahead as Jack settles back, lying down on the seat. He quickly falls asleep.

"Jack, wake up buddy." Chuck reaches over the seatback to nudge Novac. "We're at the hotel; make sure you use the Jack Stevens passport to check in. Keep your real passport in a pocket; you'll need it back home."

Jack gets out of the car yawning, stretching his arms wide. "I could eat a horse. Has this place got a restaurant?"

"Nope, no restaurant," Chuck says. "There's a good place down the street. Let's get checked in and we'll go eat on Bill's nickel."

Jack pats his stomach. "That's the best plan I've heard so far."

After dinner, Jack goes back to his room, hangs up his clothes and falls into a deep sleep as soon as his head rests on the pillow. He wakes to dawn's orange glow, the filtered light coming through lace curtains. Feeling well-rested after his days of travel, he feels the urge to explore.

After washing up, he dresses, then heads downstairs to the street. The morning is cool with some moisture in the air. Jack pulls the collar up on his coat, watching a horse-drawn cart delivering bread to a bistro on the corner. The city is still quiet, the horse's hoof beats clopping on the street almost drowning out the voices of the merchants opening their shops.

Jack sets off at a rapid pace, filling his lungs with the cool morning air. The block his hotel is on is a long triangle almost a mile around. Some of the buildings are centuries old; Jack admires the changes in the styles of architecture. The city feels special to Jack, like London, Rome or Berlin; an indescribable air of history-making events and lives that permeates the very soil. Half-way around his second tour, Jack is joined by more people on the street, shops are opening.

28

Pleased by his exercise, he stops down the street from his hotel.

At a patisserie, men with white aprons tied around their waists bring a few small round tables and wicker chairs with brightly colored cushions to the sidewalk. Jack walks into the old but bright, clean place to a long glass display counter. A woman behind the counter turns to him and asks, "Que voulez-vous, Monsieur?"

Jack hesitates a moment, then studies the items in the display and the counter behind. Holding up one finger, he points to the pile of fluffy croissants. The woman places the croissant on a plate, then asks if he wants something to drink. Jack points to a coffee urn. She pours coffee into a cup and puts the cup and plate on the counter top. Jack takes a dollar bill from his wallet putting it on the countertop. The woman looks down at the bill, smiles knowingly, tucking the dollar in her pocket.

Jack sits down at a table outside, the sun shrinking the long shadows as it ascends. More people, cars, trucks, and buses emerge; another work day begins. Jack finishes his croissant and gets up to refresh his coffee. He returns to his chair to watch the morning unfold. Chuck comes with Paul to join Jack at the table.

Jack gets up to wave at the men, they join him at the table.

"How's the chow?" Paul asks. "My croissant was so good I'd like to take one back home with me," Jack answers.

MIKE DOWNS

Paul heads for the counter, then turns back. "How'd you get it? You speak the lingo"?

"Nope, I used the international tourist language. You just stand around looking stupid and point. You might wanta watch how much money you pay. I put a buck on the counter; the lady smiled, snatched it up and stuck it in her pocket."

Paul is through the door when Chuck, grinning, puts his two cents in before following. "Or you can just speak louder and louder until they walk away or throw something at you. That's the way Paul usually does it."

Paul comes to the table with a plate full of sugary treats. Chuck follows with a croissant and a glass carafe of coffee. He looks at Paul's plate, then rolls his eyes at Jack.

"He'll be bouncin' off the walls for an hour." He pours coffee into Jack's cup, then takes a seat. Women with linen bags begin their shopping for the day. Two women with steaming cups of coffee sit at a table close by and begin chatting.

Chuck quickly finishes his croissant. "Let's take a walk when we finish, and I'll go over the plan with both of you back in our room."

"I'm ready," Jack says.

"Aw, come on, guys, I haven't finished yet," Paul complains, cheeks bulging.

Jack and Chuck get up from the table. Chuck puts some coins on the table, then taps Paul's shoulder. "Take it with you."

30

Chapter 4

Chuck spreads a color map of Paris on a table in the hotel room.

"I have several places marked I think are good ones for the hand off. We want the place to be public with multiple exits, so we can get to a car and be on our way."

Jack leans over the desk tracing the marked places with a finger.

"I know this place," he says, tapping the map. "I walked through this park when I visited Paris after I ran the Miller at Montlherey. There's a bridge that Eiffel built going to an artificial island. They made hand rails and steps out of concrete that look like tree limbs. The place is incredibly beautiful and busy. The bridge is perfect, close to a main road, too."

"Okay, Jack," Chuck says. "That's one we can try. Take a look at these other places I've marked."

Jack looks up from the map, his face set. "Hold up. We've only got the rest of this day to get the list. We don't have time to check out other places and if I'm not forceful enough, there's no telling where Goux would want to meet. No, Chuck, Buttes Chaumont is the place. We're close to it and, as I remember, there's a big train station pretty close by. We could hop a train if we had to."

"What if Goux doesn't go for it?" Chuck asks.

"What's the name of his captain? Bill told me the captain doesn't like Goux, said he'd like to see him on Devil's Island. No, Goux's gonna do this my way. I'll call 'im and set it up for this afternoon, okay?"

Chuck shakes his head. "Bill said you'd wanta do it your way. Okay, go ahead, give it a try, Jack."

Jack takes a note paper from his pocket, showing it to Chuck.

"What do you make of this signature? Bill gave me this to verify Goux's list. It's the captain's."

Paul and Chuck both look at the note.

"André Renaud," Paul says.

"Yeah, that's what I get, too. What's all the stuff on the rest of the paper?" Chuck asks.

Jack takes the paper back, looking at his notes. "I got bored on the flights over here and wrote down some formulas for weight displacements and wing configurations. I'm thinkin' of building a racing airplane; no one had any paper, so I used this."

"It looks like some odd type of code to me," Paul interjects.

Chuck rubs his chin, thinking, looking at Jack. "Well, you're right about one thing: once you call Goux, we have to make it happen today. I won't go against Robbins's orders; it's today or we're gone. But I'll tell you the train's the last thing we'd wanta try. The world cup finals are here today, the train station'll be mobbed. I'm gonna rent another car so we'll have a back up if we need it.'

Jack calls the number Chuck wrote down. Goux answers his direct line.

"Hello, Inspector Goux, Jack Novac here." He looks up at Paul and Chuck, smiling. "Oh yeah, I love you too. Yeah, okay, Goux. Listen, I'll meet you at the Buttes Chaumont Eiffel Bridge at 3 o'clock."

Jack holds the phone away from his ear. "Stop it, Goux. André told me to call him if you gave me any trouble. Why don't I just talk with him and he can tell you."

He brings the phone back to his ear. "André, yeah André Renaud, your boss. You're a hard man, Goux, I know that. Just give me the list and I'll be out of your life. Yes, I'll be alone. If you are, too, I'll take the list and be gone. 3 o'clock on the bridge. I'll see you there."

Jack hangs up the phone. "Man, that guy hasn't changed a bit—mister hard ass."

"You didn't do anything to make it easier, Jack," Paul says.

Jack slowly shakes his head. "It wasn't gonna go easy. The guy went off on a blister just hearing my name. The guy's a schmuck; that was the only way to handle him. Bill said you had the plan to get us outta here, Chuck. What do you want me to do?"

"Since you got Goux to agree, I'll take you and Paul in the Citroën to the apartments across the street from the park. That's where I'll leave the car. You can walk between the buildings; that will put you on Rue Manin. If Goux's watching, he'll see you're alone. Cross the street and you'll see the entrance to the park. Come back the same way after you get the list, and Bob's your uncle. Paul and I'll watch for trouble."

Chuck points to a location on the map. "If we can't make it back to the car, I'm going to rent another one and leave it by the square in Saint-Denis. The town's about four miles north of here and on the way to our airfield. The square has a famous old cathedral that's easy to find. If we get separated or injured, that's our backup plan. Here, take the map with you, Jack; I've got another one in the car."

"You expecting trouble, Chuck?" Jack asks. "Are you guys armed?"

"Bill said no guns," Chuck replies. "I'd like to think nothing will happen, but we need to be prepared for the worst. Paul and I are going to find another car and take it to Saint-Denis. We'll be back by one o'clock and that'll give us time to go to the park and check it out. There's a good restaurant across the street. Go have lunch. We'll meet you back there at 2."

Shortly after Paul and Chuck leave, Jack grows pensive: feeling cooped up, he goes outside to walk off his nervous tension. Thinking about his meeting with Goux, Jack decides to stop thinking. He takes his hands out of his pockets and squares his shoulders to enjoy a beautiful day in Paris.

The sun shines brightly, warming the day; people milling about the city seem to share the same vibrancy. Jack tries to enjoy the day, but his thoughts soon bring Maddy's face to mind. In his mind's eye, he sees a picture of her on the beach in Santa Monica: her long, dark hair catching in the wind rushing off the Pacific. Home is where he wants to be.

Becoming impatient to get the Goux drama over with, he has a strong urge to find a phone and call home. He walks for quite some time, hands balled in his pockets, before turning back, his mind still churning. "Stop it, Jack," he mutters to himself. A woman walking toward him on the sidewalk looks at him with concern, then hurries past. Jack turns, looking back at the woman, he smiles, then quietly, under his breath, says, "Better get some lunch."

Entering the restaurant, Jack is surprised to see Paul and Chuck already there. Chuck waves him over to the table. Jack takes a seat at the table as Paul bulges his cheeks with bread.

"We just got here," Chuck says. "We have a car in place just off the square by the cathedral: it's a black and yellow Citroën Avant. We'll meet in the cathedral if we get separated. Paul and I checked out the park. All around the bridge there's heavy foliage so we won't have any problem watching. By the same token, Goux could have his people there too.

"Be sure you take the same path back to the street. There are paths that lead to the interior that are narrow, dark, and have low tunnels. Perfect places to be ambushed, so don't stray. If you get jumped, go for the street." "Okay, Chuck," Jack snaps. "I've got it. Let's have some lunch."

After they finish eating, Chuck stands from his chair, taking out his wallet. "Lunch is on Bill. It's a little early, Jack, but I'll drive us over to drop you off."

"You guys go ahead," Jack says. "I'll walk over and digest some a this food."

"Okay, Jack. Paul and I will be right behind you when you leave the bridge. Good luck."

Jack turns into the park entrance. Not wanting to give away Chuck or Paul, he keeps his eyes focused straight ahead. Walking quickly, he turns right and then left at the bridge entrance. There are several couples on the bridge enjoying the day, walking hand in hand. Halfway across he spots Goux leaning on the railing, a sour look on his face.

"Hello Goux, you're not in uniform. I almost missed you."

"I am no longer required to wear the uniform, Novac; my position is…what do you say, raised."

"Glad to hear it. You have the list?"

Goux takes an envelope from his pocket. Jack reaches into his coat, Goux tenses, then relaxes when he sees a paper in Jack's hand.

"What do you have on the paper, Novac?"

"It's the verification André sent. It has the number and his signature that are supposed to be on the list you give me."

Goux's hand tightens on the envelope, he stuffs it in a side pocket and brings another envelope from an inside coat pocket.

"Here is your list." Goux snaps the envelope in front of Jack.

"You are in much danger here, Novac. Make sure you keep the list safe."

Jack opens the envelope to compare the signature. Satisfied, he puts the papers in his inside coat pocket.

"Why would I be in any danger, Goux? Nobody's supposed to know I'm here."

"There are spies everywhere, Novac. You are wanted by the Germans for a list of charges including murder. They can not get this list; you are a poor choice to have it."

"Au revoir, Goux." Jack turns on his heel and heads back the way he came. Goux watches for a moment, then turns away and hurries off.

Jack looks behind him as he turns on the pathway. He wipes his palms on his coat and heads for the park's entrance. 30 yards before the entrance, two rough-looking men approach. Jack looks over his shoulder to see two more men emerge from the trees. He continues toward the first men, slowing his pace. Chuck and Paul come

37

on to the pathway from behind the two guys facing Jack. Jack is relieved to see his protectors: the distance to the men is closing.

One of the men, his face contorted with fury, holds up his hand, palm out, then points to Jack. "Arrêt," the man shouts. Jack straightens, then glances about. With a surprised look he points his hands toward his chest as if to say, *'who me'?*

"Hey, you!" Chuck barks at the men from behind them. Both men snap around to see who is yelling. Jack uses the distraction to try and run past all four men as he races for the entrance. Paul tackles one of the men when he tries to grab Novac's coattail. Jack pulls his coat in and charges past.

Reaching Rue Manin, Novac steals a quick look back over his shoulder. Paul and Chuck are rolling around on the ground, arms failing, with all four ambushers. Jack crosses the road and darts between the buildings. Breaking out on Rue Pailleron, he runs for the Citroën. At the car, he yanks on the door handle. Patting his pants pockets, he utters a curse, realizing he doesn't have a key to get in the car or start it. A police whistle shrills. Jack looks up from the car to see Goux running toward him, blowing his whistle.

Chapter 5

Jack jumps out into the street, sprinting across, dodging traffic. Tires squeal, a cab driver slams on the brakes, slowing just enough for Jack to flash by. A half block behind, Goux holds up his arms to the traffic, blowing his whistle furiously. Momentarily hidden from Goux's view by traffic, Jack jumps into the back of a vegetable delivery truck as it pulls away from the curb. Goux stops traffic enough to cross the street, his eyes straining for a glimpse of Novac. Goux stamps his feet, "Merde, merde, merde!"

Jack, down between baskets of vegetables, hauls himself off the jostling floor of the truck. He thinks the truck is headed northeast but does not want to go too far and get lost or have the truck driver find him and cause trouble. When the truck comes to a stop, Jack hops out. On the sidewalk, he looks about trying to work out where he is. He turns a corner, looking around for anything familiar and trips on an uneven surface, almost going down.

A flic, patrolling the street, reaches out, snagging Jack's arm to keep him from falling. Taken aback by the uniform, Jack pulls away. The policeman, confused by Jack's behavior, reaches out for him again. Novac lashes out, punching the man hard in the face. He turns to run, gathering speed when he hears the police whistle shrilling behind him.

Still unsure of where he is, he stops, seeing only that there is a busy avenue before him. Multiple whistles sound behind him. Jack looks over his shoulder to see more police pounding down the sidewalk after him. He once again recklessly threads his way across the street, horns blare. He holds his arm out to ward off traffic; on the other side of the avenue, he turns west. Winded after several blocks, Jack slows down. He wonders why people on the sidewalk take so little notice of him. *'Is everyone in a big hurry around here he thinks?'* Just then a group of men rush to cross the street in front of him.

He looks where the group is going and sees a large gathering of people. By their manner of dress, Jack knows the majority are not Parisians. With an immediate sense of relief, Novac realizes where he is: Gare Du Nord, the train station, is off to his right. Jack quickly joins the crowd to begin threading his way deeper into the people. The soccer matches are over for the day and hundreds are going out of the city. Jack takes a quick look back to see the police stopped at the edge of the crowd, scanning people.

Threading his way forward, Jack tries to see over the crowd searching for an exit before he gets to the trains. A train departure announcement blares and the crowd surges toward the platforms. Novac, carried by the wave, struggles to veer off to one side. Taking refuge from the crowd beside a stone column, he waits for the mass to subside to look for a safe exit.

"Keep going, Herr Novac, we have a train to board."

The man's English is delivered with a heavy German accent. Jack turns to see a tall, stout man in a black leather long-coat.

Jack takes in the man and the coat before answering. "I'm not takin' a train today, buddy, and sure as hell not with Gestapo."

Producing a Luger from his pocket, the man shoves it into Jack's ribcage.

"You will find your hell either here today or in Berlin, Herr Novac. I have an arrest warrant for you: it would not make me unhappy to shoot you where you stand. My director, Herr Reinhard Heydrich, however, is quite anxious to meet you. Perhaps you have heard of the man with the iron heart?"

Jack, trying to weigh his options without being too obvious, goads the Gestapo man.

"I take it he's another one a your murder boys. You guys all seem to have cute names for each other."

"You have no idea, Novac, how stupid that remark is. Heydrich will greatly enjoy flaying the skin from your body, a piece at time. The elite of our Reich will not offer any mercy to our enemies. You are like all these French with their smiling faces; all thinking they are secure with their Maginot nonsense."

Jack smiles at the Gestapo man. "These happy people you're referring to are not French. These are Italian, Hungarian, Brazilian, hell, just about every country but France. Guys like you outta know their enemy, we know you."

"I will take great pleasure with your interrogation. Move to the trains or die where you stand."

"Sorry, Fritz, I don't have a ticket."

The Gestapo man rakes Novac across his cheek with the barrel of the Luger. "Move or die, Novac. I have the ticket or the coffin, the train will not wait."

Jack puts his hand to his cheek, looks at the blood on his hand, shrugs, then walks toward the trains.

The Gestapo man puts the Luger back in his pocket. "We are on the second platform, move down to the fourth car."

Jack uses his handkerchief to wipe the blood from his cheek. He stops at the car, not wanting to get on. "Hey, how the hell did you know I was here?"

"We have the best intelligence in the world. I've watched your every move since you came to Paris."

"No, I don't believe you. I didn't know I was gonna be here till a coupla days ago. Who told you I was coming?"

"I am tired of your talk, Novac. I will take the list now."

"What? I don't have any list. What are you talking about?" Jack stammers.

A new light comes to the Gestapo man's eyes. A grim smile forms on his face. "Not so arrogant now. You are beaten, Novac, I know everything." He takes the gun from his pocket. "Give me the list or I will take it from your dead body."

Jack hangs his head, stalling for every second he can get. He can not give up the list or get on the train; he has to make a break for it. He slowly reaches inside his coat for the list, hoping to distract the man enough to knock the gun away and run for it. Summoning his nerve, he draws the paper out. The Gestapo man lunges forward to snatch the paper out of Jack's hand. Jack can't believe the man is so fast.

The Gestapo man waves the paper triumphantly in Jack's face. Turning the paper to scan it while standing back from Jack's reach, he beams with victory. Out of the corner of Jack's vision, he catches sight of a hand cart loaded with luggage speeding toward the Gestapo man. The cart slams the German into the side of the train car; heavy luggage pommels him to the ground.

Instantly Jack sprints past the train cars, jumps off the platform and heads out the back of the station. Scores of tracks merge to the main rail routes out of the city. Trains enter and leave constantly. Jack slows to find his best avenue of escape when he hears gunfire and a round pings off a rail next to his foot.

With a renewal of energy he didn't know he had, Jack takes flight again. He runs, keeping his steps in time with the spacing of the railroad ties. One miss and he'll go down, an easy target. Another bullet, striking close by, spurs Jack to a locomotive on his right, gathering speed, exiting the station. With a burst of speed, Jack jumps on the buffer stop of the locomotive. The long mushroom-headed cylinder on the front acts as a cushion when contacting other cars.

Draped across the cylinder, Jack is out of danger from the Gestapo man's bullets. but he struggles to hang on. Sparks fly from the giant steel wheels as the locomotive's engineer pulls the brake lever. The screech is deafening, someone must have seen him jump in front of the train. His teeth bared in agony, Jack's arms are almost pulled from their sockets. The locomotive travels a long distance before slowing to a stop. Jack wearily climbs down rubbing his shoulder, then heads for the outside of the rail yard.

Novac takes the map Chuck gave him from his pocket. He remembers the road north by the railroad tracks is almost a straight shot to Saint-Denis. Crossing the wide avenue, he takes off his greasy, stained coat and folds it over his arm before continuing north. It takes a half hour of walking before he sees a small café with a taxi cab by the curb. Jack gets in the back of the cab, takes

44

out his map and points to a rail yard outside Saint-Denis.

The cabbie shrugs, having grown used to the foreign element invading his land. Shoving the gear lever on his ancient Renault to nosily engage a gear, they putter off. Jack is surprised the ride is so short. He pays the cabbie with some French coin and not wanting the driver to know his real destination, then waits for the cabbie to leave.

Jack checks his map, then walks a half mile to the Cathedral. He sees the black and yellow Citroen parked where Chuck said it would be. The car is locked just as the other one was; Jack is tempted to give it a good kick but doesn't want to raise the curiosity of the locals. Tired and frustrated, he drapes the coat over his shoulder. Hands stuffed in his pockets, he trudges to the cathedral.

"Man am I glad to see you! Thank God you're all right," Chuck exclaims.

Jack's heads snaps up to the direction of Chuck's voice.

"Yeah right, good to see you, too, Chuck; your plan was almost flawless...except for car keys."

Chuck looks puzzled, then slaps his forehead with the palm of his hand.

"Jeez, Bill's gonna kill me. That was stupid. I'm sorry Jack."

"Bill doesn't need to know, Chuck. I threw you off just wanting to get this crap over with. We just didn't spend enough time planning. It's always the simple stuff that bites you. Hey, where's Paul? Let's get outta here."

"Paul's the only reason I'm here. We were holding our own with the four guys at the park until the cops showed up. The first four guys turned out to be cops also, but that wasn't a big surprise. Anyway, we couldn't get away and two of the uniformed cops handcuffed us.

"They marched Paul and me to a van to take us to the police station. One cop opened the rear door and Paul bit down on his arm and wouldn't let go. I never heard a guy scream like that. Paul scared the crap outta the guy. The other cop tried to pull Paul off and I ran for it.

"I made it to the car and saw you jump in the back of a truck. I got the cuffs off easy and drove to the intersection, made a U-turn to come after you. I was too far behind when you got out of the truck, but I saw you turn down the street. When I got there, cops were chasing you and I had to leave the car to get through the crowd of people. I was pretty sure you were headed to the train station, so I pushed through and started looking for you.

"By the time I found you, the Gestapo man was trying to get you on the train. I ran the luggage cart into him, I'm sorry I was too late. I saw you jump in front of the train and thought you might'a gotten run over."

Chuck shakes his head, not meeting Jack's eyes. "All this and we lost the list. Bill's gonna be fit to be tied."

"We didn't lose the list, Chuck. I gave that idiot the verification paper Bill gave me. I've got the list in my pocket. I'd love to be a fly on the wall when Mr. Gestapo hands it to Heydrich, his man with the iron heart. So whatta we gonna do about Paul?"

Chuck looks at his watch. "We've got to go, Jack. We can't miss the plane, it's even more important now that you have the list. Those Gestapo people aren't gonna give up. We have to get outta here. Paul knew what he was doing when he went into his crazy act. It was meant to give me a chance to get away and get you and the list back home. Robbins has connections. He'll find a way to get Paul back."

Chapter 6

The return trip back to America is as tiring as the first trip. The English government will still not allow Pan Am to fly passengers to or from Europe. They are determined to keep the business strictly British. Both Jack and Chuck try to work the kinks out of their backs as they exit the cramped mail plane. Bill Robbins waits with armed guards by two Packard town cars.

"Good to see you guys," Robbins says. "Good job both of you. Jack, let me have the list and you and Chuck can take the car to the hotel. Get cleaned up, take a nap, I'll treat you guys to dinner after a debrief."

Jack wakes to a pounding at his hotel room door accompanied by a ringing phone.

"Get up, Jack." Chuck yells through the door. "Robbins is in the lobby waiting for us."

Jack swings his legs off the bed, knuckling his eyes. Ignoring the phone, he stretches his arms out yawning, then plods across the room scratching his butt through his undershorts. He yells back at the door, "Go on down, Chuck, I'll be down in a minute or two."

When Jack enters the lobby, Robbins is pacing; he turns to Novac and motions for him to follow. Outside is dark with rain beginning to fall lightly. A man holding an umbrella stands by a Packard with the rear door open as first Robbins, then Chuck and Jack get in.

"We'll stop by my office," Robbins says, "for your reports then we can relax and go have the dinner I promised."

The men remain quiet during the ride. The V-12 engine rumbles smoothly, the big sedan impressing Jack with the smooth ride.

"You must be in fat city, Bill. This is an expensive car."

"I told you I have a big budget, Jack. I've had some modifications done on this baby so it's a bit heavy, but that engine makes so much torque the car will jump when I need it to."

There is slight groan from the brakes as the car stops in front of Rockefeller's International Building off 5th Avenue. The chauffeur holding up the umbrella is quickly out by the rear door.

"Come on we can all huddle under the umbrella," Robbins says.

Jack gets out and walks past the chauffeur who tries to follow but then hurries back to Robbins to protect him from the rain. Jack looks up at the statue of Atlas, holding his hands above his eyes to ward off the rain. The statue seems even more majestic gleaming in the rain and bathed in the lights of the surrounding buildings.

"Come on, Jack you can see it from my office," Robbins calls as he, the chauffeur, and Chuck go by. Jack follows them into the building.

Inside the building Robbins turns to the chauffeur, "Dell, we'll be an hour or so." The chauffeur nods his head and turns away. Robbins ushers the men to the elevator, works the button panel and looks up at the display above the doors. When the elevator stops, Robbins leads the way to an unmarked office. He unlocks the door and waves Jack and Chuck in. The office is unremarkable; there are two desks on opposite ends of the room, some chairs and a row of file cabinets. Robbins takes a seat in a high-backed black leather chair behind the largest desk. Jack walks to a window to look down on the Atlas statue. Robbins watches Jack, his fingers calmly interlaced atop his desk.

"You like that statue, Jack? People protested when they put it up. They thought it looked like Mussolini."

Jack shrugs his shoulders.

"So, let's get started then. Pull up a chair, men," Robbins says. "Jack, let's begin with you. Chuck gave me most of the dope in his report."

Jack moves a chair close the Robbins's desk, then sits down shaking a cigarette out of the pack and lighting it. He exhales and watches the smoke drift, taking his time to answer. Robbins sits forward in his chair.

"What I want to know, Bill, is how in the hell did the Gestapo know I was there? How did the guy pick me up in the train station?"

"I don't have an answer for you, Jack, not yet anyway. Let's just get your take on the deal and maybe that'll help us figure out what happened. You seem a little upset, my friend."

"Upset is way too mild, Bill. I had a tough time getting away after I got the list. When the Gestapo guy got me, I was pretty damned rattled. I didn't know if he knew about the list at first, and thought I'd just make a run for it. Then he pokes a gun at me and demands I get on the train that's gonna take us to Berlin.

"I knew if I got on the train I'd have to find a way to destroy the list and kill myself before they could torture me again." Jack mashes out his cigarette in an ash tray on Robbins' desk.

"You could say I was surprised, Bill, because I thought you had me covered. Am I pissed? Oh, yeah, buddy, I'm pissed. Maybe it's because I'm tired, but I thought you ran a tighter ship than this…friend."

Robbins' hands turn to fists, color coming to his face. He looks down at his fists and takes a moment to compose.

"I am sorry, Jack; I will do anything to make it up to you. I promise I'll find out what happened and punish whoever leaked that you were coming to France. Paul is there working with Goux's captain to investigate Goux's involvement. The French police are going to drum Goux out. I want to know if he passed anything to the Nazis."

51

Jack gets out of his chair to walk back to the window. He speaks without turning to face Robbins. "I don't think Goux's your man. He tried to give me a fake list at first. When I took out the verification paper you gave me, he presented the real list. He warned me about having the list; he didn't want me to have it."

"Maybe he didn't want you to have the real one because he knew the Nazis were on to you," Robbins says.

"Okay, Bill, have it your way. I'm gonna go back to the hotel, gather my stuff and get the first plane home."

"Come on, Jack, stick around for dinner at least."

"No thanks, Bill. I'm gonna go."

Robbins stands to offer his hand. "Okay, Jack, I am sorry. I meant it about helping out with your flying; I owe you pal."

"I know, Bill; I'm more than just pissed. I'm not sure what I'm feelin' right now. It's best I go. Tell you what, why don't you come out to L.A. and I'll give you a tour of my plant and take you to Offenhauser's, the best race engine guys in L.A. Those guys are artists you can appreciate. We'll go have dinner with the stars at the Brown Derby, or the Trocadero; maybe you can recruit one of them."

Jack shakes hands with Robbins, then Chuck before heading to the door.

Robbins, with some effort, puts a game face on. "Have Dell take you to the hotel, Jack. Have a good trip, I'll keep in touch."

Chuck finds his voice after Jack leaves. "Man, I think he was really scared in Paris."

"You would've been too, Chuck. The Gestapo almost killed him in Berlin; they ended his racing career and tried to kill Maddy and her mother. He's a brave guy; I think he's mostly mad at himself for being scared."

Jack gets off the plane in L.A. Maddy runs out to meet him. Wrapping her arms around him she pulls him to her, kissing him with an urgent passion. She moves back to study him, her face clouding. Maddy traces her finger gently past the fresh scar on his cheek.

"What happened, Jack? I knew something was wrong, I could feel it. We have a strong connection; it was almost like the feeling I had in Berlin. You scared me, Jack."

"I love you, Maddy." Jack pulls Maddy back into his arms, he needs the embrace, to take in the scent of her hair almost as proof he is truly home. "I'm sorry I scared you. I'll tell you all about it when we get home. I just want to be with you at home; I've thought of little else on this trip. Let's stop on the way and get a bottle of that Rhine wine you like. We'll sit out back and watch the sunset on the ocean waves."

He looks at Maddy, hoping to see her smile.

"Don't worry, baby, the debt to Robbins is paid in full."

"We both know we have not seen the last of Bill Robbins," Maddy replies.

Chapter 7

Jack put the top down on the new '38 Ford convertible for the trip home. He figured the noise of the wind rushing by would make talk difficult. Unsure of Maddy's mood, he was not eager to pique her anger. They stopped on Washington Boulevard and Jack went in the store for wine. When he parked the car in the driveway, Maddy got out to open the trunk.

"I've got your bags, go on in and open the wine. I'll meet you out back," she said.

Jack goes into the kitchen for glasses and a corkscrew. Holding the bottle by the neck, he pops the cork then takes the wine and two glasses out to the backyard. Putting the wine and glasses on a small wicker table, he sits down heavily in a chair blowing out a breath. Suddenly very tired, he wonders how he is going to explain the whole lousy trip.

Maddy has a sweater on when she comes outside. Jack watches as she walks toward him trying to read her expression, fearing the worst. She takes the wine glass from his hand, takes a sip then puts the glass down on the table. With both hands on the arms of his chair Maddy leans forward to kiss him. She pulls back and stares into his eyes. He can see from her red-rimmed eyes, she's been crying.

"You lied to me; do not ever do that again Jack Novac. I knew you were in trouble. I called Robbins and he would not take my calls; he was always out or in a meeting."

Jack can take no more.

"Jesus, Maddy, if I make you cry it's like stabbing me with a knife. I am really sorry. Robbins said it was secret, he said I couldn't tell anyone. It won't happen again, I promise."

Hands on hips, eyes narrowed, Maddy stares down at Jack.

"I will give Bill Robbins a good painting when I see him."

Puzzled, Jack looks into the face he loves, trying to think what she could mean.

"Why would you give him a good painting? What kind of painting? Do you mean pasting?"

Maddy's brow wrinkles in thought. "Mother said she heard the midterm elections delivered President Roosevelt's party a good painting or brushing, something like that. We were both puzzled but thought it must an American idiom."

Jack thinks a moment before blurting out, "shellacking, a good shellacking, it means a good beating." He laughs, pulling Maddy into his lap.

"I will laugh too, Mister Cowboy Novac, but you have not escaped my anger yet. The next time Robbins calls for some clandestine duty—and he will—we will go together or not at all. I will not be left behind wondering if I will ever see you again. If you agree, all will be forgiven and you will receive a good roll in the hay tonight. I hope I have that one right."

"There is no way I could argue, Maddy. You're far too clever for me and the roll in the hay tonight is more than I hoped for. I love having you with me, but I will not put you in danger if it should come to that. I'd never be able to live with myself, do you understand?"

Maddy untangles herself from Jack's arms to stand up.

"I think we have had enough talk for now. I have missed you, longed for you, it is time for bed."

Jack wakes a happy man as he swings his legs from under the covers to head for the bathroom. Feeling well-exercised from his roll in the hay he grins to the reflection in the mirror. Coming out of the bathroom, he smells the rich scent of coffee coming from downstairs. Jack slips into a robe and bounds downstairs to the kitchen.

Maddy stands before the stove, turning sizzling tubes of sausage in the hot pan when Jack circles her waist with his arms. He pulls her tight to him to nuzzle her neck.

"Down Cowboy, you will have both of us burned."

"Okay, I'll just get a cup of coffee and admire you from across the room. Any closer than that and I won't be able to keep my hands off you."

Maddy slices the cooked sausage to blend it into the scrambled eggs, adds salt and pepper, then scoops some onto plates. She butters toast and brings the plates to the table.

"Mori has been calling for you. He says there is a man coming in the plant, trying to get the men to join a union. He is beginning to sound desperate."

"Damn, I wanted to spend the day with you. The employees already voted to stay outta the unions. I'd better go in for a bit to see what's up. The mob's trying to get a foothold here and a protection racket's their stock in trade. I won't be long, I promise. Tell you what: I'll make it up to you. I'll take you and your Mom to see the new Disney movie. We'll make a big night of it. After the movie we'll go to that new German restaurant in the Palisades."

Maddy smiles, studying Jack's face. "That will be wonderful. I have read in the paper that it is a wonderful movie. They say the color and the animation are magnificent. Mother used to read fairy tales to me when I was a child. Snow White was my favorite from the Brothers Grimm. I will pick up her and we can meet you here when you get back."

***

The "plant" as Jack calls it, was not his first choice as a business. The electronics business came from him wanting something secure to invest in.

When Novac returned to America after his ordeal with Baron Von Steuben, he was hailed a hero in the New York papers. His acclaim spread across the country and Jack planned great things on his arrival in California. First and foremost, he married Maddy. He bought the house in Santa Monica and land for his plant in Culver City just down the road from the old Playa Del Ray Speedway.

He had plenty of money from his Monza victory, and prices in depression-era California were cheap. There lay the problem. Jack's dream was to manufacture and sell his own racing engines. He loved the science and engineering that went into creating racing engines. The depression brought hard times, and racers were not spending money on new engines.

Jack went over the numbers; the cost to outfit a shop with the tools needed to build and test engines far outweighed any profit. Harry Miller, the best racing engine manufacturer in America, was bankrupted. Fred Offenhauser, Miller's shop foreman, bought all of Miller's tools and rights and was just making ends meet.

Two events changed Novac's direction. His old friend and investment advisor saw Jack's quandary and suggested buying land in Orange County as a long-term investment. For the business he could purchase patents for products he could manufacture. As an offshoot of the depression there were thousands of patents for sale; many with products ordered if the patent owner could deliver.

What he found was a patent for aviation instrumentation, and government interest for product, that the patent owner could not come up with funding to manufacture. Jack bought the patent, got the government order, and was off and running. With the plant churning out product, Jack's interest turned to improving existing instruments, and developing new ones in an industry that was moving fast.

Navigation was a new frontier; Jack's interest in science spurred him to hire the best minds he could find to pioneer new ideas. California's universities had the men he wanted. These men were known in the 1930's vernacular as "eggheads". Jack saw a passion for science in these men. A passion that burned, like racing had burned in him.

Precise aeronautical navigation was what the government wanted, and Jack wanted to contribute. His pilot's license set him up as an integral part of the team. He did not have the formal education of the eggheads, but he did have a natural sense of things mechanical that they did not. Testing the instruments in flight was where

Jack excelled, and he enjoyed working with his bright young men.

Chapter 8

It is almost noon by the time Jack gets to the plant. He drives with the top down; savoring the little traffic on the road, and watching the sun chase the morning overcast away. Parking in front of his two-story brick building, he pauses a moment; a train whistle sounds off in the distance. He flashes back to the Paris train yard, then shakes his head trying to get rid of the thought. Mori Able rushes out of the front door before Jack can get out of the car.

Mori trots to the car; his hands grip the door sill.

"Jack, the guy's inside, he's making everyone nervous."

"It's okay Mori. I'll take care of him. Where's he now?"

"He's back in the drawing office. The guy just wants to intimidate everyone. The draftsmen are all huddled on the other side of the room."

Jack walks into the building and down the hallway to the swinging doors of the drawing office. Going through the doors, Jack sees a man swivel around to face him. The man's white shirt under his open sports coat spreads over his beltline. He's of medium height with a wide-brimmed hat pulled down low. He is looking at a small gauge in his hand.

"You want somethin' here, bub? Wait over there with the others; I'm waitin' on Novac an' I'm runnin' outta patience."

"I'm Novac, what can I do for you?"

"It's what I'm gonna do for you, bub," the man says juggling the gauge.

Jack swells with anger as he walks over to the man and takes the gauge from him.

"You aren't here from a union are you, buddy?" Jack asks.

The man's face goes hard. He lashes out without warning punching Jack in the stomach, then hammers Jack's shoulder when he doubles over. He yanks Jack up by the shirt front, popping buttons off that scatter across the floor.

Jack grabs the gangster's arm. Then still holding the gauge in his hand, brings it down hard on the man's head. The metal edge tears through the felt of the gangster's hat making a bloody gash on his head. The man goes down in a heap. Wide-eyed draftsmen press themselves into a corner as far from Jack and the other man as possible. Not realizing just how fast his anger overcame him, he sets the gauge down, his hand shaking with pent-up adrenalin.

"Hey, Lou," Jack calls out to one of the men, "why don't you and the others go have some lunch; this guy won't bother you again. Mori, give me a hand here; you take his feet, we'll move 'im to the bathroom and put a bandage on his head."

Mori takes the man's feet. "Jeez, Jack, I thought you killed the guy."

"It's just a scalp wound Mori, looks a lot worse than it is. He'll have a king-sized headache, but he'll be all right."

They lay the man on the bathroom floor. Jack takes the man's hat off to inspect the wound while Mori goes to a sink to run water on a towel.

"Hold on a minute with the towel, Mori."

Jack goes through the gangster's pockets and takes a wallet out to remove the driver's license. He finds a .38 Colt in a coat pocket and puts it in his own back pocket.

"Okay, Mori, you can wipe his head, I'll get a bandage. If he comes to, stand away from him."

The man groans as Mori cleans the wound. Jack pulls the little red strings from two Band-Aids and applies them to close the wound. The man's eyes flutter, then one hand goes to his head wound while the other goes to the pocket where he had the gun.

"Where am I? Where's my gun?

"You're in the bathroom at my plant. I just put a bandage on the cut on your head. You'll have a headache, but you're not hurt bad."

"You're a dead man, Novac. Nobody messes with us. You just made the biggest mistake of your life. Gimme my gun back."

Jack stands up, looking down at the man. "Man, that wallop musta' made you stupid. You can rest here till the cops come for you."

"Cops ain't gonna do nothin'; I'll be home for dinner. When I tell the boss about this, your life won't be worth spit."

Jack shakes his head. "Tell your boss this plant is involved in government work. We don't pay protection and tryin' to collect extortion money from us is a federal crime."

The gangster scowls as his eyes go dead. "Sure, I'll tell him. The feds ain't got no say. Benny can make anyone in this town do whatever he wants."

Jack extends his hand to the man to help him up. The man slaps Jacks hand away, then struggles to get to his feet.

"Okay, come on tough guy, I'll walk you to your car."

Jack walks behind the man outside the plant to a big late model four-door Buick.

"Gimme back my gun," the man snarls.

Jack throws the wallet he took into the Buick.

"No chance. I'm giving the gun and your driver's license to the FBI. You can explain to them how tough you are and how well connected your boss is."

The man gives Jack the finger, grinds the transmission into gear and lurches out onto Jefferson Boulevard.

Jack goes to his office with Mori trailing behind him. He opens a closet to get another shirt.

"I'm gonna call the FBI and have them come by to pick up the gangster's gun and license."

Mori's brow wrinkles with concern.

"Um, will you be in tomorrow? Do you think we should get a security guard?"

"I'll ask the FBI man to station some men to watch the plant, and I'll be in first thing tomorrow. If I'm not here, just make sure to get some I.D. from the FBI man before you hand over the gangster's stuff. I don't expect any more trouble from those guys, Mori."

Jack calls the FBI office to report the extortion attempt. He asks if they could send someone to watch the plant for a couple of days. He begins to sort through the paperwork from his in-box. After lunch he goes into the drawing office to talk with the men there, then to the machine shop to see what the men are working on. Jack stacks his paperwork, calling an end to his day. As he leaves, he looks into Mori's office.

"I promised Maddy I'd take her to the movies; is there anything else you need before I go? Don't worry, Mori. I'll see you in the morning."

"No, I don't need anything right now. Have a good evening, Jack. What time will you be in tomorrow?"

"I'll be in early; I want to get a full day in before the weekend."

Jack changes his clothes when he gets home then goes out to the backyard. Maddy and her mother are sitting in deck chairs, a carafe of iced tea on the table between them.

"Hello ladies, are you ready for a big evening?"

"Mama's a little under the weather, Jack," Maddy says. "I want her to see the movie with us, but we'll have to do the town another night."

"I'm sorry to hear that Mrs. Rosen. Is there anything I can do?"

Mrs. Rosen smiles up at Jack. "Thank you, son, but my stomach is a little unsettled. I am looking forward to the movie, but I would like to get to bed before too late."

Maddy grins mischievously. "Mama was playing bridge last night with her Palisades ladies' group and had too much schnapps."

Mrs. Rosen's cheeks color. "Oh, Madeline, you little imp. You need not add to my torment."

Jack chuckles watching the mother-daughter exchange. "It's okay, Mrs. Rosen, we both know Maddy's got a bit'a the devil in her. I have to be at work early tomorrow anyway, so we'll see the movie and take you home. The movie's at the Cathay Circle Theater. I think you'll enjoy the theater as much as the movie; it's really a grand place."

On the way home from the Disney movie Maddy and her mother bubble over talking about Snow White. They stop at a diner for coffee and pie, the two women still chatting excitedly about characters in the movie. Jack sits back contentedly sipping his coffee, watching his wife and her mother enjoy their banter before taking Mrs. Rosen home. When they return home, he tells Maddy that he is looking forward to Saturday and going with Ross to the valley to look at some planes.

Chapter 9

The overcast sky makes the air heavy with humidity as Jack drives to Clover Field to meet Ross early Saturday morning. He hopes the sun will soon be able to chase the gloom away. Novac is eager to try out a real high-powered aerobatic plane. He studied the manuals for instrument flight Ross wanted him to read. After he finished those, he read many firsthand accounts of aerobatic flying to learn the best tricks. His self-confidence took a knock in France; flying a powerful stunt plane is just the tonic he needs.

"Hey Ross, you ready to go?" Jack calls out as soon as he opens the door to Ross's business.

"Hold your horses, Novac, it's too early to be gettin' excited. Let's go get some breakfast. It'll give the weather time to clear. I'm hungry anyway."

"The weather'll be clear by the time we get there, Ross."

"Look, Jack, you can't be stunt flyin' when you can't see land or the horizon. So just take it easy and I'll let you buy me breakfast."

Jack has toast, then fidgets with his coffee cup during breakfast. Ross takes his time eating a tall stack of hot cakes, paying no attention to Jack until he finishes. "You gonna play with your coffee all day or do you wanta do some flyin'?"

By the time they get to Van Nuys, the mid-day sun has sent the overcast out to sea. The airfield bristles with small planes. Ross points to a large hangar to their right. "Park over there by the big truck."

The smell of old gas and oil that have soaked into the ground permeate the air inside the dirt floor hangar. Bi-planes in various stages of disrepair share the space with engines, propellers, wings, tires, car parts, and assorted junk.

"Hey, Julie," Ross calls out. "You in here, man?"

Emerging from the gloom at the rear of the hangar, a heavyset man hollers, "Who's yellin?"

"Ross Elmore here, Julie. I brought Jack Novac to try out that Bellanca you've got."

As Jules Hacket comes into the light, his heavy-jowled face has the pasty pallor of a man unwell. Ross goes to him with his hand extended, they shake hands and Ross introduces Jack.

Ross looks at Hacket with concern. "The place is lookin' a little run down since I was here last, Julie."

"Yeah, well I ain't been gettin' a lot done around here lately. The doc says I got ulcer

69

problems an' I jus' ain't got much energy. This depression, recession, or whatever they're callin' it we're havin' ain't helpin' either; I laid off most of my guys to try an' make ends meet."

"I'm sorry to hear that, Julie. Jack's willing to pay top dollar to rent the Bellanca. How 'bout we get started?"

Hacket's eyes narrow as he looks Jack over. "I'd like to see him in my Jenny first, Ross; that Bellanca cost me a fortune. I can't afford a smashup."

"I thought we had a deal, Julie. So you're tellin' me you don't trust me?" Ross barks.

Jack quickly interjects. "It's okay, Ross, I don't mind; the man's got a lot at stake. Why don't you look over the Bellanca and I'll take the Jenny up?"

Jules shrugs as if it makes no difference to him, then motions for Jack to follow him. "The Jenny's out-front. I had Junior look it over after the movie guys finished with it. Wait a minute and I'll get Junior to go up with you. Bring my boy and the Jenny back in one piece, just show me you know what you're doin."

Jules returns, followed by a younger version a head taller and 50 pounds heavier than senior. Jack and Ross have been looking over the Jenny. Ross tells Jack in loud voice not to work the old plane too hard, then goes with Jules to inspect the Bellanca Flash.

"You been up in one'a these before?" Junior asks Jack.

"Yeah, quite a few times. Is it ready to go?" Jack asks.

"I gave it the once-over," Junior replies, pulling on a leather flying cap.

Jack steps toward the rear cockpit.

"You take the front," Junior says. "I wanta see a real ace in action."

Jack shrugs, then steps up on the wing and into the front cockpit. He pulls on his cloth helmet as Junior yanks the propeller to start the engine.

Junior climbs aboard and Jack takes off. After gaining altitude Jack circles the field, then drops down to land.

Jules and Ross hurry to the Jenny as Jack shuts off the engine.

"What's the matter?" Ross asks.

"There's way too much rear weight. If I tried to do a spin, or anything else, we'd never get out of it."

"You sayin' Junior's too heavy?" Jules asks. "Why are you sittin' in the back anyways, Junior?" Jules asks Junior who has just gotten out of the plane.

"I wanted to see the ace fly, Pop. I guess the ol' Jenny scared 'im."

Jack climbs out looking at the rear of the Jenny. "It's not just Junior. What else is in the back of this thing? I had to use a ton a elevator to keep the tail up."

Jules thinks for a moment, then speaks sharply to Junior. "Did you make sure the movie guys emptied that oil smoke tank they put in?"

71

Junior smacks his forehead with the heel of his hand. "I guess I forgot, Pop."

Jules shakes his head. "Well, I guess this guy knows enough not to get the both of you killed, boy."

Jules turns to Jack. "You can go on and take the Bellanca up, Mr. Novac. I see you know what you're doin; just don't take the life outta it."

"I'll go up with him, Julie," Ross says, "just so you won't have to worry."

The Bellanca is a sleek two-seater mono-wing plane painted a brilliant bright blue with a yellow lighting bolt stripe down each side of the fuselage. Jack follows Ross, closely inspecting the plane as Jules watches. When they climb into the cockpit, Jules, standing on a wooden ladder alongside, goes over the controls with both men.

"We'll keep in touch on the radio," Ross assures Jules. "We'll be gone a coupl'a hours out near Rogers Dry Lake. Don't worry. Like I said before, Jack's a good pilot. Let's go, Jack."

Jack revels in the plane's power as he opens the throttle to take off. The 960-horsepower radial engine hauls them off the runway, rapidly gaining altitude. Jack banks right, heading for the desert. The Bellanca feels solid and responsive to the controls, bolstering Jack's confidence. He is anxious to put the plane and himself through a thorough test while proving to Ross that he isn't going to cowboy the plane into ruin.

Arriving over the dry lake bed near Rosamond, Jack takes his time to pick out landmarks to give a base to his mental list of maneuvers.

Jack talks to Ross on the plane's radio. "I'm gonna start with some slow rolls to get a feel for this baby. Let me know if you see mistakes or have some suggestions, okay?"

"I like it so far," Ross answers.

Jack rolls to the right, using the ailerons, elevators, and rudder to go inverted, then continues the roll to bring the plane back to level flight.

Ross's calm voice comes through the headset. "You let the nose dip, Jack; you need to use more rudder."

Jack nods his head, then talks into his microphone. "You're right, Ross; I also missed comin' back on track. I'll try a few more."

Jack brings the plane back to where he can line up his landmarks and goes again, remembering to use the rudder more to keep the nose up. After a few more, Jack is satisfied he has the feel he needs to progress.

"That'll work, Jack. Tell me what you're planning from here," Ross asks. "Julie's wantin' to know when we're comin' back."

Looking forward under the clear canopy Ross can see Jack shake his head. "Jeez man," Jack says, "we just got here. Tell Julie it's going well and I'm really enjoying his beautiful baby; and I need at least another 30 minutes."

"Okay Jack, Julie says you've got a half-hour, but he doesn't want you to do any steep dives."

Ross doesn't need to see Jack's face to know he's annoyed.

"I gotta get my own plane, Ross."

"Don't worry about that now, Jack, you haven't got the time. What do you want to try?"

"I'll do barrel rolls and Immelmans. Keep your eyes peeled for any traffic, will you? I just wanta concentrate on gettin' these two tricks right."

"Go to it, Jack. I'll keep watch."

Jack pulls back on the stick, gaining altitude. With his land bearings and horizon placed, he rolls over the top but has to use the rudder to pitch the tail. He returns to his starting place to continue performing the maneuver until he and Ross are satisfied.

"We need to get back now," Ross says.

"Let me try one Immelman and we'll head back," Jack replies already putting the plane in action.

As they approach Van Nuys, Ross calls out to Jack. "Don't screw this up by buzzin' the airport, Jack. Julie's seen it all and he'll just take it as an amateur showin' off."

"Well, how 'bout a slow roll?" Jack says as he starts the bank.

When Jack stops the Bellanca by the hangar, both Jules and his son are beside the plane before the propeller stops.

As Jack and Ross climb out of the plane, Jules reaches out to shake Jack's hand. "So whatta you think of her, Mr. Novac?"

Jack gives Ross a questioning look. "Ah, I think she's a fine ship, Jules. Very good power and most of the controls are responsive. The rudder cables are a little sloppy would be my only complaint."

"Fair enough," Jules replies. "I'll have Junior take care of that. When do you want to take her up again?"

"I'm not sure, Jules. I'm havin' my own plane built, and I want to do some racin'. I'm curious to know why you changed your mind. You really didn't want me to fly the Bellanca earlier."

"When Ross radioed that you were over Roger's Dry Lake, I called a friend of mine to take a look at you. She watched you with some field glasses an' said you handled the ship real good. She's flown the Bellanca for the movie's an' knows how it flies. If Pancho says you can fly, that's good enough for me."

"Is that Pancho Barnes you're talkin' about?" Jack asks.

"Sure is," Jules replies. "You know her?"

Jack grins, "I'd like to. I've heard stories about her. There's no doubt she's got flyin' in her blood."

"Well, you let me know when you wanta take her up again. If the movie studios don't have her scheduled, she's all yours."

On the way back to Clover Field, Ross asks Jack about flying the Bellanca.

"You surprised me, Jack. You were real easy with the Bellanca. I thought you'd try your death dive, see if you could peel the wings off'a her like you did with my Stag."

"I didn't try to hurt your Stag, Ross. That's the last thing I'd do. I was tryin' to show you with the Bellanca that I could do the right thing an' not cowboy it. Maddy's always kiddin' me about cowboyin'. I spent a lotta time flyin' the Stag, Ross. I knew what she could handle."

"Well I'm beginning to feel better about helpin' you out, Jack. Maybe you've got enough sense to keep from killin' yourself. You know what they say about pilots; there are bold pilots and there are old pilots, but there aren't any bold...old pilots."

"Very funny, Ross. I'm not lookin' to mess up; besides if I got myself killed, Maddy'd murder me!"

Ross just shakes his head.

Chapter 10

Jack is up and out early Monday morning, still buoyed by the thrill of piloting a fast plane. He felt good in the Bellanca, in control from the beginning. The aerobatics were a very similar rush to the auto racing he missed so much. His good right hand was all he needed on the stick. The sky is still dark with some stars evident on the way to the plant. Alone in the deserted parking lot, Jack stops for a minute looking up at the clear sky. The Big Dipper is just visible against the silky blackness.

Entering the building he flicks on the lights, then heads to the lunch room. Brewing coffee is the first order of business. A steaming mug of coffee in hand, Jack goes to his office determined to wade through the stack of paperwork on his desk. He plows through the paperwork and, after his third mug of coffee, he hears people coming into the building. Mori enters Jack's office carrying cups of coffee and donuts on a tray.

"Morning Jack, you musta come in with the sun."

"Sun hadn't come up when I got here, Mori. You gonna eat those donuts by yourself?"

"Naw, I thought I might share some." Mori brings the tray over and, after Jack takes a donut, he sets the tray down to take seat.

"Looks like you've made a pretty good dent in the paper pile," Mori says before taking a bite of his donut. "What's on your agenda for today?" he asks, brushing crumbs from his shirt.

"I want to see how we're doin' gettin' out the current orders, and what's come in," He pauses to sip his coffee. "I wanta talk to the guys in the experimental department about the electric gyro drives. We need to concentrate on those. We need the best accuracy and reliability possible to put ourselves on the map. The electric gyros are gonna be used for all kinds of guidance systems. I'm convinced that's gonna grow into being our bread and butter product."

After going over business with Mori, Jack goes downstairs. He walks down the sparkling white hallway to the experimental department at the back of the building. There is a bright blue border, waist high, painted on the walls. Each office has a large window to the outside to bring in sunlight. The clerical and managerial offices maintain an open-door policy.

Jack waves and acknowledges greetings from both sides of the hallway as he goes past. At the end of the hallway is the experimental department on his left and a doorway to the machine shop on his right. The experimental door has a red and green light above it to indicate the level of danger of work there.

Jack pushes open the heavy door that whooshes closed behind him. Here the walls on the sides are windowless. The wall on the rear expanse has high mounted glass panels and forced-air fans at the top of the tall ceiling that turn lazily. Men in lab coats are at benches, some working on delicate instruments, others seated are soldering electrical components.

Scattered around the room, blackboards covered with chalked figures and formulas sit on mobile bases. Cork boards with dozens of pages of notes and schematics pinned to them festoon the walls.

At the whoosh of the door, a couple of the men turn to see who entered.

"Good morning, Mr. Novac." A man approaches Jack with small bearings in his hand. "I've been anxious to show you some new bearings we're working on for the gyro axles."

"Good man, Scotty," Jack says. "That's just what I came down to talk about." Jack holds out his hand. "Let's see what you've got."

Holding the center of the little bearing with his fingers, Jack spins the outer case. "It feels smooth; the seals don't seem to have much drag. I hope it's an American-made bearing. Have you done any testing on it?"

Scotty takes the offered bearing back. "We're building a testing rig now. I wrote letters to some of the European bearing manufacturers, but I have not gotten anything back yet."

Jack puts two fingers in his mouth blowing a loud whistle. He waves his hand above his head. "Hey, men, huddle up for a minute, please."

The six men that comprise the department gather around Jack.

One man in the group speaks out. "Is this where you tell us we're being laid off? We heard a rumor that you're going to be building airplanes."

Jack shakes his head. "I don't know where you heard that, and as long as you do the work I want, your jobs are safe. The reason I want to talk with you is that we will not seek any vendors from outside of this country for the foreseeable future. I know most of you guys are immersed in your own world; but here's the deal. Since the beginning of '38 Germany is making no bones about ramping up for war. We could be fighting a world war very soon."

The men shuffle about, their eyebrows raised in disbelief, mumbling to each other. Then one of the men speaks. "We don't want to fight Europe's war, Mr. Novac. President Roosevelt said that we are going to stay out of it."

"I'm not gonna argue the point with you," Jack says. "I'll just lay this out for you. If you want to work for me, we will plan for the future to bring out instruments and guidance systems that will help keep America safe. You guys are the best educated and brightest generation of Americans yet; I am proud to work with you. Most of you guys are dedicated to your work. You eat, drink, and sleep thinking of new ways we can advance.

"Scientific advances are our key for survival. We need to have the best engineering in the world; you eggheads are some of the best. Caltech graduates only the best. Germany, as you may know, marched into Austria; they won't stop there. Japan is massacring thousands in China and telling us we can't stop them. So, even if you don't believe we're gonna have to fight, what I want is the best from you.

"We won't use vendors from outside the US. We will do everything possible to help America defend herself. I know you guys don't want war, and I'm not asking you to produce bullets or bombs. I'm asking that you use your big brains to bring us innovative technology now. Our gyros have to be smaller, lighter, and spin faster. As to your jobs, they're secure: we have plenty of government orders to fill."

Jack slaps Scotty on the shoulder, then grins at the others.

"Think ahead, you bunch a eggheads, and get back to work."

"Scotty, give me minute, will you?" Jack asks.

They turn back toward the door before Jack begins. "I worked at a good little shop some while ago that was ultimately destroyed by malicious gossip. One disgruntled guy turned a few others sour, the work got sloppy, and the place folded. I'd like you to tell me who's spreading rumors."

Scotty looks down at the floor, choosing his words before making eye contact with Jack.

"I don't want to be the palace rat, Mr. Novac. How about I have a word with the man first? If that doesn't work, then I'll let you know, okay?"

Jack looks into Scotty's eyes with a newfound admiration.

"That's a good plan, Scotty. You're the head of this department, the men respect you. I do want to know the outcome because there are some gangsters that are trying to horn in. They could be at the bottom of this."

Scotty brightens, his anxiety relieved. "I heard you took care of the guy; knocked him cold."

"That's the only thing they understand," Jack says. "You let 'em in and they'll milk you forever."

"I'm glad you're running the show, Mr. Novac. By the way, how's the plane coming? Are you still planning to make your own test plane?"

"You bet," Jack says. "I've received some funding to help the process and secured a hangar at Clover Field. Offenhauser is doin' the engine and I'm lookin' for a designer to get the build goin'."

"I know a guy from Caltech, named Ben Jackson," Scotty says. "He's working at Douglas and is really sharp. Airplanes are all he thinks about and I'm sure he'd love to have a chance to do some work for you. He knows stress and load formulas that you'll need to have to make a good design. Want me to set up a meeting with him?"

"You mean he'd be moonlighting?" Jack asks.

"Yes, sir. He has Saturdays and Sundays off, but he still hangs around the airport, helping people out. He's been at Douglas as an engineer since we graduated from Caltech. He knows build procedures from drawing board to completion. A few of us have rooms at an old Victorian in Santa Monica, so I'll be seeing him tonight."

"Okay, Scotty, that sounds good. I've got plans for tomorrow, but I could meet him Sunday. Let me give you my home number; if we can meet, I'll come out to Clover Field."

"Mind if I tag along, Mr. Novac?"

"Please do. When the plane's done, it'll be the test bed for all of our instruments. It'll be good for you to be familiar with the plane as it comes together. Give me a call tonight if you can put us together. Thanks Scotty, I'm lookin' forward to the build, and even more to the test flying."

"You're going to fly it?" Scotty asks.

"Damn straight. That's the part I'm really lookin' forward to. There's a lot of mechanical engineering to do and I love that stuff, too. I'm tryin' to talk my old racin' mechanic into helpin' out."

"Jeez, I didn't know we'd have the boss's butt on the line. We're going to have to be extra careful."

"I would appreciate that, Scotty. I'll talk to you tonight. Keep me posted on the rumor mill."

Chapter 11

Jack decides to drop by Carl Sanders burger joint. He always enjoys trading stories of their racing adventures with his old race mechanic. Some of Carl's regular customers join the table, and the stories begin to grow wilder. Empty beer bottles clutter their table when Lulu, a jovial Chinese woman and Carl's partner, prods Carl to get back to work. Before leaving, Jack phones Maddy to tell her he is bringing dinner home with him.

"Hi, Maddy, I'm home," Jack calls as he enters the front door, carefully cradling dinner. He sets the grease-stained brown paper bag, bulging with Carl's mini hamburgers and fries, on the kitchen table. Maddy comes in the kitchen as Jack washes his hands at the sink.

"Carl wouldn't let me leave without takin' some burgers and fries. How about grabbin' a coupla' a beers and we'll go out back and chow down. I mean we'll eat ourselves silly; he gave me enough to choke a horse."

Maddy shakes her head giving Jack a puzzled look. "I thought I had learned English but almost every day I hear new things. Americans speak with so many idioms it must take years to understand what they all mean."

Jack takes the bag outside to the table as Maddy follows with two bottles of beer. "The German language probably has the plenty of idioms too; you just grew up with 'em. I know one thing about German; the words are so long I don't know how to say 'em. I'd hate to have to spell 'em."

Maddy hands Jack a beer bottle to open. "In English you use many words to describe something," she says. "With German, in some cases, we just use one word. It is more efficient."

"Wow, did you say efficient? Okay, I'm tryin' to think of a word Neubauer was teasing me with. Something about a chimney sweeper. He'd say it, then try to get me to pronounce it; he got a big kick outta that."

"The word is bezirksschonsteinfegermeister," Maddy fires the word out smiling at Jack. "It means district chimney sweeper. Herr Neubauer is a funny man, I miss him."

"Yeah, that's it," Jack says quickly, trying not to bring up sad memories. "What a tongue twister, and that means it's hard to say. I don't doubt learnin' English is tough; I never got much past taco and cerveza with my Spanish. Listening to me talk doesn't help you much either. My speak is pure workin' class American; that's what I grew up with."

"I love listening to you. I love you, my American hero." Maddy opens her beer, then takes a sip. "Let's chow down, Cowboy."

After working their way through most of the burgers and fries, both lean back in their chairs.

"I ate too much," Jack says rubbing his stomach.

"It is a beautiful night, Jack. It makes me feel guilty that I am able to enjoy this life when so many suffer in Germany."

Jack moves to cup Maddy's face in his hands, looks into her eyes, then kisses her. "I love you, Maddy; we can't change the world tonight. Let's go listen to some music on the radio."

Jack twists the radio dial, settling on a jazz station before joining Maddy on a sofa. Maddy kicks off her shoes, puts her feet up, then lies down with her head resting in Jack's lap. He runs his fingers through her hair enjoying the moment.

Jack grins looking down at Maddy. "I know. Let's take a trip out to Cornero's big gambling ship tomorrow. It'll be fun. I'd like to see what all the fuss is about before the district attorney closes it down. The thing's three miles out to sea but the DA still wants it shut down. I knew Tony Cornero years ago when he was in the bootleg business. He's not a bad guy as far as gangsters go. The booze was the real stuff; he smuggled it in from Canada.

During our wonderful experiment with prohibition, there was a lotta poison liquor killin' people: if you bought booze from Tony, you knew it was good. I read in the paper Tony says all the gambling on his ship is honest too, no gimmicks; he'll pay $100,000 dollars if anyone can find something rigged. There's a French restaurant on board that's supposed to be first class. We can have a good meal and give the wheels a spin. I don't think Tony's gonna win this one. Eventually the cops are gonna sink the SS *Rex*."

Jack and Maddy are both napping when the phone rings.

"I'll get it," Jack says. Maddy stirs, lifting her head to let Jack get up. "I asked Scotty from the plant to call. I forgot all about it."

Jack returns to the couch after taking the phone call to hold his hand out to Maddy.

"Let's go to bed."

Jack walks down the hallway behind Maddy with his hands on her shoulders past framed pictures of his race cars and her magazine covers. He steers his drowsy wife into the bedroom at the end of the hall. Sitting on the edge of the bed, he pulls off his shoes.

"I'm gonna meet Scotty and a friend of his at Clover Field on Sunday, but I'll be home for dinner. I'll make us breakfast in the morning and we can walk down to the pier in the afternoon to catch a water taxi to the Rex."

Maddy wakes the next morning, hearing pans rattle and low-toned grumbling coming from the kitchen. She enters the kitchen rubbing the sleep from her eyes.

"Jack! What on earth are you doing? The kitchen looks like a hurricane struck."

Jack turns to Maddy, the front of his pajamas covered with flour and egg. "I couldn't find any hot cake mix so I tried to make some from scratch. I've run outta eggs so after I take a shower we can go out for breakfast."

Maddy stands with her hands on her hips surveying the mess. "Before you go to shower you can help me clean up this mess."

"Aw, let's just go have some breakfast in town. I'll help you clean up when we get back."

"No Jack, we clean now before you track flour all over the house."

Jack brushes a cloud of flour from his pajamas, looking around the kitchen as if seeing it for the first time. "Well, all right boss, I didn't know hot cakes were such a pain."

Maddy grins mischievously, then gives Jack a peck on his cheek. "You do the washing, I'll dry."

Outside is another beautiful Santa Monica day. In the 1930's Santa Monica was a city teeming with corruption: Raymond Chandler's Bay City. Having a place above the bay to enjoy the ocean view is a vision Jack has had for a long time. He has been around long enough to know the city's pitfalls and the people and places to avoid.

After breakfast they decide to do some window shopping and walk off the meal. They peer in the windows of some shops but find little of interest. Maddy asks Jack where the Merle Norman shop is.

"It's on Main Street but it's a couple a miles from here. You wanta go home and get the car?"

"I like to walk, and we can use the exercise," Maddy says. "My brother and I used to hike in the mountains for days. Now I work at home on my book or drive my mother somewhere and think about those days."

Jack is quick to change the subject. "We could go up to Big Bear next weekend. It's up in the mountains with lots a trees. There might be some snow left if you like the cold."

"Oh, Jack, I would love that. Can you get away from the plant?"

"I'll make sure I can. We'll drive up Friday and come back Sunday; that'll give you all day Saturday to roam the wooded wilds."

Maddy pulls Jack close, looping her arm through his. "This is like living in a fairytale. Your California is truly magnificent; I do love it here."

"This is our California, Maddy. We belong here together."

Just north of Ocean Park Boulevard, Jack and Maddy stop to admire the much-publicized new Merle Norman building.

The bold, streamlined Art Deco design signifies hope and prosperity, defying the years of depression.

"Boy, I really like it," Jack says. "That makes me want to rebuild the plant with that look. I'm gonna go up the street to Tommy's bar while you're getting' your beauty treatment. I haven't seen Tommy in a month a Sundays. I'll meet you here in a half hour and we can hike back home. By the time we get home, we can grab a snack and then head out for the *Rex*."

They both nap when they get back home. Feeling rested, they dress for a night on the gambling ship, SS *Rex*. Jack parks the car off the Santa Monica Pier and goes around to open the passenger door for Maddy. She is wearing an off the shoulder royal blue taffeta dress Jack bought her in London. Jack wears a navy blue suit with a crisp white shirt and red tie.

Jack takes a coat from the back seat. "Let me help you with your coat, its liable to be chilly out on the water."

With the water fairly calm, they can watch, in relative comfort, the lights of Santa Monica recede as the water taxi takes them out to the SS *Rex*. Men dressed in tuxedos help them from the boat to the stairways. They ascend to the main deck, then to the entrance of the huge gambling room.

"Hi ya, Jack, or is it Mister Novac now?" A man with a snap brim Stetson hat smiles broadly as Jack turns toward him.

"Hey Tony, good to see you," Jack says, shaking the man's hand. "Just call me Jack, that will be a welcome change from when you used to call me kid. I'd like you to meet my wife, Maddy. I've told her how we used to do liquor business."

"I am very pleased to meet you, Mrs. Novac." Tony Cornero takes her hand in both of his. "Has Jack told you all of my terrible past?"

Maddy smiles radiantly looking into Cornero's eyes. "Why, no Mr. Cornero, he said you were not a bad man for a gangster."

Cornero laughs heartily. "I like her, Jack. I know you're here for dinner but I'd like to give you some chips to use later."

"Thanks Tony. I'd like to have a word if you have some time."

"Sure thing, Jack, I'll make time after you eat."

Jack approaches the maitre d' passing him a ten-dollar bill. "I made reservations for Jack and Maddy Novac." The maitre d' carefully folds the bill with a practiced hand before it vanishes.

"Ah yes, Mr. Cornero has selected your meal and wine. You are to be his guests. Please come with me."

He takes Maddy's coat and Jack's hat away after they are seated.

"This is very nice, Jack," Maddy says. "Mr. Cornero must really like you."

"Uh yeah, he's either ridin' high or he wants something," Jack answers.

"What is ridin' high, Jack?"

"It just means he's doing well, maybe showin' off some. He's always been a man of grand gestures."

After a sumptuous meal, their waiter brings a bottle of fine champagne. Jack toasts Maddy, then excuses himself. After washing his hands, he exits the bathroom to return to the restaurant when he feels something roughly poke him in the back.

"You're a real dandy ain't you, Novac?"

Jack turns his head to see the gangster he laid out at the plant. "Hey, tough guy. I see they'll let anyone on this ship. You plannin' on shootin' me in front of all these people?"

"Naw, that ain't the plan but I will if you make me. You're a smart guy, ain't you? I just wanta see if you can swim to shore. Let's go on outside."

Jack walks ahead of the gangster trying to come up with a plan.

"Don't doddle. Head for that door bright boy," the gangster says playfully.

Jack turns toward the door, knowing he has to do something before they get outside. They go a few paces with Jack slowing his steps. Flexing his hands, he readies for the door: he'll have to use the door in some way to get away from the gangster.

"Keep stallin' if you wanta get it here." The gun barrel digs harder into his back. "You can swim, can't you bright boy?"

The door looms a few paces away when Jack hears a dull thud; gone is the pressure from the gangster's gun. Jack slowly turns to see the gangster slump to the floor.

"Help me get this drunk to the sick bay will you, mister?"

Jack lets out a breath. Tony Cornero grins as he kneels over the gangster, tucking a worn black leather sap away in his pocket.

"Get his gun will you, Jack?" Cornero says under his breath.

"I'll get a coupla boys to take the bum down to the storage room. Why don't you finish your dinner? I'll join you later."

"Thanks, Tony. I'm afraid I'll owe you for this. I don't know what I've got to repay you."

"It's okay, Jack. I've found it never hurts to have a favor owed. Don't worry, you're not gonna regret it." Tony cuffs Jack's shoulder. "You can depend on that."

Jack watches as two men in wide-lapelled suits materialize to whisk the woozy gangster away. Cornero gives Jack a jaunty salute and returns to the gambling tables. Novac looks around for someplace to leave the gangster's gun, then jams it in his pocket before returning to Maddy.

Maddy looks relived as Jack approaches the table. "I thought you started gambling without me."

Jack squeezes Maddy's shoulder before sitting down. On his way back to the table, he decided that he would tell Maddy the truth about being waylaid.

"I got nabbed by the gangster that was giving trouble at the plant. He stuck a gun in my back and was gonna try and make me jump off the ship. Cornero appeared like magic and knocked the guy out. I was thinkin' the guy was lucky you weren't there. You'd a hurt 'im a lot worse."

Maddy sighs in mock exasperation. "Jack Novac, I do not know what to do with you. A trip to the bathroom on a ship out in the sea and you find trouble. I really must keep a better watch on you."

Jack wiggles his eye brows in his best Nick Charles/ William Powell imitation while he pours champagne into their glasses. "That's fine by me, mommy."

Maddy nods toward the restaurant entry. "There is your friend."

Tony Cornero stops to speak to the maitre d', then proceeds to their table. He sits down facing Jack and Maddy.

"Here I am with the world-famous Jack Novac. I've been readin' about your adventures in the papers. I kinda wondered at times if the guy I was readin' about was the same kid I sold liquor to. You've come a long way, Jack. From winnin' Indy to fightin' Nazis man to man. I hear you've got a big new building in Culver City."

Cornero thumbs back the brim of his hat. "So, what can I do for my friend?"

Jack raises his wine glass in a salute to Cornero. "Well, first let me say thank you for the fantastic meal and then for the rescue. You seem to be doin' pretty well yourself."

Maddy reaches across the table to pat Cornero's hand. "I would also like to thank you on both accounts, Mr. Cornero."

"Your sentiment is certainly a fine reward, ma'am," Tony says.

"What I'd like to find out," Jack says, "is what you might know about the guys that are tryin' to shake me down. The guy you sapped came to my plant workin' the protection racket. Some of the stuff I'm doin' is for the government so shakin' me down is a dumb act. I took the guy's gun and driver's license to the FBI. I'm wonderin' if the guy's a loose cannon or part of an outfit?"

Cornero pulls his eyes from Maddy to rest on Jack's face.

"I'm sure you've heard of Hollywood's new gangster darling, Benny Siegel. The man I tapped is part of his crew. I thought he was here to watch my action and report to Benny. Siegel has been trying to horn in but hasn't got enough muscle yet. He's part of the mob back east with Lucky Luciano and Meyer Lansky.

"Don't think he's dumb, Jack; they don't call Siegel "Bugsy" 'cause he swats flies. He's," Cornero pauses to look at Maddy, then continues. "put a lotta guys down, and hasn't been convicted of any murders yet. My advice is to keep your distance."

The conversation stops when a waiter comes to the table to pour each of them an expensive cognac in fine crystal glasses.

Jack lifts the glass to his nose, then takes a sip. "You have outdone yourself, Tony, this is fantastic. The food, the ship, all first class; I hope you can keep it."

"If you mean the DA, I beat him once in court. I'm three miles out in international waters; the guy ain't got no legal right to hassle me. On the other hand, when Benny gets tired of milkin' Hollywood's finest he may take another run at me. He's got some county cops on his payroll, but he lives big, attracts a lotta attention. Lansky doesn't like that, but Lucky is staying away since

MIKE DOWNS

the Thelma Todd thing. So, while he's without the heavy hitters, I'm okay for now."

Maddy has watched the two men talk without interrupting. The mention of Thelma Todd has her wanting to know more. She looks from Jack to Cornero.

"Does this Lucky man have something to do with the movie star, Thelma Todd's, death?" she asks. "I read in the papers her mother claims Thelma was murdered."

Cornero takes a sip from his glass; his expression changes from enjoyment to a grimace, having to speak about subject that is without any enjoyment for him.

"There's been talk of the cops covern' up what happened. The Hollywood rags say Thelma liked rough men an' Luciano likes it rough. Her mother has a whole list a guys that coulda had reason to kill her. I don't like bums involving women in mob business. Luciano and Siegel'll take a fall one a these days, Lansky's the only one that's liable to skate."

Cornero seems to have had enough of the current conversation. He sets the empty glass of cognac down and stands up holding out his arms in a grand gesture. A smile returns to his face.

"Come on, you two. Let's go have a good time. The SS *Rex* is a good-time ship; it's time to go spin the wheels of lady luck."

Chapter 12

The gentle rocking of the water taxi in the early Sunday morning ride back to Santa Monica put Maddy to sleep, her head resting on her husband's shoulder. Jack shrugged the gangster's gun from his pocket to drop it in the water. Back at home, the sun is high by the time they knuckle the sleep from their eyes. Jack slips from under the covers to go make coffee. Maddy in a robe and slippers, pads across the Spanish tile floor to commandeer the kitchen, banishing Jack to the living room to read the thick Sunday morning newspaper.

Cooking smells has Jack's stomach growling, he puts down the paper to join Maddy in the kitchen. Maddy dishes eggs scrambled with peppers, and onions on plates with fried potatoes.

Jack pours coffee in his cup and sits down at the table. "Wow, that smells good. My stomach's growlin' like mad."

MIKE DOWNS

Maddy sets the plates down, then goes back to the coffee pot to pour a cup for herself before returning to the table.

"I had a good time last night, Jack, even with the drama. Dinner was very elegant and delicious. Your Mr. Cornero is a smart man; he has given the ship a very Monte Carlo kind of atmosphere. The people were interesting, too: movie stars in fancy dress, gangsters, and everyday folks all mixed together and having a good time. By the way, you were winning a lot of money to begin with, how much did you lose?"

"I lost $200 dollars. That's what I figure the meal and the $100 dollars in chips Tony gave us came to. I don't want to be too beholdin' to Cornero. You never know when he'll want to collect a favor. He could put me in a bad place if he gets squeezed. I'm sure he knows all about my government connections.

"He's supposed to be makin' $300,000 bucks a month on that ship. I hope he takes the money and runs when the DA closes him down. I'm pretty sure he'll be callin' when they close in on 'im. I had a hell of a time losin' that dough. That's why I went to the Black Jack table and kept gettin' more cards to go bust."

"Do you think he will know what you lost?" Maddy asks.

Jack grins at her. "Oh yeah, he'll know to the penny."

Maddy puts down her coffee cup and smiles back at Jack. "What about the man who tried to make you swim? Will he, um, hurt him?"

"Nah, thatta'd be bad business. Tony'll probably feed the guy a good breakfast before he puts him on a boat to go home. He doesn't wanta start a war with the Luciano mob."

The phone rings and Maddy goes to answer it.

"That was Mother. She wanted me to take her shopping today but her friends in the Palisades are forming a book club. She wants to help them get started. I don't want to sit at home alone today, Jack. Can I go with you to the airport?"

Jack pauses with his fork full of eggs to answer. "You bet! As a matter a fact, I've been wantin' to take you up in a Beechcraft Staggerwing that I rent. It's a honey of a plane, big engine, fast and comfortable. After I meet with the Caltech boys, we'll fly up the coast to Santa Barbara, have dinner and be home before dark."

Jack drives them to Clover Field off Ocean Park Avenue where, even on a Sunday, the place is busy. Scotty waves from outside of the Douglas plant where he and another man wait for the couple to join them.

"Hi, Mr. Novac," Scotty says. "This is Ben Jackson."

Jackson is a medium height, heavy-set man, with horn-rimmed glasses. He rather shyly extends his hand to Jack.

"Hi ya, Ben." Jack shakes the man's surprisingly firm hand.

"Scotty, Ben, this is my wife, Maddy.

Maddy has already captured the Caltech men's attention. She is wearing tan slacks, a white blouse, and a brown sweater with the sleeves tied loosely around her neck. She smiles brightly shaking both men's hands.

Jack watches the two men fidget while steeling glances at Maddy.

"Is there someplace we can talk?" Jack asks. "I've got a list of design parameters that I'd like to show you both."

Scotty elbows Ben. "Um, yes, of course," Ben stammers. "There's a little office in the parts hangar we can use." He points to a small wood-framed building. "It's right over there."

"I'll meet you guys there," Jack says. "I'm gonna take Maddy over to the flight school to meet Ross. We're gonna take the Stag up later."

Jack walks with Maddy toward the west end of the airfield. When they get out of earshot of the two Caltech men, Jack puts his arm around Maddy's shoulder.

"Those kids can't take their eyes off you, not that I blame 'em. But I need those guys to pay attention to me today."

"I want to be a part of this undertaking with you, Jack," Maddy says.

"You will be, Maddy, and I'm lookin' forward to doin' this with you. I'd like you to meet Ross anyway. I know I talked to you about him when I was gettin' flight lessons from him. The guy's a pilot's pilot. He puts you at ease as soon as you get in a plane with him."

They walk into the flight school office that has pictures of early aircraft lining the walls. Two pictures are of a young man in uniform grinning into the camera standing beside a WWI airplane.

Jack points to the picture. "That's Ross in the picture; he was an ace in the great war."

Jack knuckles the counter. "Hey, Ross, you asleep man?"

A middle-aged man with a slight paunch comes to the counter from a back room.

"Jeez, Novac, you could wake the dead. Oh, hi, Maddy…er, Mrs. Novac. My, oh, my, your picture doesn't do you justice. How'd a fine lookin' woman like you get hooked up with a rascal like, Novac?"

Maddy looks at Jack, then asks Ross. "You have my picture?"

"No, no, nothin' like that ma'am." Ross holds up his hands defensively as his face colors. "Jack always puts your picture by the instrument panel when he flies."

"Maddy this is Ross Elmore. Best damn flight instructor…" Jack stops and grins, "on this airfield."

Ross comes to the counter to shake hands. "Best damn flight instructor in the world is more like it...buddy."

Maddy shakes hands. "Thank you for telling me about the picture, Ross. I didn't know Jack did that."

"Ross, can I leave Maddy with you while I talk to the two eggheads I told you about? I won't be gone long. Show her the Stag will you? I can trust you to act like a gentleman for that long, can't I?"

"Get the hell outta here, Novac. Your wife will be fine here and you know it."

"Okay, okay," Jack raises his hands in surrender. "I'm goin'."

Scotty and Ben are looking over a drawing table when Jack enters the building. As Jack moves to the table, he sees pictures of aircraft taped across it. He places his notebook on the table and opens it to a typed page.

"Okay, men, here's what I've got. This is gonna be a one-off plane that will mainly be used for testing instrumentation, but I also wanta race it. What I want is the best plane possible. I have specs for the Curtiss P40 that we can go over later. We have a budget of $65,000.00 dollars, which doesn't include the engine, to complete the plane and I will be making sure we stick to that.

"My design criterion is to spend the time necessary to make the build as simple as possible. I don't want a complicated structure. A good engineer will find simplicity over complexity is always the best design. To that end I have a few parameters: the craft will be an all-metal construction monoplane with flush riveting."

Jack looks up from the notebook to see the eager faces of the men nodding happily.

"It will have a single V-12 inline water-cooled engine. I want it to be light weight, have a low frontal area, retractable landing gear, and be highly maneuverable. The wing has to have a high load rating. We need to design the construction to be easy and simple and with an eye out for ease of maintenance.

"I'm not Howard Hughes so I'm serious about the budget. On the other hand, when you need a decision, you'll get it. I won't meddle unless I see something I can't deal with. So, are we good?"

Scotty is the first to speak. "Do we have a place to work?"

"Yes," Jack answers. "I've rented the back of Ross's place, and when we get to the build, I've got some of the best racecar metalworkers in the business to help us."

"When can we get started?" Ben asks.

"Now would be good," Jack says. "I'll pay for the design work, and after we agree on it, we'll go ahead with the build. I don't wanta go hog wild here. I want a good solid plane we can all be proud of. I'll leave the P 40 specs and prints with you but please don't let 'em out of your sight. They're not classified but I promised I wouldn't spread 'em around, okay?"

"Yes, sir," Scotty says. "Ben and I are both really looking forward to this. Thanks for the opportunity."

"That goes for me too, Mr. Novac," Ben says. "I do have some questions I would like to ask."

"Fire away, Ben," Jack says.

"Why are you using a V-12 liquid-cooled engine? Why all metal, and why racecar metalworkers?"

"In answer to your first two questions, our plane will be evaluated by the Army as prototypical for future fighters. V-12's are making good power now and have a smaller frontal area than a radial engine. All metal means it can take more punishment as it is inherently stronger for the weight than wood and fabric according to the Army.

"Racecar metalworkers because they have been shaping metal for decades and they are used to small runs, or one offs. They also know the riveting and welding techniques we need. These guys are tough men who are used to long hours and gettin' the job done."

Ben looks at Scotty, then, with some reluctance, seems to have to gather himself to question Novac. "Will they be…um, hard to manage?"

Jack grins back at Ben. "You don't look like a head-knocker Ben, so if it comes to that I'll take care of any problems with 'em. Let's take a look at the P40 stuff, then I need to take off. I'm lookin' forward to your designs."

Ross and Maddy walk out onto the airfield to a brilliant yellow airplane. The sleek-looking plane is bi-winged, the lower wing forward of the upper wing hence the stagger-wing title, or Stag for short. Ross opens the door for Maddy to look inside. The interior is in beautiful brown leather with duel controls and impeccably clean. The sun has warmed the interior bringing out the rich scent of leather.

"This is a beautiful machine, Ross. You must be very proud of it."

Ross' face lights up with pride. "I am very proud of her, Mrs. Novac. She brings me a lot of happiness, not to mention a mighty nice income."

"Please call me Maddy, Ross."

Ross' smile grows. "I'll be pleased to, ma'am. Don't you let ol' Jack scare you, Maddy," Ross points up at the sky. "I know he'll try some fancy stuff to impress you up there."

A frown of concern crosses Maddy's forehead. "Do you think him dangerous, Ross?"

"No, that's not what I mean at all. The guy's a natural; he's got a feel for flyin' few people have. He knows what the plane's gonna do before it does. He's a damn good pilot ma'am; the problem is he knows it."

The frown lines on Maddy's face disappear. "He was a damned good racing driver before that was taken from him, Ross. He is like the American movie cowboy, full of himself, but I can sometimes rein him in."

"It's good to know someone can, ma'am," Ross says.

Maddy watches Jack stride across the airfield toward them. He smiles confidently, Maddy's heart swells, as for an instant she remembers his broken body lying before her in Berlin. Jack seems to sense her pain. He quickens his pace to encircle her in his arms and kiss her cheek.

Jack feels Maddy tremble slightly and looks over at Ross who is embarrassed to be odd man out. Jack smacks Ross' shoulder. "We'll be back before dark, Ross. I'll take good care of the Stag."

He takes Maddy's hand to lead her back to the plane. "Are you ready for a deluxe trip to the skies with your favorite captain of the air?"

"I am ready, Cowboy." Maddy turns to Ross, her eyes glistening. "Thank you, Ross. I will make

105

sure the wild one behaves with your beautiful baby."

The 450-horsepower radial engine quickly pulls them into the sky. Jack rocks the plane side to side, then sets the throttle forward to power north.

Jack raises his voice to be heard over the roar of the engine. "This baby'll do over 200 miles an hour, so it's a short flight to Santa Barbara. I'm gonna go east to show you the mountains, then the desert. From up here you get a good idea of how diverse California is. We'll come back down the coast; it's really something to see when the sun is low."

Maddy enjoys the sensation of speed and the clear view of the landscape. Her grin reflects Jack's as they bank back northwest to Santa Barbara. Jack has the plane in level flight near the coast out of any turbulent air.

"Take the wheel in your hands, Maddy."

She looks over at Jack, her eyes questioning.

"Go on, it's okay. You can get a feel of what it's like to fly."

Maddy tentatively takes the wheel in front of her, smiles at Jack, then focuses forward. She feels the vibration of the engine through the wheel. The plane immediately responds to any small movements of the wheel. After a few minutes she relaxes her grip on the wheel to enjoy the sensation of flying. When she gains the confidence to look over at Jack, he is sitting back in his seat, grinning wolfishly with hands behind his head.

The plane's nose drops, and Jack's hands instantly come away from his head. Maddy very gently pulls the wheel back toward her to bring the nose up. She then looks over at Jack. "You want me to land it, too?" she says, smiling proudly.

After a seafood dinner in Santa Barbara, they fly back south above the coastline. A sinking sun glorifies the colors of rugged shoreline, small villages, orange groves and vineyards on their return to Clover Field.

Back at home, Jack and Maddy sit quietly listening to the radio. During a commercial, Maddy goes to the kitchen to return with two glasses of red wine.

"I had a lovely weekend, Jack," she says handing Jack a stemmed glass. "The more I see of California, the more I understand why you love it here." She sips from the wine glass, looking at Jack over the rim. "So, when can I start taking lessons from Ross? You knew I would want to, didn't you?"

"I hoped you would," Jack says. "It's something we can share. There are places all over the state we can fly to in a day. Why don't I ask Ross if we can take the Stag to Lake Arrowhead next weekend? Would you like that?"

"Only if you let me try the rudder pedals," Maddy replies.

Chapter 13

The following week goes by in a rush. After Jack returns from the long Lake Arrowhead weekend with Maddy, he is recharged and eager to get back to work. Sitting at his desk, he relaxes with a morning coffee. As he watches the steam rise from the cup, he thinks of Maddy in her hiking gear enjoying the clean crisp mountain air.

She loved the forest; pine trees left a heavy scent that seemed to free her of any dark thoughts. Jack reaches down now to rub his calf. They had walked for miles around the lake until his breath had come in heavy billows in the chilled air. Maddy turned to him, smiling into his face. "Has the cowboy had enough?"

Jack grins behind his desk, raising the coffee cup to take a drink, savoring the rich flavor. Mori enters the office and sits in a low-backed chair across from Jack.

"How was your weekend, boss?"

"We had a good time, Mori. Maddy walked my legs off, but she really enjoyed the mountains. I think it reminded her of hiking in Germany when she was a kid. All that walkin' was more exercise than I've had in a while. I ate a huge steak one night that I gobbled up and wanted more. What did you and the missus do?"

"We went to Gilmore Stadium Saturday to see a dog show. I talked Dot into staying to watch the midget races. I'm glad it was a clean race day. Nobody got hurt and we both really got a kick out of the show those boys put on."

"Was that Dot's first race?" Jack asks.

"Yeah, you know the papers have been full of horror stories about midget racers getting killed. The danger of the thing, I have to admit, is in itself a thrill, but I don't want to see them getting hurt. Those guys drive hard, man."

Jack shakes his head. "If the do-gooders manage to kill midget racing here, the guys'll just go somewhere else. Most a those guys are tryin' to make a livin' racin'; it's in their blood. Before I get too riled up, what's on the plate for today?"

"Bill Robbins will be in today before lunch," Mori says.

Jack looks up from his note pad. "I didn't expect him. Does he want me to pick him up at the airport?"

"No," Mori replies. "He called Friday, and I told him you were out of town. He asked if you would be back today; I said you would be available before lunch. Harry Van will be in this afternoon. He said he spoke with you at an air show about making instrument panels for his planes."

"Yeah, that's right, I remember him. I think it would be good for us to able to be able to provide the whole instrument panel. We could make 'em for the small plane manufacturers with the basic six-pack instruments, to the more complicated ones for the big commercial guys. Van's job would help us pay for the tooling we'd need to buy. I'd like to have the boys make the entire panel, with gauges, wiring, lights, switches, ready to go.

"We're pretty busy now, Jack," Mori quickly adds.

"Yeah, I know Mori, but if war starts I want us to do our part. Airpower will decide the victor and small specialized manufacturers like us will be called on to perform like never before."

"Okay, Jack, we've got a good profit margin this year, we can afford it. Maybe I'm just too conservative or just afraid of this war everybody's going on about. I hope it doesn't happen."

"I hope so too, Mori, but look at what's happening in Japan and Germany right now. They want the world and will commit any crimes to get what they want. Get ready, be prepared: that's what I think's the best policy."

Mori solemnly nods his head. "I hate reading about what the Japanese are doing to the Chinese, but that's not our war damn it." Agitated, Mori turns to leave, waving his hand in the air. "I'll leave you to your paperwork."

Jack is hunched over the paperwork on his desk when Bill Robbins comes in.

"Hey, Bill, good to see you." Jack comes around his desk to shake hands. "So, what brings you to town?"

"I just wanted to see how the golden people are doing. You've got sun, beaches, sea, and movie stars. What more could you ask for?"

"Yeah, we've got it all, Bill." Jack goes back to his desk. "Take a load off, have a seat."

Bill pushes the office door closed before pulling a high-backed upholstered chair close to Jack's desk. Slouching down in the chair, his legs drawn up, he seems on edge.

Jack gives Bill a quizzical look. "Somethin' eatin' you, Bill?"

"No Jack, you know I'm just more comfortable with the door closed. I've got some news for your ears only, and the next installment for your plane."

Jack clears the paperwork on the desk to shove it in his out-box. "Okay, Bill, I'm all ears."

"First of all, the Army wants you to use an Allison engine. Stay calm, Jack, let me finish. The deal I made is that they put some money in and provide the engine. They'll leave you alone, so you can play with the engine to get what horsepower you can out of it.

"Actually, I think that's pretty smart for those guys. They get to find out what kind of power you can get out of the Allison, without a government contract and all the red tape, plus you'll get it done a lot faster. You'll have the engine this

111

week. I took time this weekend to talk with the Offy boys. They'd be six, eight months at best to deliver an engine and it would be a one-off. Then you'd have to make it work.

"So, you've got an engine and money…"

The office door crashes in, swinging back on its hinges, slamming, with a bang, against the wall. A broad-shouldered man, dressed in a loud sport coat, barges into the office. A broad-brimmed hat shades a handsome but deadly menacing face. He stops his march a pace from the desk, his eyes boring into Jack with murderous intensity.

"I'm Ben Siegel, and nobody gets away with roughin' up my boys. You're gonna pay double the goin' rate or I'll plug you where you sit, you two-bit pissant."

"You don't want to do that, Benny."

Startled, Siegel snaps his head around to see Bill Robbins seated in the chair.

"What the hell are you doin' here, Robbins? This ain't got nothing to do with you. It'd be best to keep your nose outta my business."

"Benny, Benny, this is my business. Trying to extort a defense contractor, not to mention a personal friend of mine, will finally put you behind bars. That's a federal crime, Ben, and not very smart. Tellin' a man you're going to shoot him when he has a gun trained on you is not smart either."

Jack lays a heavy-framed pistol on the desk top.

Siegel advances toward the desk. "Gimme that," he demands, his hand out to take it. "Nobody pulls a gun on me, pissant."

Jack picks the pistol up, pointing it at the gangster's face. Siegel stops, his eyes glowering down at Jack.

Jack returns the look, cocking the pistol's hammer. "Only if you wanta see how big a hole it makes."

Robbins gets up from the chair to face Siegel. "Be smart, Ben, we just ran you outta New York. You can keep doing business here if you keep your nose clean. If anything happens to Jack or his business, I'll bring the whole federal government down on you. That's a promise. You're too smart for this racket, man. You've got the looks and the personality to make it big in a legitimate business. The Hollywood crowd is at your feet; they could bankroll it."

"I don't like havin' a gun pulled on me."

Jack lays the pistol down again. "I don't like bein' shot. I see you came loaded for bear. That's a damned big bulge under your arm."

Siegel, for a second, seems to be at a loss for words. "Why'd you bust up my man, Novac?"

"Didn't he tell you he sucker punched me first? I'm not liable to lay down for that."

"That's not what he told me. How 'bout on the boat?"

Jack shakes his head. "He stuck a gun in my back and said he was gonna make me swim. The next thing I know is he's lyin' on the ground, then two guys drag 'im off."

"Who hit him? Cornero?" Siegel asks.

"I didn't see who hit the guy. I'm just happy they did," Jack replies.

"Let it go, Ben," Robbins says. "I mean what I say. If any harm comes to Jack or this business, I'll call in the cavalry."

Siegel pulls his eyes from Jack to bore in on Robbins. "You're right about one thing, Robbins. This guy's penny ante shit. I'm wastin' my time."

Without another word, Siegel leaves, cleaving a path through the crowd of people in the hallway.

"Whew." Robbins passes the back of his hand over his brow as if wiping sweat away. "When did you get that cannon, Jack?"

"I bought it new a coupla weeks ago, I haven't even shot it yet. It's Smith and Wesson's .357 magnum. The gun's got hell of a lot more power than a .45, and I'd be willin' to bet that's what Benny had under his arm."

"Well, you're right to be cautious," Robbins says. "He's been implicated in a dozen murders and no one's been able to pin a thing on him. We had him on a murder charge in New York that could have stuck but the witness...died."

Jack thumbs the hammer down on the pistol. "He's a tough lookin' guy all right, but I've seen guys at some little bullring racetracks that'd eat 'im for lunch."

Mori comes in sheepishly looking around the office.

Jack grins at Mori and winks at Robbins. "Lose somethin', Mori?"

"No, I just wanted see if there was any blood on the carpet. That was Ben Siegel, the big east coast gangster, wasn't it?"

"The man himself," Jack says. "You can tell everyone you've seen 'im in person."

"What did he want?" Mori asks.

"He came to have Bill tell him how smart and handsome he is, and to see my new gun. He got bored and left."

Jack locks the gun in the desk, then gets up to smack Robbins on the shoulder. "Come on, Bill, I'll treat you to lunch."

Chapter 14

When Jack arrives at the plant the next morning, he settles into his chair with a heavy sigh. Mori comes into the office with purchase orders, taking a moment to look over his boss before speaking.

"Ah, rough night, boss?"

Jack looks up at Mori, his eyes red from lack of sleep. "Well, I'm here, Mori. That's as good as it's gonna get today. The night's festivities with Robbins didn't go as planned. Maddy was gonna make dinner for Robbins but he reminded me I'd promised him a night on the town. We had dinner at the Brown Derby before going across Wilshire to the Coconut Grove and that's where it all went south.

"Bill's been under a lotta strain runnin' the cloak and dagger department back east and I guess he just wanted to let his hair down. We had beer at lunch, then wine with dinner. Bill started on those

116

rum fruit drinks at the Grove and kept orderin' more of 'em. Turns out Sonja Henie was havin' a birthday party and Bill's a big fan, so to make a long story short, we got thrown out.

"By the time Maddy and I got him back to our place, he was sick as a dog. Maddy an' I spent the rest of the night tryin' to keep Robbins from throwin' up all over the house. I'm glad I started orderin' club sodas early in the evening. Maddy's takin' care of him now and not very amused. We owe the guy, but we're thinkin' the debt's about paid up. I'm takin' him to the airport tonight, so he'll be outta our hair, an' back in New York."

Mori clucks his displeasure. "Well," Mori waves a folder in the air. "Can we look at these purchase orders?"

"Sure, we can go over that stuff in a minute. I'm gonna go shave and get some coffee."

Jack looks better on his return: he brings a pot of coffee back with him and he and Mori spend the morning pouring over the purchase orders. Hours later Jack arches his back, spreading his arms wide.

"Okay, Mori, we're good on all that stuff except the vacuum pumps. I don't wanta use that company anymore, we've had too many problems with their stuff. I've got another company in mind but I wanta talk to 'em first. Let's get some lunch; I'm thinkin' that hot dog place at the beach."

Scotty raps on the door frame. "Do you have a minute, Mr. Novac?"

"Sure, Scotty, I was just on the way to get hot dogs at that place on the beach. You wanta come along?"

"You bet," Scotty says, unable to conceal his excitement. "We can meet Ben there if it's all right with you. We've got the plans ready for the plane."

Jack rubs his hands together; a wide grin spreads across his face. "Yeah, that's what I've been waitin' for; you go call 'im, then we'll go."

"Dot made me lunch, Jack; I'm going to eat here okay?" Mori asks.

"Sure thing, Mori, I'll call if I'm gonna be late gettin' back."

Jack drives at a quick pace to meet Ben at the little hot dog shack on the beach. A salty wind coming in from the Pacific blows sand and trash around the tables outside of the hot dog shack keeping the lunch business to a minimum.

"Let's order and go back to Clover Field. It's too windy here to look at your drawings," Jack says.

In the hangar behind Ross Elmore's, Ben spreads out his drawing plans on a bench top.

Jack rewraps his hot dog laying it down a corner of the bench. He hunches over one of the drawings, then lifts the top drawing to see the one under it that denotes mechanical features. His finger traces lines of control cables. Scotty and Ben have not touched their food, both men watch Jack anxiously waiting for some sign of his thoughts.

118

Jack reaches for the hot dog without taking his eyes away from the drawings. He unwraps the food, then steps back from the bench to take a bite. He looks over at the two men. "You guys aren't eatin', your dogs are gonna get cold. Go ahead, eat; I like what I see. You guys did a lotta detail work that shows good engineering. Oh, and before I forget, we'll have an Allison engine this week."

Both men grab their hot dogs and tear open the wrappers.

Jack grins as the men chew furiously, then points at the drawings. "I want the fuselage as tight to the engine as possible and from there back narrow in section with a simple shape. The aluminum skins will be full sheets down the length, flush riveted. The plane needs to be as stiff as you can make it. I wanta feel every vibration the machine sends.

"The main wing needs to removable without disassembling the central structure. If we need to change wing profiles or lengths, I don't wanta tear the whole thing apart. The radiator and oil coolers will be under the wing with low drag ducting. I like the P40's cockpit but without the high metalwork behind the seat. We want it lightweight but very rigid—no wing buffeting."

Ben gulps down the last of his lunch. "We've got an engine? I thought it'd be months before we had one. We're really going to do it, Mr. Novac?"

Jack grins, then winks at Scotty. "You can bet your butt on it, Ben. We'll have a brand-new

Allison engine, maybe this week. You're up for it, aren't you?"

Ben glances over at Scotty, then squares his shoulders trying to look confident. "You bet I'm up for it, Mr. Novac. It may be a little heavier than you want, at first, but once we prove it in the air, we can pare some off it. I'd rather build it with a safety margin than risk a failure."

Jack lightly punches Ben's shoulder. "That does make good sense, Ben. I don't wanta fall outta the sky, but I wanta be fast."

Will the Allison engine give enough power?" Ben asks. "I think it's only rated for about 900 to 1000 horsepower. The German record planes have got over 2000 horsepower."

"Me, and, I hope, Carl Sanders, my mechanic from the Miller days, will be working on the engine as soon as it gets here. I'm hoping with hot fuel and lots a supercharger boost, we can make big power for short bursts. The Allison is a good design, a strong bottom end and good cylinder heads. For low altitude races and records I think we can make it work.

"Let me know what you need to get started. I don't want to invest in heavy machinery, so that work will get subbed out. When you complete the final drawings, I can do some machine work at my plant. The Allison engine should take a lotta guess work outta the project, so we're ahead a the game there."

"I need to hire a model maker," Ben says. "We need to have a scale model to put in Caltech's wind tunnel first thing. That will determine the final design." Ben nods to Scotty. "A few of our professors are interested in this project and are willing to help us with their time and knowledge."

"I'll write you a check," Jack says, "when I get back to the plant. Just let Scotty know how much you need. I'd like to see the wind tunnel, and how our plane is evaluated in it. That technology is very interesting to me. Meetin' your professors would be good, too. I hope we'll be doin' more business with 'em in the future."

One hand casually steering the car, Jack glances over at Scotty on the way back to the plant. "You look worried Scotty. Something wrong?"

Scotty's lips thin, his jaws set in decision. "What do you think about Communism?" he asks.

Jack lets out a breath. "If you're thinkin' a joinin' up, you're not gonna like my answer. I can see why people think it's a better way of life when they're down an' out in this damned depression. It does surprise me that some highbrows are talkin' like it's a good idea.

"The theory of Communism in my opinion is for people that lack ambition. Regardless of that, what I see in real practice makes it pretty grim. Writers and poets keep harpin' on Russia, but if you read the news, Stalin's killin' thousands of people over there. Russian workin' class is starvin' when the Communists here are preachin' that all Communists are the same class and treated and cared for equally. No, I don't buy it. Fat cats will always rule the roost."

Scotty looks over at Novac, with a shy smile forming. He notices that the car is going by telephone poles lining the edge of the road at a much faster rate. Novac, while still steering with a relaxed hand, has a determined jut to his chin. "I see you're not reluctant to share your opinion."

"No, I'm not," Jack says. "Maybe that was too much up on the soap box, but I'm tired of hearing the Communist line. I've seen first-hand what happens when fanatics take over a country."

Jack, realizing the car's excessive speed, looks up at the rear view mirror, relaxing the pressure on the gas pedal. He glances over at Scotty. "You're grinnin', so what's the deal?"

"You asked me to let you know about who is behind the rumor mill at the plant," Scotty answers. "It's not gangsters that are trying to get in, it's one man who's a Communist party member. He's preaching to anyone that'll listen."

Crunching across the gravel at the curb, Jack turns into the driveway of his plant, parks and shuts off the engine. "I don't want one bad apple spoilin' the rest of our employees. Whatta you think of this guy? You wanta keep 'im on?"

Scotty rubs one hand over a clinched fist. He watches his hands as if they belong to someone else, then answers. "I have talked to him several times, Mr. Novac. His work suffers from inattention; he's more interested in his Communist activities than work. I think it's time to let him go."

"That's good enough for me, Scotty. I'll go up to the office and bring Mori in; he can cut a check and you can have the guy come see me at the end of the day. Your department is very important to this business; we need bright people in a good environment that are dedicated to our innovations. So, let me know if there are any more disruptions."

"I don't think there will be any more problems, Mr. Novac," Scotty says. "The rest of the men are all good workers. We all understand the value of having a good job that pays well in these times. Ben and I are really excited about building your airplane and the guys in my department will be, too."

Chapter 15

Jack puts down the report papers he has spent hours working on. As the business has grown so has the paperwork. The increase in government contracts tripled the amount of paperwork. He taps the papers square, then puts them neatly atop a corner of the desk.

Speaking into the intercom, he tells Mori to bring him the severance check and send up the man he has to fire. After a heated argument with the unruly young man, Jack has to call his security manager to escort the young man from the plant.

Fingering the intercom lever, Jack calls Mori.

"Mori, I've had it for the day. I'm gonna' go see the man at the vacuum pump company in El Segundo first thing in the morning. I'll be in before lunch, have a good evening."

"Okay Jack, sorry about the young man. I could hear him yelling from my office. See you tomorrow," Mori replies.

Jack's mood quickly lifts as he walks to his car. It is a warm cloudless Southern California day. A fresh wind has blown the L.A. basin clean. The San Gabriel Mountains are clear in the distance, some still with spots of white-capped snow. The raucous sound of a loud motorcycle blasting down Jefferson Boulevard spoils the moment of serenity.

The bright red machine must be going ninety; Jack hears the rider downshift and watches as the bike decelerates. The rider leans the bike over hard sliding his foot across the road to keep the bike upright. The exhaust note rises furiously, dust and gravel fly up from the bike's rear wheel as the rider jockeys to make it into Jack's parking lot.

The rider, bent over the handle bars, is headed right for him. Jack's head flashes back and forth, looking for the best place to dive out of the monster motorcycle's path. The rear wheel of the beast suddenly locks up, the big red machine, chrome flashing in the sun, screeches to stop just at Jack's feet. The rider pulls the goggles down, grinning at Jack like a mad man.

"Howdy, Pard, like my new machine?"

Jack smiles, shaking his head. "Jeez Carl, that's one hell of a entrance, I thought you were gonna run me down. I shoulda known it was you when I saw you dirt-track it in here. When did you get this beauty? L.A. ain't gonna be safe with you ridin' this bullet."

Carl Sanders worked alongside Jack during his entire auto racing career. Carl raced bicycles, then progressed to motorcycles as a teenager until he had a bad crash. He couldn't afford proper care for his broken leg which was badly set and left him with a permanent limp. He is still wickedly fast on a motorcycle and loves riding fast.

Jack takes his eyes off the bike to look at Carl. "You look like you've lost weight, Pard. There's somethin' else too; you either just got lucky or that bike's doin' you wonders."

Carl flicks the kick stand down with the heel of his boot. He grabs his pant leg to lift his bad leg over the seat. "I bought it for a song from a guy down on his luck. This is the fastest thing on two wheels; I had the cylinders bored out to give a little more power and just put it back together the other day."

"Man, she's somethin' Carl. I saw an ad for these Crocker bikes. They're really a masterpiece of style and engineering. Is Lulu mindin' the store? You're usually makin' your little burgers by the bushel about now for the dinner crowd."

"We just sold it for a ton a dough, Jack. You still need a wrench for your air racer?"

"You bet I do, Pard. I was just on my way home," Jack says. "You wanta come over to the house an' talk it over?"

"Sure thing, Jack, wanta race?"

"You gotta be kiddin', Carl. You'll be there before I've gone a coupla' blocks. Let me run back inside an' tell Maddy you're on the way over."

NOVAC'S WAY

***

Jack gets out of his car, admiring Carl's bike in his driveway, noting the way the bright chrome work reflects in the sun's late-day rays. He goes through the front door heading for the backyard. Carl and Maddy are sitting in the wicker chairs, drinking dark bottle beers. Maddy gets up to give Jack a kiss, then hands him cold bottle of their favorite Rainier beer.

Jack sits down and takes a sip of the cold beer. "So, what's the story, Carl? How come you sold the store?"

"Well, I'll tell ya, Jack, I did have some fun an' we did make some money. But I was gettin' bored stiff. I was puttin' on too much fat, an' tired a payin' out money ta all the creeps."

Jack stops, the bottle half way to his lips, to look at Carl. "Whatta ya mean, 'payin' out ta all the creeps?"

"When me an' Lulu first started, we were just makin' enough to pay the bills. Then we came up with the idea for the five cent mini burgers an' business took off. It didn't take long for the creeps to horn in. Health Department inspectors wanted a cut; cops started comin' in for free meals, lately tough guys were comin' in wantin' protection dough. Lulu beaned one a 'em I was tusslin' with, with a fry pan, then when the cops came, they wanted protection money too.

"We had an offer to sell from a guy that said he could take care a the guys tryin' ta muscle in. He wants to open a bunch more places like it an' said if we'd sell an' not tell people we came up the original idea, he'd pay big money. When the guy said 'big money', Lu grinned that goofy look a her's an' we sold it then an' there. We went to the guy's bank next day an' got cash money. I bought the Crocker the next day."

"Where is Lulu, Carl?" Maddy asks.

"She's managin' our friend Roy's restaurant downtown," Carl replies.

Jack looks to Maddy who knows what he is thinking and nods her approval.

"Why don't you give her a call an' you two have dinner with us?" Jack asks.

"Sounds good to me, Pard," Carl says. When Carl returns, he seems reluctant to talk. Jack and Maddy trade glances before Jack speaks.

"What's up, Pard? You look upset; everythin' okay with Lulu?"

Carl shuffles his feet before replying.

"Well, Jack, I really came to see you today 'cause—well, I was kinda' wonderin' if you'd be my best man."

Jack and Maddy both jump up from their chairs to congratulate Carl. Jack slaps him hard on the back, grinning ear to ear.

"Of course I will, Pard. I'll be delighted. You couldn't find a greater gal in the whole world."

"I'm so happy for both of you, Carl," Maddy exclaims. "Is Lulu going to be able come here for dinner? I haven't seen her for quite a while."

Carl, grinning like a maniac, nods his head yes. "She said she'll be here in a jiffy."

Maddy turns her head back on the way to the house. "I'll put some champagne in the ice box."

When she returns Maddy asks Carl if fish will be all right for dinner.

"That'd be perfect, Maddy. Me an' Lu are both tryin' to get rid a some a the fat we've put on. We've been eatin' rabbit food for seems like forever."

"Rabbit food?" Maddy's face contorts, her lips curling up. "Is that a diet food now? It sounds awful."

"Naw," Carl says, a big grin spreading across his face. "I mean we eat lots a salads, you know, green stuff like rabbits eat."

Maddy's hand covers her heart. "Thank goodness. I couldn't imagine you and Lulu eating those pet store rabbit pellets."

Jack chuckles before putting in his two cents. "I think Carl just likes pullin' your leg, Maddy. You shoulda seen the look on your face when he said rabbit food. So, when's the big event, Carl?" Jack asks. "Where are you two gonna tie the knot?"

"We may just go to the beach an' have one a them sidewalk preachers say some words. I just wanted you an' Maddy to be there 'cause I think that'd make Lu feel better about it, make it special, you know what I mean?"

Jack shoots Maddy a puzzled look. "Why do you wanta do that? I mean maybe it's none a my business but are you sayin' you don't wanta make it legal?"

"I'd like to do it right Jack, but Lu's got no birth certificate. I went to the county office an' the guy said, 'No birth certificate, no marriage license. Then he asks why I wanta marry some chink anyhow. I hate the way some people look down at Lu. She can work harder'n most men an' she's a lot more honest too.

"I just want somethin' nice an' simple. I want Lu to be happy an' have a great day. I don't care if it's legal or not, we've been livin' together for quite a while anyways. She's got no family an' neither do I, so we don't need a big fuss."

Jack's fist taps Carl's jaw playfully. "We're your family, Carl."

Maddy reaches out to Carl also. "You and Lulu will always be part of our family, Carl. My mother thinks the world of you and Jack's mother and father are grateful to you for all the years you brought their son home safely. I'm grateful to you for that, too. We both adore Lulu; I hope you will both think of us as family."

Jack squeezes Carl's shoulder. "How 'bout a real church wedding with all the trimmins'? I just happen to know a justice a the peace up in Monterey. I met 'im at a flight school an' he owes me a favor or two. His wife is Chinese an' they're both doin' what they can for the Chinese war relief effort.

"Maddy an' I can fly us all up there on a weekend; you can get married in a real church, all legal. We can stay at the Del Monte hotel, that's the deluxe place up there. I've been wantin' to take Maddy; we just haven't found the time. It's a beautiful place; lot's to see and do. If you and Lulu want to enjoy your honeymoon on your own, you can fly back with us Sunday evening, or come back later.

"You guys don't have to worry about trippin' over us. There's plenty for us to do. Maddy and I really enjoyed Steinbeck's Tortilla Flats novel: it's all about Monterey. I hear they're gonna make a movie of it, so it'll be interestin' to find the places he wrote about while we're there. I'll call the JP guy tomorrow and let you know when he can set it up, okay?"

"That sounds great, Jack. I'll tell Lu when she gets here."

Maddy goes into the house to answer the door bell and returns to the backyard with Lulu arm in arm. "Look who I found. Doesn't she look wonderful?"

Lulu looks bright and happy; she has lost weight and let her hair grow. Her pretty round face is framed by the shoulder-length straight black hair. The flower printed dress she wears is pure American in style. She carries a small patent leather purse that has the same high blue-black gloss as her hair.

"Jack, can you help me in the kitchen?" Maddy asks.

"Uh, sure Maddy." Jack gets out of his chair to hug Lulu then follows Maddy into the house.

"I thought we should give Carl and Lulu a minute to talk," Maddy says. "While you're here, you could peel some potatoes for me."

When Jack and Maddy return to the backyard they find Carl with his arms around Lulu who is smiling broadly and dabbing her reddened eyes with a hanky.

Carl looks perplexed; his eyes search the faces of his hosts. "She says she's cryin' cause she's so happy." Shaking his head, Carl continues, "Women are a mystery to me."

Jack laughs. With a brief glance at Maddy, his eyebrows arched, he turns his attention back to Carl. "They're a mystery to all mankind, Pard."

Maddy, arms crossed on her chest, smiles at Lulu before speaking to Carl. "You have never shed a tear when something grand happened to you?"

"Sorry, Maddy," Carl says. "The only time I can remember sheddin' a tear was when I was a kid an' tore up my leg after crashin' my motorcycle. The tear wasn't for me either, that bike was a mess."

Lulu lifts her head, light comes to her dark eyes. Her face radiates with a playful smile on her lips that she directs to Maddy. "You can't live with 'em and you can't live without 'em," she says.

Maddy arches her eyebrows at Jack laughing, then reaches out to Lulu.

"Let's go to the kitchen and talk while the men talk about engines. Jack can hardly wait for Carl start on the engine he got the other day."

At dinner Maddy and Lulu talk about fashion and movie stars. Maddy mentions that she read in the paper that a woman witness in a Los Angeles assault trial was threatened with arrest by the judge if she did not leave the court room. The woman dared to wear slacks.

Jack and Carl are still engrossed in their conversation about the Allison aircraft engine.

Lulu helps Maddy clear the dinner table after they eat. Maddy brings the now-chilled bottle of champagne for Jack to open. He pours four flutes of the golden bubbly. He and Maddy hold up their glasses to toast Carl and Lulu. Jack clinks his glass to Lulu's, then Carl's. Maddy joins in with her glass.

"Here's to you, Pard" Jack says. "I hope you have as much happiness with Lulu as I have with Maddy. You'll feel like you're the luckiest man alive."

After a flute of champagne, Carl yawns, pats his stomach and says it's time for them to leave.

"I'll meet you at the airport hangar for lunch tomorrow, Pard. I'm pretty anxious to see that engine. If we can have Offy make us some pistons, an' maybe rods, we can crank some more boost in it an' put some hot fuel in an' see what we get."

Jack shakes Carl's hand at the front door, then gives Lulu a hug. "Take care goin' home, you two."

Lulu hugs Maddy then walks to the motorcycle with Carl; she pulls him to her and kisses him before going on to her car. Carl's face goes red as he sees Jack and Maddy watching. Jack grins back at him and waves.

"I'll see you later, Carl. Try to stay outta trouble on that monster motorcycle."

Chapter 16

Jack wakes in the morning and reaches for Maddy. The covers on her side of the bed are thrown back and she is gone. As he heads to the bathroom, he hears typewriter keys clacking against paper. When he finishes shaving, Maddy comes to the doorway.

"Coffee is ready and I'm starting breakfast."

The smell of hot cakes is in the air and Jack's stomach growls. He hurries into his clothes and makes a beeline for the kitchen. Nuzzling Maddy's neck while she turns the hotcakes, he steps back, then pours a mug full of coffee. Maddy places a few hot cakes on a plate and takes them to the table. A wisp of sweet melting butter haze rises from the top of the cakes. The butter runs down the cakes onto the plate.

"Do you want grape jelly or syrup?" she asks.

"Jelly, please," Jack says.

Maddy brings her plate to the table, sits down and pours a little syrup onto her cakes.

"You make the world's best hot cakes," Jacks says chewing a mouth full. "Were you up all night?"

"No, I woke up about 5 o'clock with an idea for another chapter. I knew if I went back to sleep, I would lose it."

She looks up from her plate, processing another thought, a wrinkle on her brow.

"Sometimes I think I have a wonderful idea, but when I write it out it does not look as good as I thought it would."

Jack smiles at Maddy, reaching his hand out to touch hers.

"Well, I can see how that could happen, but your work is always good. I think it must be a tough one to write; you have a lotta emotion wrapped up in it. You don't have a deadline on this, so you can take your time and get it just the way you want. I hope it wakes some people up."

Maddy takes Jack's hand in hers. "I can have some underlying emotion, but it has to present facts. If it is too emotional people will not take it seriously. I have to *knuckle down* as you say and get the work done. I have a flying lesson this afternoon to look forward to, so I better get back to the typewriter."

Jack takes his plate to the sink then returns to the table to kiss Maddy. "I've gotta go to El Segundo this morning, but I'll be at Clover Field to meet Carl for lunch. If you're busy with your lesson I won't bother you. Have fun, okay?"

"I will," Maddy says. "I love flying. I'm so happy here, Jack, I'm so very lucky."

Jack winks, using his thumb to poke his chest. "I'm the one that's lucky, lady. See you later."

Jack drives down Vista Del Mar past sun–baked beaches and a sparkling Pacific Ocean on the way to visit the vacuum pump manufacturer in El Segundo. The offices of the plant are very close to the somewhat odorous oil refinery the town is named for. After outlining his concerns with the quality and delivery of the pumps Jack is satisfied with the plant owner's promises.

It is a little after 10 o'clock when Jack gets to his office. Mori and Scotty both are waiting for him.

Jack pauses before sitting behind his desk. "Whatta you guys up to?"

Scotty is the first to speak. "Someone stole our prototype gyro, Mr. Novac."

Jack hangs his coat on the back of his chair but does not sit.

"I'm listenin', Scotty, tell me about it."

"It's the finished demonstrator we made for you to take to the Army Air Force committee. Mr. Able and I both inspected the doors and locks here and found no evidence of a break-in. Someone had the keys to get in. Should we call the police?"

"Not yet," Jack says. "I know everyone that has keys and there's nobody that would steal from us. My keys are in my pocket. Where do you keep your keys, Mori?"

"Oh, come on, Jack, you don't think…?"

Jack waves his hand in dismissal. "No, I don't, Mori. I'm just tryin' to see if our keys could be somewhere that someone could get at 'em. How 'bout you, Scotty?"

Scotty's serious face clouds with anger. "I keep my keys in my locker when I'm at work. I guess it would have been easy to make a wax copy. We don't have locks on the lockers."

Jack watches Scotty's face. "And I take it you know who that somebody might be?"

"I think it was Mark Drum, Mr. Novac. I hate to say it, but it's got to be him. We just finished it and made a wood box with Novac Engineering lettering on the top. He knew we wanted it to be perfect. He didn't want to do the finish work on it because he said it was just for war-mongering elitists. I did the finish myself."

"That's the guy we just fired, isn't it?" Mori asks. "I'll call the cops."

"Hang on, Mori," Jack says. "Call that bank security alarm company your brother in-law works for. I shoulda put an alarm system in when we got those government contracts."

Mori nods in agreement. "I'll go call. What do we do about Mr. Drum?"

Jack sits down in his chair, opening a desk drawer to take out a writing pen. "Do you know where he lives, Scotty?"

"He's got a little house off Venice Boulevard in Mar Vista. I don't remember the address."

Mori stops on his way to the door. "I have it on his employment form. We better let the cops handle it, Jack."

Jack shakes his head. "If we do that there's no tellin' if we'll ever see the gyro again. I'll nose around tonight and see if he's still got it. If I don't find anything, we'll call the cops tomorrow. You guys can get back to work. I've got some stuff to catch up on before I head off to lunch."

Jack makes several phone calls; the first is to Bill Robbins in New York. Robbins is in good spirits and they laugh about crashing Sonja Henie's birthday party. He hangs up the phone satisfied that Robbins is back at it in New York and doing well. The other calls are to customers and vendors. He flicks down the lever on his intercom to tell Mori he is going out to Clover Field for lunch.

Ross is walking with Maddy to the Stag when Jack drives into Clover Field; they wave in passing. Jack watches as Maddy and Ross climb into the plane before heading to his hired hangar to meet Carl. The hangar's sliding doors are open, the sounds of wood cracking and splintering echo from within. Jack hurries around the corner to see Carl levering a crowbar under a section of the Allison engine crate.

When Carl catches sight of Jack he beckons for him to help. "I been starin' at this crate for an hour. Ross had a crowbar, so I went to work."

Jack gets his fingers behind the crate's side panel that Carl has levered back. He pulls hard, the nails securing the wood screech as Carl follows the opening with the crowbar until together they get the panel free. They both let the panel drop to the floor in their eagerness to see the engine.

The engine is a massive V-12 weighing almost 1400 pounds. Carl puts down the crowbar to reach into the crate. He runs a hand over the beautifully smooth surface of the long nose that supports the propeller shaft.

"It's bigger than I thought, but it's got a lot nicer finish than I expected. This crate's like a big Christmas present: I couldn't wait to rip it open. Besides I figured I'd work up an appetite, so you could buy me a big lunch."

Jack takes a moment looking over the engine. "I'll give you a hand gettin' the rest of the crate apart first, then we'll have a quick lunch. I've gotta scoot back to the plant and get some work done today."

Carl taps the top of the crate with the crowbar. "I was kiddin' about lunch, Pard. Lu made enough lunch for both of us. I got it in a lunch pail she bought for me. Gimme a hand gettin' the top a the crate off and I can take it from there."

With the top of the crate off the men sit on a bench out in the sun as Carl takes foil wrapped tacos and two bottles of beer out of his lunch pail.

"Lu says you get everything you need in a taco; meat, cheese, lettuce, onion, tomato, bread, or corn. She's got a way a makin' 'em different every day."

Jack takes a taco from Carl spreading the foil wrapper on his lap. "You're a lucky man, my friend. I called the J.P. I told you about. He's in Sacramento at a Chinese relief meeting, he'll be back in a coupla days. I won't let you down, Pard. You an' Lulu are gonna have a great wedding."

"Thanks, Jack, you've always been good to me. I don't forget that you know. I appreciate you and Maddy bein' good to Lu too. She told me Maddy's mom called to say that she an' Maddy were gonna make her weddin' dress. Lu's pretty damned excited."

"You know what I'm thinkin', Carl?"

"Not a clue, Pard."

Jack waggles his eye brows. "It'll be a Lulu."

Carl shakes his head. "Jeez, I shoulda known; eat your taco."

Jack takes a big bite out of the thick flour tortilla taco; juices splatter down on the foil. Carl looks over at Jack grinning, a little bit of lettuce on his front teeth.

"Like ol' times huh, Pard?"

Jack studies the face of his friend, snippets of a lot of good memories instantly flash across his mind.

"We did have ourselves a time, but we've got plenty more on the way. I'm glad you're the man on the engine. If anyone can make fast, it's you. If you need help Ross is in the front if he's not givin' flyin' lessons and Ben Jackson, the guy that's doin' the plane design, is across the way at Douglas. That's a big engine, so if you need to hire a hand to help, let me know okay?"

"Will do, boss."

Chapter 17

Jack returns to the plant yearning for the days when he and Carl thought only of racing. The two men together worked the Miller front drive race car into a weapon to destroy the competition. Racing was their life; they devoted all of their energies to it. Jack shakes his head before sitting down behind the desk to get on with the dreaded paperwork. Hours later he leans back in the chair, rubbing his eyes with the heels of his hands. Getting up from his chair, he goes downstairs to the lab-workshop to talk with Scotty.

Scotty looks up from his workbench as Jack comes through the lab's doors.

"How long would it take to build another gyro if I can't get the one Drum took?"

Scotty rubs his jaw. "Maybe a week. I have to remake the molds to sand cast a couple of parts. The big problem is bearings. The ones I showed you were prototypes; it's going to take a while to get more."

Novac scowls. "Okay, do what you can. We outta have a spare anyway. I'll see if I can get my hands on the original." Jack looks around the workshop: the place hums with activity which seems to lighten his mood. He smiles at Scotty. "It's almost five, I'll see you in the morning. Maybe I'll have good news."

Jack climbs the stairs back to his office floor. Tapping the door jamb, he steps into Mori's office.

"Did you get that address for me?" he asks.

Mori looks up from his desk, the handle of an adding machine in his hand. "I wrote it on a note paper and put on your desk. Don't get jammed up, Jack, it isn't worth getting killed over."

Jack shrugs. "I don't intend to get killed or kill anyone. I think Drum is just an impressionable kid who's in over his head. Some kids just wanta rebel against older generations; you and I did the same thing. We thought we knew better than our parent's old-fashioned ideas. These Communist organizers aren't stupid, they've got the unemployed and some pretty smart people eatin' outta their hands.

Jack turns to leave. "I'm gonna call it a day, Mori. I've gotta coupla things to pick up on my way home. See you tomorrow."

Stopping at a large Army-Navy store, Jack goes down narrow aisles past long, tall, wooden shelves looking for a watch cap and leather gloves. He finds the watch cap, then the gloves, pays the man at the counter and heads home. When he walks into his house, Maddy is loading her camera equipment into a bag.

Jack crosses the room to kiss her cheek on his way to the kitchen. "Are you off to take some pictures tonight?"

Maddy buckles the flap down on the camera bag, then turns to face Jack. "I'm getting ready to go with you tonight. Mori called to tell you that he looked up Drum's address on a Thomas map. There is a Barry Avenue and a Barrington Avenue right next to each other. We are looking for the house on Barrington Avenue."

Jack stops and turns around, an annoyed look pains his face.

"What else did Mori say?"

"He said you were going after a man you fired that you think may have stolen a gyro. Before you get mad at Mori, remember I said that I won't be left behind. I am going with you. I can take photos if we find something and can't get at it."

Jack is still for a moment, then puts his hands on Maddy's shoulders. "Promise me you'll do what I say, and we'll go together, okay?"

Maddy reaches out to Jack. "I just want to be with you, I want to help. We got out of Germany together, you know I can help."

"I'd a died in Berlin if you hadn't taken care of me. The Nazis woulda killed you and your mother if they caught you helping me. We are a team, you and me, the best team. I won't stick my neck out and I don't think we're gonna have any trouble tonight anyway. I just wanta see if Drum's got the gyro."

At a little past midnight, the Mar Vista neighborhood they are in is mostly dark and doesn't have street lights. Jack finds the address and parks the car across the street. The small house looks unkempt even in the dark. Dry weeds grow in patches around the house.

"Stay outta sight, Maddy. If you see anyone coming to the house, honk the horn a coupla times."

"Be careful, Jack," Maddy whispers.

Jack switches off the interior light and gets out of the car, silently shutting the door. Wanting to first check out the neighborhood, he walks down the street farther away from Drum's address before crossing. Most of the small homes are completely dark, the occupants in bed for the night. Jack takes the watch cap from his pants pocket and pulls it down on his head. His tennis shoes make no noise as he slips behind some shrubbery getting close to Drum's place.

Kneeling, Jack watches the house for any movement. He pulls on gloves and takes a flashlight from his back pocket. Crouched down, he creeps around to the back of the house to find the back door standing open. A closed screen door protects the interior from insects. Getting closer he peers into the kitchen; a dim light from a hallway is enough light to see most of the room. He sees a table littered with plates and flatware is only a few feet away from the doorway. Jack looks around the room, then back to the table.

Over the top of a stack of dirty dishes, he sees the lid of his gyro box.

With his head close to the door, Jack listens to the stillness of the house, trying to pick up a sound of anyone stirring. After a minute or two all he hears is his own heart thumping. Hand on the screen door handle, he gently pulls the door open, waiting for any sounds the door or its hinges might make. Inside he gently closes the door, then creeps past the hallway to the table.

With his eyes on the prize, Jack reaches for the box.

"Stop right where you are, Mister high-and-mighty Novac."

Startled, Jack turns his head to see Mark Drum holding a pistol.

"I hoped you'd come after the gyro. You think you can take anything you want." The pitch of Drum's voice grows higher.

"Well, now, I can just shoot you. I caught you trying to burn my house down because you hate communists. That's what I'm gonna tell the cops."

Jack regains his composure to talk with a very calm voice.

"Just give me back my property, Mark, and I won't press any charges. You shoot me and nobody's gonna believe your story. People at the plant know I came here to see if you had the gyro."

The pistol begins to tremble in Drum's hand.

"I have a right to protect my house. The gyro will be gone before I call the cops."

Jack pulls his eyes away from the shaking gun to look into Drum's eyes.

"The gyro's not worth anything to you, Mark. Why don't you just let me have it and we can both forget this?"

"I'm giving it to my party leader to take to Russia."

Jack's stomach suddenly lurches. Over Drum's shoulder he sees Maddy carefully opening the screen door. Jack can't warn her to stay back without alerting Drum. Fear grips him; the nervous young communist could turn and shoot her at any moment. He takes a step toward Drum, raising his voice.

"You're a fool if you think your commie buddies are gonna hang a medal on you for stealing my property." Shouting now, Jack continues. "You're a stupid goddamned fool anyway."

Drum's eyes widen, his hand shakes so badly he grips the gun with his left hand to steady it. He raises the gun slowly, a seething rage overcoming his fear. Maddy holds her camera up for Jack to see, the flash adapter is snapped into place. Maddy points to the flash disc, Jack readies to shield his eyes. Drum senses the movement behind him and begins to turn. Maddy thrusts the camera forward, then clicks the shutter button to set off the flash.

Blinded, Drum's left-hand flies from the gun to shield his eyes. Jack pounces forward using the heavy flashlight to smash down on Drum's exposed wrist. Drum screams in shock and pain: the gun clatters down on the linoleum floor.

Jack hugs Maddy, then steers her away from Drum. "You scared me to death, Maddy. I thought this jerk might shoot you."

He sees a flash of anger in her eyes and quickly adds, "But you saved me again. You're braver than Dick Tracy, but you still scare me silly. How 'bout takin' some pictures in here? We might need 'em if Drum kicks up a fuss."

Drum slumps with his head against a wall holding his arm, tears run down his face. Jack picks up the gun and shoves it in his pants pocket. He kneels beside Drum.

"Let me see your arm, I'm not gonna hurt you." Drum twists away. "Come on, don't be a baby. I don't think I broke it; just let me feel your wrist. If you're really hurt, I'll take you to the hospital."

"I don't want your help," Drum screeches. "Get outta my house. You'll be sorry for this, Novac; my friends will make you pay."

"Have it your way, Drum, you're sure as hell not gettin' any smarter. Let's go, Maddy."

Maddy bends down to take a picture of Drum, then another of his arm before leaving. Jack is right behind carrying the gyro box.

Chapter 18

Jack gets into his office early the next morning. He pauses a moment to study the pictures arrayed on the wall behind his desk. It seems to him that they were taken in another lifetime. His favorite is a photo Maddy took at his Nurburgring test with Mercedes. He stands by the W25 Grand Prix machine looking confident, his driving suit displaying the American flag. He sets the gyro box on his desk, then calls Mori and Scotty to the office. Mori is the first to enter, he stops before sitting down, pointing at the gyro box. "Do I want to know how you got that, Jack?"

"Probably not, Mori, but I don't think it's gonna come back on us. I asked Scotty to join us so let's wait a minute for him to get here."

Scotty enters, looks at Jack, then Mori and takes a seat. As soon as he sits down Jack points at the gyro box on his desk. Scotty pops out of his chair going to the desk. "You got it. Is it okay?"

Jack smiles and pushes the box toward Scotty. "It's good as far as I can tell. Take a look."

Scotty opens the box to inspect the gyro. "Can I take it downstairs to test it?"

"It's all yours," Jack says.

Scotty takes the box but stays at the desk. "Did Mark have it?"

"Yeah," Jack says.

"Did you have to…ah, is he okay?" Scotty asks.

"His arm's probably sore," Jack says. "He pulled a gun on me. If Maddy hadn't been there he'd a shot me. He said he wanted me to come after the box so he could kill me. I thought the American Communist was supposed to be compassionate, you know, kinda brotherly. He must be the Russian kind. He said his leader was gonna take the box to Russia."

Jack's face takes a more serious set. "I don't want any more break-ins; I want to make sure the place is buttoned up tight when we leave at night. Mori, have you got security taken care of?"

"The security company is here today doing the wiring. The alarms for break-in and fire will go out to their office and to the police and fire house. As of tonight, we will have a bonded night watchman from 6 pm to 8 am. I'm going to interview the night watchman later today."

"Excellent, Mori," Jack says, "you're a good man. If there's nothin' else, let's get to work.

"Ben would like to see you today, Mr. Novac," Scotty says. "He has a model maker ready to go and wants to get your okay."

"Sounds good to me, Scotty. We can meet here after lunch."

Scotty rises to leave. "I'll call Ben."

***

"Two hundred dollars a model? You guys think I'm made a money?"

Jack Novac with his airplane crew, Ben, Scotty, and Carl, gather around the desk studying Ben's detailed drawings and a list of costs.

"Douglas had twenty models made and spent over $200,000.00 at Caltech," Ben Jackson bursts out. Jack sends him a menacing glare. Ben somewhat sheepishly continues. "Caltech doesn't want something coming off a model and wrecking their wind-tunnel. So, Douglas Aircraft had a new model made for almost every modification."

"How many hours did they spend in the wind tunnel?" Jack demands.

Ben's posture straightens: this is his area of knowledge.

"They spent hundreds of hours in the wind tunnel and this was after they thought the plane was going to be good right off the drawing tables. As the plane was developed it gained more rear weight. The tunnel showed that it lost longitudinal stability. They had to sweep the wing tips back to regain the balance. The DC-3 was in the tunnel for even longer and it's renowned for being the world's most stable aircraft. The wind tunnel staff at Caltech learns from every aircraft they test. Their aeronautical knowledge grows almost daily."

"That's good, Ben, 'cause I don't have the money to make a lotta models or spend a lotta time in their tunnel," Jack quickly cuts in. He turns his attention to Carl. "How's the engine comin', Pard?"

"I just finished installin' the new pistons. The cylinder heads are done, an' I'm workin' on boost control. The intake manifolds need workin' on, so me an' Ben are makin' sure what I make will fit under the engine cover. I used some a the wood from the engine crate to make a test stand. Maybe next week we'll fire her up."

Jack smiles at Carl's news. "That's the best thing I've heard today. I wanta be there for that." He pauses to look at the faces of his crew. "Look, I know you guys are bustin' your humps on this deal but I don't have an unlimited bankroll. We'll do as much wind tunnel work as I can afford, then it's gonna have to be seat-a-the-pants testing that gets the job done.

"I've got some irons in the fire for sponsorship but people want to see the plane. Not a drawing, or a model, but the real thing. I know that's not a big help now, but it could be down the road."

Jack looks over the faces that, to a man, are more relaxed, all looking eager to get to work.

"Ben," Jack says, "the next step is to get the model done and in the wind tunnel. I'd like to see us get started on the main fuselage as soon as possible."

"I have a meeting tonight with two of my Caltech professors," Ben says. "I want to show them the drawings Scotty and I have done to see if they have any suggestions. I'm hopeful we can get started on the internal bulkheads right away. I have the NACA wing profiles and, as soon as we are sure they will work in the wind tunnel, construction can begin."

Jack gets up from his chair to pat Ben's shoulder. "That's good news, Ben. I can't wait to get behind the stick. You guys have a good weekend. I'll probably see you out at the airfield. I'm gonna take Maddy up for some touch-and-goes. She'll be goin' for her license pretty soon."

Monday morning Jack is just settling behind his desk when Mori bursts in. "Did you hear the news, Jack? Hitler invaded Austria!"

"Yeah, I heard it last night. And yes, I believe war's on the way. Maddy's upset, her mother's upset, hell, I'm upset."

The phone on the desk shrills; Jack leans forward to lift the receiver to his ear.

"Hello, hey Robbins, what's cookin', or do I want to know?"

Jack winks up at Mori. "Say, that is good news. You can tell 'em I'll do everything I can to accommodate 'em. When they send the papers, I'll get a bid ready pronto. I'm thankful, Bill. It's too bad it took that creep invadin' Austria to wake 'em up. Yeah, we've got a model goin' to the

Caltech wind tunnel, I hope, this week. Thanks again, Bill, talk to you soon, bye."

"Mori, Robbins says we're in the running for fighter and bomber instrumentation. I want you to get an estimate on building a 5000 square-foot extension to the back of the building. That means a 2500-square foot floor and two levels. I want plenty of natural lighting, and fans for ventilation. On the second story we need a storage loft. I wanta see if we can put the cost into the bid."

"Do you think we've got a chance, boss? I'd think guys like Sperry would get the nod over us."

"You're right about that, Mori; but I've got an idea about ready-to-install complete instrument panels that might just sway the bid our way. I'll talk it over with Scotty. If we can come up with a complete standardized package, then we've got something the other companies are gonna have to catch up with.

"See what you can do on the building costs. I think the panels we're doin' for Harry Van are gonna pay off better than we thought. If we get this deal, we're gonna have to hustle, but it will most likely take a year or so for the government guys to actually get it goin'. After I talk to Scotty, I'm gonna work on gettin' my plane underway and do some flyin' myself. I may not have time for that stuff if we win; and I plan to win."

***

At home that night Jack tells Maddy about Robbins's call and his plans to win the bid.

"I talked to the Justice of the Peace guy in Monterey. So, if you're ready, I'd like to call Carl and go up there this weekend. Carl's special to me and I think, like I said, we're gonna get real busy. I don't wanta lose the opportunity to give something back. When we were racin' he'd do anything for me; I don't want anything to stop me from keepin' my word to him an' Lulu."

Maddy smiles, nodding her head. "We have Lulu's wedding dress ready, she cried like a baby when she tried it on. She and Carl are, as you say, salt of the earth. Can we take the Stag?"

"I'll call Ross right now," Jack says.

Jack hangs up the phone and goes to the kitchen to get two beers for him and Maddy.

"Ross's got a charter for this weekend so I rented a Lockheed Vega for him to fly his charter, so we can have the Stag. Carl and Lulu are ready an' Carl said as soon as he talked to Lulu, she started packin'."

Maddy puts her beer down on a table and hugs Jack fiercely. "While they honeymoon, you and I can explore the coast in the Stag. It will be a very special weekend for all of us."

"Sounds good to me," Jack says. "When we get back I want to make sure we're ready to get your license, and I'm plannin' to do some local air races. Ross knows a guy that needs money to finish his racer. If I lease his plane for a few races, he'll get it ready. Ross says it's a good solid plane and plenty fast. It's smaller and lighter than our plane will be, but Ross says it can take wins if I learn to fly it right."

Chapter 19

Carl and Lulu stood rigidly while the Justice of the Peace performed the wedding atop a sandy dune overlooking Monterey Bay. Standing behind Lulu, Maddy held the bride's wedding dress down from the wind off the bay. Jack stood behind Carl, ready to hold him up. After pronouncing the nervous couple man and wife, the JP turned their attention to the whales broaching the water, frolicking in the bay.

"May your lives together be as happy and carefree as those magnificent whales are today."

After the ceremony they go back to the Hotel Del Monte to celebrate in a room off the dining area Jack rented for the occasion. In the center of the room is a table piled high with wedding presents. Carl looks at Lulu, then turns to Jack and Maddy.

"Did you two buy all this stuff?"

157

"This stuff," Jack says, "came from guys we raced with and people you and Lulu know from your diner. I just asked them to send the gifts here. Both of you have a lot of friends that wanted to show how much they appreciate you."

"Uh-oh," Carl nods at Lulu, "here comes the water works." Carl yanks a handkerchief from his pocket to give to Lulu. Her almond eyes fill with tears in contrast to her beautiful smile. He steers Lulu gently over to the gift table. "Don't cry Lu, rip open some presents. That'll make you happy."

Lulu, dabbing her eyes, turns to Carl, then punches his arm. "I am happy you lunkhead, that's why I'm crying."

Carl turns to Jack rolling his eyes. Jack smiles back, nodding his head in agreement. Maddy elbows Jack's arm; he turns to her with an innocent questioning look on his face. "Lunkhead," she says.

Sunday at breakfast, Carl tells Jack that he and Lulu want to take some time and see San Francisco. They will take the train back to L.A. later in the week. Jack and Maddy pack their bags and after lunch take turns flying the Stag back to Clover field.

Monday, Jack goes back to the plant and gets busy preparing for the Navy bid that Robbins recommended. Congress, cajoled by the president, granted the Navy a 20% budget increase to revive its strength. The instrumentation they require would be a huge undertaking for Jack's business. He is banking on winning the bid by including in it his custom panels with the instruments mounted, wired, and ready to be fitted.

He knows he will have to put up money himself to expand the business, hire more help, and acquire the necessary machinery. Jack, sure that a world war is on the way, is going to gamble that the US government is going to need plenty of defense contractors. If he gets the contract, he wants to prove that his company can perform, and can put profit aside to help win the war.

Helping Maddy ready for her pilot's license while concentrating on the Navy bid has left Jack little time to ponder the progress of his airplane. The model for his racing plane is at Caltech in the queue for wind tunnel testing. Ben's professors have studied the model and plans. They were quite pleased with his work, having only a few suggestions for what they thought might be improvements.

Jack receives a phone call from Ross that afternoon. He tells Jack that the racing plane he leased is ready for him to fly. They plan to look the plane over on the weekend at the Van Nuys airport. Ross is very enthusiastic about the quality of the plane's construction. Carl is next on the phone saying that he's ready to fire up the Allison engine.

"That's great Carl, I'll call Maddy and we'll be there in an hour. If you want, call Lulu and we'll go get some dinner after we watch your baby run."

Lulu is with Carl at the hangar when Maddy and Jack arrive. Carl makes last minute checks on the Allison engine as Lulu wipes grease smudges off it. The big V-12 rests on stout 10x10-inch timbers with a water radiator and oil tank on one end and fuel tank, batteries, and an instrument panel at the rear.

"Hey, Pards," Carl calls to Jack and Maddy. "The engine's about ready to fire up, I've spun her over to register oil pressure, and fuel pressure. So, Jack if you'll stand by to work the throttle and watch the gauges after she gets runnin', then I'll check for leaks. She'll be loud and probably smoke some till the new rings seat, so hold onto your hats."

Jack moves to the rear of the engine where Carl points out the gauges and what they should read. He shows Jack the controls and the engine and fuel cut-offs in case of a fire or oil pressure loss.

Carl flips a switch that produces a loud whine. "Okay, here goes." He pushes the starter button; the engine coughs, then belches fire from the exhausts. Maddy and Lulu jump as a loud backfire echoes in the hangar.

"Sorry, I gotta prime it more," Carl says.

He runs through the procedure again. The engine seems to catch, then just turns over on the starter motor. Carl keeps the starter going and adds more throttle. Bang! Bang! Long streams of orange flames shoot from the exhaust stacks; the engine roars. Carl reduces the throttle and the engine lopes along unevenly. Thick oil smoke plumes from the exhaust for a minute before clearing as the exhaust note changes to even

160

running. Carl revs the engine several times, then slowly eases the throttle back to a low setting.

When he is sure the engine will stay running, he yells over the noise for Jack to take the throttle. Carl grabs a flashlight and goes to inspect the engine: he scans for water, oil, and fuel leaks. Finding the engine's systems sound, he feels the crankcase sides, then the tops of the rocker covers with his hands. With a long screwdriver held to his ear that he uses like a stethoscope, he touches it to various places on the engine intently listening. Standing back, he nods to Jack holding his hand up with an okay sign.

Jack can't help himself, with a huge grin he works the throttle revving the engine. Carl stands close to Jack looking over the gauges, then leans to Jack and yells to keep the revs at 1500. "I don't wanta put too much heat in it yet. Let me check the exhaust stacks real quick, then we'll shut her down." Carl moves back to the engine. He licks his finger before touching each exhaust stack. He draws a thumb across his throat to have Jack shut the engine off.

"She sounds great, Pard," Jack says. In obvious delight he cuffs Carl's chin. "Let's get cleaned up and we'll take the girls down to the Galley an' celebrate."

They are still early for the dinner rush when they arrive at the Galley restaurant and go to a booth away from the noise at the bar. Steak and seafood are the specialties here; it's a good-time place with outstanding food and service. A waitress with a sailor hat perched on the back her head, pencil behind her ear comes to the table.

"Hiya, Jack. Where ya been keepin' yourself?"

Maddy gives Jack a quizzical look. "Hi Doris, how've you been?" Jack asks. "When did you start workin' here?"

"I've been here since the flood; I don't think Steve's place is gonna open again."

"That's too bad," Jack says. "This is my wife, Maddy, and my ol' Pard, Carl Sanders, an' his wife, Lulu." Jack turns to Maddy. "Steve's was a great little breakfast and lunch place in the canyon that got wiped out in the flood. I hope he's okay Doris, I haven't heard."

Doris nods to them. "I'm glad to meet you all. We all got out before the big water hit, but Steve was tired a slingin' hash anyways. He's down by Oceanside enjoyin' the weather."

She takes the pencil from her ear. "What can I start you all off with?"

Jack looks around the table then orders. "Bring a bottle of champagne and we'll look over the menu to decide on dinner."

Maddy looks across the table at Carl over her menu. "What kind of fuel are you burning in that engine? It smells like something the Mercedes team used in the Grand Prix cars. I like the smell but it makes my eyes water."

"It's an alcohol-gasoline blend right now. We'll run straight alcohol and a ton a boost for record attempts," Carl replies.

Lulu is holding Carl's hand, looking at his fingers. "I've got a question too," she says. "Why did you touch the hot exhausts? Didn't that burn your fingers?"

"I licked my finger before I touched the exhaust stacks to keep from gettin' burned. I can tell how each cylinder runs by feelin' if the heat in the stacks is all the same. A stack that's cooler means it's not runnin' as well as the rest."

When the conversation lulls, Jack speaks up. "The racer I leased is finished and I'm gonna go fly it Saturday."

"I'd like to come see it, too," Carl says.

"Okay," Jack says, "But I don't want to show up with an entourage. The guy I leased the racer from was happy to get the money but he's already grousing to Ross about me racin' the thing. Ross said the guy won't make any changes to the plane for me. If I'm gonna race it, it'll be as is. I know Maddy wants to go, and so do Scotty and Ben. The best thing I think to do is show up in different cars and let me and Ross feel the guy out."

Doris comes to the booth with the champagne and glasses.

Jack pops the cork, pours all the glasses full, then raises his glass. "Here's to you Carl, best damn mechanic in the game."

They toast Carl, then enjoy dinner and plan for the weekend.

Jack drives Ross and Carl to the Van Nuys airport. Maddy drives in with Lulu; Ben and Scotty come together in Scotty's car. After he parks the car, Ross directs Jack to the plane that is parked among other small craft. It is much smaller than Jack expected and painted a brilliant red. The plane's owner and builder, Jerry Maharris, is the short thin man standing by the plane. He has a high forehead of receding gray hair and petulant look on his face.

Ross advances to the man with his hand out offering a hand shake. "Hi Jerry, the plane really looks good. Is she ready to go?"

"Which one's Novac?" the man asks.

"I'm Jack Novac. Like Ross said, your plane looks good."

"Look, Novac, I built this plane for me to race; you may not even fit in the cockpit. Why don't we make a deal and I pay you back your money from my race winnings?"

Carl is on the far side of the plane looking it over and doesn't hear the conversation.

Jack's face clouds, Ross quickly steps in. "Look, Maharris, you're not gonna welsh on this deal. You came to me looking for money; I thought it would be good deal for my friend Jack, and for you. He gave you what you wanted, no questions asked. If he doesn't fly the plane, you won't either. Jack will take out a mechanic's lien and I'll go to the contest board."

"Okay, okay," Maharris puts his hands up in surrender. "You don't have to go savage on me. I just wanted to race it before Novac cracks it up."

"If Jack cracks it up due to his flying, you are insured," Ross snaps, poking Maharris's chest with his finger. "If he cracks up because the plane isn't sound or you didn't do the maintenance, then it's on you. He paid for a brand new Menasco Super Buccaneer engine, I'm gonna look it over and make sure. You piss me off Jerry. We made a deal, and I expect you to keep your end of it."

"I don't want you mad at me, Ross," Maharris says. "I'll keep my end of the deal. Why don't we get Jack in the plane and see how it fits?"

Jack climbs in the cramped cockpit, takes the control stick in his hands, puts his feet on the rudder pedals, and scans the instruments. The canopy is an inverted V shape that slides back over the pilot's head.

"I'll need get the seat down about three inches to get the canopy closed, and back a couple inches to get comfortable."

Maharris rolls his eyes, then notices Ross's glare. "That might be more than I can get. Let me take the seat out and see what I can do."

After several hours of modifications, Jack gets back in the plane. He feels the controls, looks out over the front of the plane, then pulls the canopy back over his head. He pushes the canopy forward to adjust the seat belts across his lap and the belts across his shoulders. "My head's kinda wedged when the canopy's shut, but I'd like to try it out."

Maharris watches nervously as Jack goes out to the runway. Jack pulls the little red plane off the runway quickly, then gains 500 feet of altitude before circling back. He wiggles the wings of the small craft up and down pulls up and banks steeply then heads west. Before going out of sight, Jack rolls the plane over and points the plane's nose up before disappearing in a cloud.

Carl, Ross, and Maharris are watching in front of one of the hangars. Ben and Scotty with Lulu and Maddy are watching from beside their cars behind a wire fence.

"Jesus Christ! Is that guy nuts?" Maharris exclaims.

Carl grins looking over at Maharris. "Stick around an' you'll get used to it. He ain't nuts, he's just that good. You shoulda seen him before the Nazis got him."

Maddy shades her eyes with her hands, searching for Jack in the sky. "There he is," she yells, pointing out his location.

The cloud cover is breaking up allowing a view of Jack making shallow dives and hard twisting turns. He circles the airport dropping altitude, then lands and taxis to where Ross and Maharris stand.

Jack climbs from the cockpit to walk around the plane. He reaches out to test the control surfaces before asking Maharris to remove the engine bay panels. The men gather around the engine bay. There are some signs of small oil leaks in the nicely laid out and clean compartment.

"You've done some very nice work here, Jerry," Jack says.

"Looked like you were gonna rip the wings off her," Maharris retorts.

Jack slaps Maharris's back. "There was some minor vibration but we're gonna need hard turns to win races. She's a good plane, I need more time in her and a place laid out to simulate a race course. Let's go talk it over."

Chapter 20

In the weeks following Jack's first test of Maharris's airplane, he works diligently at the plant during the week, and is out in the racer every weekend. Maharris comes to admire Jack's abilities and even allows Carl to help with the plane's maintenance.

The desert heat has beads of sweat running down Maharris's face as he wipes away an oil stain from under the plane's engine as Jack watches. "How many times are we gonna be out here practicin' Novac? You're wearin' out the machinery."

Jack lays his hand on Maharris's shoulder. "I'll pay for the repairs, Jerry. We need to make sure the plane's ready for the races and I need the practice. I just wish we could do something with the canopy."

"I know, I know," Maharris says, "You can't turn your head to see behind you. You musta said that about a thousand times. I'd have to change the whole damned plane to gave that big head of yours more room. Just worry about what's in front of you, will you?"

During the next week Jack hosts the first of the Navy personnel that have come out from Washington to inspect the plant. They were noncommittal giving Jack no idea what they thought of his plant or his contract bid. Ben calls with good news; Caltech is ready to put the model in the wind tunnel.

Thursday night Jack and Maddy meet Ben and Scotty at Caltech, and are introduced to the professors and staff at the wind tunnel. When they peer into the tunnel Maddy turns to Jack with a puzzled look. Jack looks back, then turns to Ben. "Why's the model upside down?"

"Sorry, I should have told you," Ben says. "The scales that measure the various forces are above the tunnel in the balance room. The connections from the model run up to the scales and are recorded there. Here comes Professor Millikan. He said he wanted to talk to you before we get started."

A tall, trim, bespectacled man with a spring in his step extends his hand to Jack. "Hello Mr. Novac, Mrs. Novac, I'm Clark Millikan. I just wanted to speak with you for a moment before we start tonight. We have done the setup work and are ready to begin testing. I believe you have the basis of a good plane and I will help Ben and Scotty as much as I can. However, we now have a government commitment that means we have to rush your project along."

Jack nods to show his acceptance. "I imagine that must have something to do with Hitler's advance into Austria. Hopefully you can point us in the right direction before you have to stop. I appreciate any time you can spare. I see the place is filling up with military. Can we watch a run or do we need to leave?"

"That is very understanding of you, Mr. Novac," Millikan says. "I have planned to do this run with a smoke wand to give you a visual of the airflow. The military are eager to begin their setup so after the runs are finished tonight, they would like to take over. I will run your model until we have good data but I'm afraid you will have to go after this run."

The platform they stand on to give access to the viewing window tingles with the vibration of the huge fan that powers the ten-foot tunnel. The model is held in place by a series of stays that attach to the wings and aft portion of the model. These are the connections that run up to the balance room. Jack and Maddy press forward to watch the model. There is some discernable movement of the model as the wind speed increases. When speed becomes constant a thin trail of white smoke from a wand passes over various surfaces of the model.

Ben looks intensely at the smoke trail, his hands braced on the viewing window's sill. He talks to Jack without taking his eyes off the model. "What we want is a smooth trail of smoke passing over the surfaces. If you can see a disruption where the smoke breaks up, particularly at a join or the after part of a wing section, it means there will be a loss of lift and an increase in drag. It could also mean that the downstream airflow could negatively impact control surfaces."

As the test ends Clark Millikan approaches. "It looks pretty good, Mr. Novac. Ben has done a very fine job. The wing sections he chose are good for high speed, low drag. You will need to be very careful with your construction however. These wing sections depend on a very smooth surface. Commercial constructors usually can't afford the time and money to make these wing sections work properly."

"Thanks for your time, Mr. Millikan," Jack says, "I have some of the best metal fabricators in the business ready to go. She'll be smooth as a baby's bottom."

Millikan chuckles. "Best of luck. I look forward to seeing the finished product."

Jack asks Ben and Scotty if he can buy them a beer on the way home.

"Maybe another time," Ben says. "Scotty and I are going upstairs to the balance room to go over the calculations. Professor Millikan wants to do several more runs before we have to stop. As far as the Army's concerned, Scotty and I are part of the staff here."

"Good job, you two," Jack says. "Let's have lunch tomorrow, I'm buyin."

Late Friday morning Scotty calls Jack to say that he and Ben have been up all night running tests on their model. "We have one more before the Army guys throw us out, so we're not going to make lunch, okay?"

"Take all the time you need. You two rest up, Scotty. I'll see you Monday."

On the weekend Jack wins his first air race at a county fair air show near Indio. His plane is far superior to the other planes there and the other pilots grouse about a wealthy playboy stealing their prize money. Jack gives the prize money to Maharris, saying he wants to find more races to run with tougher competitors. The big race at Mines Field in Los Angeles is scheduled in three weeks and Jack wants to be ready.

Monday morning when Jack turns into the plant's parking lot he sees the night guard outside cleaning off a fire extinguisher.

"What's goin' on?" Jack asks.

"Hiya, Mr. Novac. I caught a coupla guys tryin' to start a fire in the back early this morning. I chased 'em for a while but I wasn't catchin' 'em so I thought I better get back an' put out the fire."

"Do you know who they were?" Jack asks.

"No, can't say I would know 'em. It was still dark when I found 'em. They ran fast as deer though."

"How'd you know they were back there?" Jack asks.

"I was just doin' my rounds an' went into the back room when I saw a light flash up at the tall windows at the rear of the room. I heard a crash

171

and went out the back door to see what was goin' on. Two guys were there an' one of 'em had a bottle with a rag burnin' in it. He threw it towards me and ran. The thing went off like a bomb when it hit the ground, I ran after 'em but couldn't catch 'em."

"Let's go around back an' take a look," Jack says.

The night guard points up to the back wall where just below a window is a black stain. "That's where the bottle smashed then dropped to the ground an' caught the grass on fire."

Jack walks around the land in back of the plant, then comes back to the guard. "I don't see anything that would help to find out who the firebugs are. I'm glad you were on the job; you kept this from being something far worse. Can you carry a weapon?"

"Yes, sir, I used to be a military cop," the guard replies. "You'll just have to okay it with my boss."

"I'll do that. Thanks again." Jack turns to walk away, then turns back. "I'd like to have you do a walk around the outside of the plant a couple times at night; I'll add ten bucks a week to your paycheck."

"Yes, sir, will do," the guard replies. "Thanks, that ten bucks will come in mighty handy."

Back at his desk, Jack is writing a memo to Mori Able when Scotty knocks on the door frame.

"Hey, Scotty, come on in. How'd it go?"

Scotty sits down on the edge of the chair his hands on his knees eager to talk. "We had a great

172

time. Professor Millikan was there the whole time and instructed Ben and me to make changes to the model. We learned a lot; the Army guys were interested and didn't leave until after midnight. We cut the drag down by reducing the wing span and adding more molding around the wing root. That was really interesting because we reduced the wing span until we started to see instability.

"We glued two inches of wing back on and went out for coffee to wait for the glue to set up. When we ran the next test, we had the stability back and no increase in drag. That really quantified the testing."

Scotty bubbles over, his excitement is infectious. Jack leans forward over his desk enjoying the dialog.

"An Army pilot was there and liked the cockpit canopy. He told this big Army guy that it afforded much better visibility. The Army guy said it didn't offer enough pilot protection and that he heard you were some used-up race car driver. He went on saying that you are blind in one eye and had to crane your head around to see. He didn't like it…"

Jack rears back in his chair. "Who the hell's this Army brain?"

"I don't know," Scotty says. "He's a General, or Major, or Grand Pooh-bah, for all I know. He was there after you left strutting around like he owned the place. He told anybody that listened that some government big shot had the Army buy you a toy plane."

Jack scowls, shaking his head. "Well, it's no secret that Bill Robbins got the Army to give me the Allison engine. They were supposed to put some money up so that they could use any information we gather. That's why it's all metal. You know, that really doesn't matter; I appreciate you guys doin' an all-nighter to get the job done."

"I wouldn't have traded a night's sleep for the knowledge we gained," Scotty says. "Those guys at the wind tunnel are very dedicated. They know exactly what to do, and they get results. We had professors coming in to look over the data at 3 o'clock in the morning. It was exciting for both Ben and me. Hopefully we'll have all the final data next week."

Mori Able knocks, then enters the room. "Hi ya, guys. Am I interrupting?"

"Come in, Mori." Jack says. "We're just talkin' about the wind tunnel tests. He and Ben pulled an all-nighter gettin' the work done before the Army moved in."

Scotty gets out of his chair. "I better get going. Can Ben and I have lunch with you today?"

"You bet," Jack says. After Scotty leaves, Jack talks to Mori about the fire and outlines the list he made to keep the plant safe in the future.

Chapter 21

Jack leans back in his chair at the plant, hands clasped behind his head, thinking about the problems with the engine in Maharris's plane. Oil and cylinder head cooling system glitches have ruined the last two outings. The next race is a big one at Mines Field on the west side of Los Angeles. It will be the first time Jack will race against the top air racing professionals. Frustrated with Maharris's maintenance and preparation, Jack has resolved to fast track his own plane.

His ringing phone breaks the tension of his thoughts. "Hey, Robbins," Jack says into the phone. "What's up in the cloak an' dagger world?"

After the initial banter, Robbins says he called to wish Jack good luck in the upcoming race, and to ask about the Navy contract. Jack thanks him for the good wishes and says that the Navy always wants more information, more paperwork.

Robbins tells Jack that as long as the Navy wants information it means they are interested and not to give up.

"Thanks for the pep talk, Bill. I'll give the Navy boys everything they want. I get that I'm the new boy on the block. I'll be outta the plant on Thursday to get in some practice at Mines Field. I think we've gotta real shot at winnin' it. Take it easy, pal. I'll call you Monday and let you know how it went."

Thursday morning Maddy and Jack are on Mines Field airport by Maharris's plane. She, along with Carl, Lulu, and Jack are drinking coffee out of paper cups, the coffee's steam billowing up in the morning's chill.

"I found out yesterday why we've had the overheatin'," Carl says. "Maharris had the oil cooler duct blocked. After we argued for a while, we took the panel out that had the cooler blocked. But I still didn't think we were gettin' enough air through to cool the rear cylinders. I went over to some of the other guys runnin' the big Menasco engine an' looked at their setups. Anyways after Maharris left last night I got out the tin snips an' opened up the inlet an' made ducts on both sides of the engine cover for the air to get back out. I went home, got a boost gauge an' just finished puttin' it in.

"Maharris is stompin' around here somewhere, mad as a wet hen. Pard, the guy's a savvy plane builder. I get that he don't want to hurt the plane, but I think it's more like he knows he's not the pilot you are. He doesn't wanta get shown up."

176

Jack cuffs Carl's shoulder. "I'm glad you're here, Pard. It's just like you to work all night to make it better. I plan to run his plane as hard as it'll go if that's what it takes to win here. I'm pretty sure we'll part ways with Maharris after this race anyway. I'm lookin' forward to our own plane so we can do what we want with it."

The tiredness goes out of Carl's face replaced by his big grin. Maddy and Lulu are busy waxing the plane. They have started at the back to give Carl room to work. The wax is Carl's own special concoction that he developed for Jack's Miller race cars years ago. All racers have their own 'speed secrets' and a slippery smooth surface for going faster through the air is but one of many.

Jack sees Ross Elmore walking toward them with Maharris in tow. They stop at the front of the plane to inspect Carl's metal craft on the cooling inlet. Carl starts over to them and Jack calls him back.

"Let 'em talk it over, Carl. Ross seems to be able to get through to the guy. I'm gonna tell Maharris this is the last race we'll do, but I want it understood I expect everything the plane has to give."

Ross comes over to where Carl and Jack are, Maharris hangs back.

"Howdy, boys," Ross says. "That's a nice bit of metal work, Carl. Jerry's pissed 'cause you didn't ask him before you did it."

"I'll be happy to apologize to 'im, Ross," Carl says. "But he wasn't around last night an' it needed to get done before practice this mornin'. It

177

took me most of the night to get that an' the boost gauge installed."

Ross's looks puzzled. "It didn't have a boost gauge? How'd Jerry know what boost he was running?"

Carl shakes his head. "I don't think he's much of a engine guy. I've never seen him look at the spark plugs or make any change to the fuel mixture. I moved the cylinder head temp gauge hook up to the rear cylinder too. We were gettin' high temps with the gauge hooked up to the front cylinder. I haven't told Jack, but the throttle cable was set so the engine only got three-quarter throttle. I know Jack's gonna run this baby hard, so I figured we better get on top a the cooling."

"Three-quarter throttle!" Jack exclaims.

"Take it easy," Ross says. "Blowin' up's not gonna help. You said you wanta win this race, Jack. With the course this tight it'll be best chance you'll ever have in this plane. Let's just get our heads together and make it happen. You're mad an' Maharris's mad so yellin' at each other won't get the job done. Tell me what you want to do, and I'll talk it over with Jerry."

Jack's face is contorted in anger as he spits out his ultimatum. "What I want is for Carl to be in charge of the engine. Jerry can take care of the rest of the plane, and if he agrees to that I'll give him all the prize money. If he's smart, he could learn a a thing or two from Carl that could help him in the future. You can tell him if you'd like that this will be the last race. He can do want he wants with the plane after this one."

Jack turns away shaking his head. "Three-quarter throttle, Christ almighty, amateur hour."

Ross comes back from talking with Jerry Maharris. Carl and Jack have their heads together planning the day's practice sessions.

"Jerry says he'll do it if you throw in money for an engine rebuild after the race."

Jack looks at Carl whose eyes roll, then addresses Ross.

"Sorry about all this, Ross, but here's the deal. He can have the prize money if I win or place with Carl as chief mechanic. Or he can have nothing but his plane back as was the original deal after this race. I gave him the prize money from the first race and paid him for his maintenance. Thanks for intervening, but I've had enough. Carl and I are like brothers, we think alike, and I trust his work. He's the best man to make the plane a winner. Right now, we'd both like to concentrate on this race."

Ross returns to Jack and Carl after giving the ultimatum to Maharris.

"He says he's going home and you two wizards can run the plane by yourselves. He'll be back after the race to inspect the plane for any damage you cause."

Jack slaps Carl's shoulder. "That's the best news I've heard today. I'll call Scotty an' Ben, we'll have our whole crew for this race. Thanks Ross, we're gonna rip'em up, man."

When Jack returns from the first practice session, Carl is there with his journal to write down the report Jack gives him. After writing down the information, Carl tells Jack that a Menasco engine representative gave him a spec sheet for the race engine. Ben and Scotty join the group as Maddy and Lulu get back with coffee and sandwiches.

Jack looks at the engine sheet over Carl's shoulder. "I'd like to get outta the wind and sun a minute so we could study this thing."

Ross takes a coffee from Maddy, says thanks, then has a look at the paper Carl is holding with both hands to keep the wind from rippling it. Pointing his thumb in back of them, he says, "We can go to that hangar behind us and get out of the wind. I know the guy that keeps his plane there."

Jack takes coffee and a sandwich from Maddy and kisses her forehead. Taking a sip of the coffee, he motions for all to follow Ross to the hangar. Carl spreads the Menasco spec sheet out on a workbench. "Wow," Jack says. "We can't get that kinda boost outta the engine. If I go a lap at full throttle, the cylinder head temp is way too high. Oil temp's slower to rise but it's goin' up too."

Jack and Carl nod, grinning hugely, they both come to the same conclusion. "First call for alcohol," Carl says.

Ross looks puzzled, then nods his head. "You mean for fuel to knock the cylinder head temperature down, don't you?"

"Yep," Carl says. "Me an' Jack love that stuff. We've been makin' power with that stuff since the Miller engine days. The alcohol runs a lot cooler and can pull temp outta the heads but I'm still concerned with the oil temp. The back of the engine compartment is a flat sheet of aluminum, an' I think it's killin' the air circulation. We don't have time to rebuild the whole plane though."

Ben puts his sandwich down taking a note pad from his pocket. "I saw that too, Carl." He starts to draw on the note pad. "How about we form an aluminum panel in a shallow V shape. We put that behind the engine and enlarge the cutouts you made in the side panels. I think the air will have a much smoother path to exit. We'd get more air past the back of the engine, which will help cool the supercharger and carburetor too."

Carl looks at Jack, nodding his head. "That's good thinkin', Ben. If you can get on that, I'll start figurin' on how much alcohol we can add to the gas. We can't run on alki alone 'cause the fuel tank's not big enough, you gotta run a lot more alki than gas 'cause it burns faster. Is there anything else you want done, Jack? How's she handlin'?"

"Well, I gotta say that little plane does fly. I can just about pull the wings off her roundin' the pylons. Maharris is a pain in the butt—but he built a damn good plane."

Carl looks up from the tech sheet in thought, his fingers pinching his lower lip. "Ben, how 'bout you let Scotty work on that panel an' you do an inspection of the plane. I'd feel better if you went over it to see if you can find anything suspect. If you find anything, we've got some time to fix it. Jack'll pull the wings right off the thing if it's got a weak area."

"Sounds good to me, Carl. Scotty and I can pull the removable panels off to get a good look at everything."

Maddy winks at Lulu, then cuffs Carl's shoulder. "That's mighty good thinkin', Pard," she says, her voice lowered to imitate Jack's. "I'd like to keep the cowboy healthy."

***

The next practice is in the afternoon. The team of men has worked flat out since the morning. After Carl finished enlarging the carburetor jets, Jack sent him and Lulu home to take a nap. Carl was reluctant to go but Jack convinced him by saying he wanted him fresh for the afternoon practice.

Carl returns that afternoon with a fresh shave and renewed energy. He and Jack go over the plane, checking the new modifications before Jack taxis out to the runway. Jack makes a few laps before another racer tucks in behind him. Jack doesn't want to show his hand but needs to do some laps at full throttle to find out about the temperature issues. He pulls up and throttles back to let the other plane go by.

After the other plane pulls away, Jack opens the throttle and continues to lap. Six laps more and he lands to taxi back where Carl and the rest of the team wait eagerly to hear how it went. Jack climbs out of the cramped cockpit, pulling his goggles off.

Carl touches the back of his hand against the engine cover. Jack talks to the group as they gather around. "She's much better. It took six hard laps before the temps got up. That's a whole bunch better than before and the power's up too. I'm pullin' another 400 revs. Let's give it a good close inspection and we'll all go home for a good night's sleep."

Friday has two more practice sessions. More pilots and planes arrive to fill up the field. Carl calls the group together to show them a check list he made up.

"When we go over the plane, check each item off with your initials so we know who checked what. If you have something to add to the list write it in at the bottom. I'm gonna drill the carb jets out some more today and add a fresh set of spark plugs.

"We need to get a handle on fuel mileage today. Adding more alcohol helps the temperatures but we can only go so far with the fuel tank capacity we have. Lulu and Maddy agreed to start timing the competition today so we know where we are there. We have two practices before we qualify this afternoon. After the last practice, we'll have a better idea of where we stand."

Jack works on the cockpit. He's not wearing a parachute so he can sit lower. He takes the aluminum seat out, finds a fairly soft grassy piece of ground and hammers a bulge on the seat bottom with a big ball peen hammer. He sits in the seat squirms around a bit then gets out of the seat to hammer more.

Carl wanders over to have a look at what Jack's doing. He wipes his oily hands with a rag studying the hammer work before Jack notices him.

"You mad at that thing, Pard?"

Jack stops the hammering. "I'm tired a bashing my head in the cockpit. I'm all cramped up in it and maybe a little more room would keep me from murderin' my neck."

"I don't think Maharris's gonna like that much," Carl teases.

Jack huffs a breath. "I'll make him a new one. I haven't forgotten how to work metal, you know."

"Really," Carl grins, "I thought you fat cats just lounged around with your feet up on a desk orderin' other people to do all the work."

"Did you need somethin' here, Carl, or are you just in a mood for needlin'?"

"Boy, you're kinda tense aren't you, Pard?"

Jack puts the hammer down to wipe his brow. "Yeah, Carl, I guess I am. I like this flyin', you know? I can do this pretty good without havin' to think about my hand or my eye. I'd really like to win this one, Pard."

"You're lookin' good up there to me, Jack; we'll get 'em. I just finished puttin' in the carb jets. I don't wanta go any bigger. We've done about all we can to keep it cool, the rest is gonna be up to you. Your gonna have to lay back early on to keep the temps down, just go to full throttle the last few laps if you can. The guy in the silver job that tucked in behind you yesterday is the hot dog around here; we'll put a watch on 'im next practice."

Chapter 22

Each time Jack stops the plane after the practice laps Carl drains the fuel tank to measure the amount left. Ben and Scotty have worked out an inspection ritual that covers the check list Carl made out. Maddy and Lulu keep the plane clean, wiping it down with rags while Jack readjusts the seat belts in the cockpit.

When Jack climbs down from the plane, Maddy picks up her notebook before going over to Jack. "Let's get out of the noise, Jack. I've got the times from the last practice if you want to go over them."

"Sure thing, Maddy. I'll tell Carl we'll be in the car."

Seated in the car, Maddy passes the notebook to Jack.

"There are two men who have times close to or a little better than yours. The silver plane is the fastest, then the white plane, then you. The other planes are quite a bit slower; one of them crashed just after he got off the ground."

Jack looks up from the notebook at Maddy. "It didn't look like a bad crash from what I could see. What are these other notes?"

"I'm going to send a report to the sports magazine I used to write for in England. I wrote to ask if they wanted some articles on the American scene."

"Good for you Maddy, I'm glad. I always liked readin' your stuff about the Grand Prix races. Besides bein' the world's best lookin' woman you've got a real talent for describin' things so a reader can visualize it."

"Here comes Carl," Maddy says.

"What's up, Carl?" Jack asks.

"Ben an' Scotty found a crack in the wing spar. Ross's askin' the guy that has the hangar if we can borrow his stuff to weld it up."

Jack opens the car door to get out. "Let's go have a look."

Carl and Jack are under the plane looking up inside the fuselage.

"I agree, Carl, we can sleeve it easy, but I'd like to weld in two ¾" inch tubes to triangle it to the rear tube."

"Ben had the same idea, he's roundin' up the tubes. He an' Scotty are pretty savvy, Pard. I say we let them do the work. We've got time before you qualify an' it makes 'em a real part a the team."

"You're the boss," Jack says.

187

Ben and Scotty return from their scavenger hunt with the tubing needed to repair the plane. The four men are all on their backs under the plane. Jack and Carl have wet rags and fire extinguishers at the ready. Ben pulls on his dark green goggles to use an acetylene torch to preheat the sleeved join on the cracked tube. Scotty helps Ben with positioning the new tubes while Ben does the welding. Ben continues with a post-weld normalization much to Carl's approval.

"He knows what he's doin', Jack," Carl says, "That's a nice job; it's stronger than it was before with very little gain in weight. I like your work, Ben; you and Scotty are good guys to have on the team."

The men crawl out from under the plane, dusting off their coveralls. Carl turns off the welding tanks while Ben and Scotty gather up the torch and tools.

"We'll let the tubes cool off, then give the plane a final look-see before we qualify. Lulu and Maddy have been timin' the planes an' we're pretty fast. Two other guys are as fast then the rest a the guys are a good bit slower. We can easily qualify third without havin' to use up the engine so that's my advice. It's up to you Jack, but if you take too much now you might not have it when you need it, comprende?"

"Okay, Pard, I'll take it easy."

Mines Field, located close to the Pacific Ocean on Sepulveda and Century Boulevards, is clear and bright for qualifying. Jack takes off, then uses enough throttle to bring the temperature to midpoint on the gauges. He concentrates on gaining altitude in order to dive down turning into the pylon to not lose too much speed in the turn. The last pylon before the start finish line must be taken on a tight line so as not to go over the boundary line marked by the race's organizers.

Jack has watched the other planes in practice and noticed that only the best flyers use a line that gives them the best speed away from the pylon. He quickly realizes that this could be the crucial point in his race and practices his points for turning into the pylon, then freeing the plane up to gain speed to the finish line.

Carl waits with his note pad by the plane for Jack to climb out.

"So whatta you think?"

"She's good, Pard. The plane feels like it's more stable and easier to bank than before. You guys do good work. Let me give you the readings real quick, I'd like to watch that silver plane qualify."

Jack joins Maddy and Lulu in the grandstands to watch the end of qualifying. The man flying the silver plane shows confidence and speed; Jack notes that the pilot is using the plane and engine hard; he knows they both use the big Menasco engine. The silver plane flashes by the grand stands, the engine screams gaining revs, then Jack hears the engine miss.

The pilot immediately throttles back, pulling off the race course to land.

Maddy clicks her stop watches off and lowers her clipboard. "He's two seconds a lap faster than we are, Jack. That last lap was a bit slower; I think I heard the engine miss."

Jack looks at the times on Maddy's clipboard. "I think you're right. He ran it as hard as he could. From what I hear the Menasco engine starts to miss when it's badly overheated."

Jack reaches past Maddy to pat Lulu's knee. "I hope the guy in the silver job hasn't got a guy as clever as Carl on his crew. That could make all the difference."

Lulu nods her head. "You and Carl are a good team; he loves this stuff. It really is exciting, and I'm glad he's happy. The burger joint we had was getting him down; now all he talks about is engines and racing."

"I'm lucky to have him workin' on this, Lulu," Jack says, "We're gonna take a look at our plane, then call it a day."

***

Jack is up early, waiting for the coffee to brew. Books and magazine articles about airplanes and racing litter the kitchen table. Maddy pads into the kitchen, rubbing the sleep from her eyes. She fingers her long dark hair back to pour two mugs of coffee, then clears space on the table to place the mugs.

"Are you nervous, Jack? I don't think you slept well last night."

Jack smiles back at Maddy "Yeah, I guess I am. I'm tryin' to get a handle on this kinda'

190

racing. I wanta race these guys clean but I wanta win, too. Watching the air race films doesn't give a good picture of guys really battling. I've been readin' Jimmy Doolittle's articles on how to race the pylons but there's nothin' about passin' guys."

"I never read that you did anything but race clean, Jack. You are fast, clean, and most of all, my cowboy, I know when the race starts you will be fine." Maddy kisses his cheek, then starts clearing the table. "Help me clear off the table and I'll make breakfast. Carl is probably at the airport now fussing over every little detail. I want to take some pictures of the planes for my article, so we can go as soon as we finish eating."

Carl has the engine cover off the plane when Jack and Maddy arrive. His head is inside the compartment: a rag hangs from one rear pocket, wrench and screwdriver in the other.

"Whatta ya see, Pard?" Jack asks.

Carl backs out and turns to face Jack. His almost unlined boyish face, the blond hair and his infectious grin hide the fact that they have known each other for almost twenty years. "It all looks good to me, Pard. You ready ta rip?"

Jack runs his hand down the leading edge of the wing. "Ready as I'll ever be. Where's Lulu?"

"She'll be here soon. I wanted to get a early start so I rode in on my cycle."

"Maddy's off takin' pictures. Let's go see if we can find some coffee."

By the time Jack and Carl return to the plane, Ben, Scotty and Ross are there. The grandstands fill up with people eager to be thrilled by the morning's schedule of events. Aerobatics, inverted flying, parachute jumping, simulated aerial dogfights, keep the customers happy. After a lunch break the day's races begin.

The planes for Jack's race are lined up at the start line. Jack climbs into the cockpit as Carl and Maddy look on. Jack buckles his seat belts, Carl slaps the side of the plane giving Jack the okay sign, Maddy blows Jack a kiss before they move away.

Novac is all business now, waiting for the flag to drop. Engines rev, dust billows up behind plane's propeller wash. The starter's flag waves, then drops.

Jack is first off the ground. Mashing the throttle open, he pulls up, then roars down the straight rounding the first pylon taking a lead of fifty yards. He knows he can't keep this pace for the entire twenty laps but is determined to lead the first lap. Flashing past the finish line he counts down the laps. Two more laps and he sees the temperatures going up fast: he has to throttle back to save the engine for the last laps. Before the end of the fifth lap the silver plane flashes past. Two more laps and Jack is passed by the white plane.

Inching up the throttle Jack tucks in behind the white plane and counts down the laps. He can see that the silver plane is beginning to distance both him and the white plane. The temperatures are just moving above mid-range. Two more laps and the silver plane has gone out of Jack's sight on the main straightaway.

Carl, Ben, Scotty, and Ross are on the field watching. Maddy and Lulu are in the main grandstands. Ben watches with binoculars. He lowers the glasses to glance at Carl, he looks at Scotty and shrugs his shoulders. He raises the glasses again watching for a lap, then lowers them to glance at Carl. Fidgeting, Ben can no longer contain himself.

"What's he doing, Carl? You think he's overheating again? He's getting too far behind; I don't think he's going to get that silver plane. I wish we had a radio in the plane. We could tell him he's too far back now."

Without taking his eyes off the race, Carl offers his opinion. "Jack's a pretty cool customer. I've watched him do this before. He knows we can't run full throttle the whole way and finish the race. He's gotta bide the time till he can open her up. I don't think the other planes can run full throttle all the way either."

At fifteen laps Jack needs to get by the white plane. He opens the throttle more to go under the plane in front. He goes past and skins by a pylon. Leveling up on the straight, the white plane goes past on the outside. Jack has no choice now: he has to get past this plane to catch the silver plane before too many more laps go by.

He opens the throttle more to get by. The white plane hugs the bottom line around the pylons now to make it hard for Jack to get through. On the straight section Jack opens the throttle all the way to get by the white plane; he just edges by before banking hard into the pylon. Back on the straight

193

he can see the silver plane ahead again and figures this pilot also has throttled back trying to keep the Menasco engine cool. It takes two more laps for Jack draw even with the silver plane. He quickly dives under the plane to take the lead.

Jack hugs the low line to keep the lead, throttling back just enough to stay ahead. Going into the next pylon, the silver plane streaks above Jack, then dives gaining speed. He is out of Jack's line of vision. Jack is on level flight heading for the pylon when the silver plane dives in front. Jack instinctively ducks his head as the rear of the silver plane almost takes the propeller off his plane. His determination grows as he follows the silver plane around the pylon.

"Man, that was an eye-opener," Jack says aloud. "That's very clever my friend, let's see how you like it."

The temperatures are inching into the red zones. Jack shoves the throttle full open. With only a few more pylons to go before the finish, he gently pulls the plane up to gain altitude. He has to time this just right, but time is running out. The dive has to be made before the pylon; Jack quickly realizes he's too late for this one. He dives down, skins around the pylon with all the speed he can muster, then pulls back up. With the silver plane under him Jack has to judge when to make the move. It's now or never. The next three-story-high pylon is coming up fast.

Jack pushes the stick forward and dives. He's so close the silver plane has to pull up to keep from crashing into the back of him.

Both planes roar onto the last black and white checkered pylon. Jack can't move his head around enough under the tight canopy to find the other plane. He knows the guy is there, he can feel him. He can't let the other plane get under him. Jack dives even lower to get the last bit of speed into the final pylon. He banks hard, the stick forward, centrifugal force pulls at his body, mashing his head hard against the canopy.

Jack feels the plane tremble as he pushes harder than ever before, the inside wing skims the ground, throwing up rocks and lumps of dirt. Past the pylon he frees up the plane letting it drift out to gain speed, he can hear the banshee roar of the other plane now. Jack's grip on the stick tightens as the engine bucks, then backfires just before he flashes by the checkered flag. The silver plane's nose is at his wingtip, its engine misfiring, and belching flames from the exhaust pipes.

Ben and Scotty jump up and down hugging, pounding each other's backs. They both reach out to shake Carl's hand. Ross slaps him on the back.

Carl motions the men to follow him. "The man's not lost any of his speed or guts. That was a damn fine bit a flyin'. Let's head up to the announcer's booth."

Maddy and Lulu run to meet the others; Jack taxis the plane from the runway. He climbs from the plane, pulling off the leather helmet and goggles bushing away his hair wet with sweat. He moves his head side to side, then rubs his neck. The soreness and fatigue vanish when he sees

Maddy running toward him her arms outstretched. Tears of joy stream down her face.

Jack hugs Maddy fiercely, trying to keep his own emotions in check. The rest of the group hangs back to give the couple a minute, then rush forward. Much back pounding and hugging commences before Jack announces that they should get the plane back to the hangar and depart for a big party. News reporters nudge Jack to the announcer's booth for the prize giving.

"The party's on me," Jack calls over his shoulder, "We'll meet you at The Galley. Maddy'll call and reserve the big table."

Happy hour is still going strong at the Galley by the time Novac's group arrives.

Jack stands up by the table with his champagne glass raised. "Thanks to everyone for all your help this weekend. I really wanted to win that one for all of us."

Carl touches his glass to the others around the table before standing. "Well, Pard, I think that was purely evident to anyone that watched the finish. You ain't lost a bit a knowin' how ta get the job done."

After midnight Scotty gets up to go home. "Hey, Scotty," Jack calls out, "Tell Mori I'll be late getting in. Thanks again for the help; we couldn't have done it without you guys."

Jack, Carl, Lulu, and Maddy party on into the early morning.

Chapter 23

It is early afternoon before Jack gets to the plant. Mori follows Jack into his office.

Mori has an armful of papers he offers up, bending at the waist playfully paying homage. "Hail to the conquering hero. Have you seen the papers yet?"

Jack takes a seat behind his desk, slowly shaking his head.

"No, I had a hard enough time gettin' outta bed. We partied till morning and I didn't get much sleep."

"You've gotten us some really good publicity; the scribes loved the battle you had with the other pilot. The local papers gave you a big build up also. I spent the morning talking to people that either wanted to congratulate you or know more about Novac Engineering.

"Your race sounded pretty exciting. I snuck away from our raffle a few times with a couple of the other guys to listen to the radio reports. I wish I coulda been there."

"You were doin' good work, Mori. How much money did you and Dot raise for the flood victims anyway?"

"It wasn't just us, pretty much our whole church group helped put the raffle on. We sold that old Ford you donated for $400.00 smackers. We got mounds of food and clothing, too.

"Are you feeling up to going over my cost analyses for next month? Scotty wants to talk to about bearings for the new gyros, too."

Jack rubs his hand across his face. "Sure Mori, but it might take me a minute or two to catch up."

"I'll go get you some coffee. Want anything else?"

Jack smiles up at Mori. "If there's any donuts left that'd maybe help soak up some of the alcohol."

Fortified with strong coffee and sugary donuts, Jack works with Mori on cost increases that will affect their product prices.

Mori points out a line on his cost sheet. "Bearing prices are rising again, and Scotty says the bearings he needs are getting harder to find. My advice is to buy the bearings we need now before the prices go up and the availability recedes. Stockpiling bearings now could also give us an advantage over our competitors."

"I'd say you're right on the button, Mori. Send Scotty up and we'll decide which bearings we'll need and see if we can project the quantities."

Scotty enters Jack's office. "Morning boss. How long did you guys party after we left last night?

"It musta been after four when they kicked us outta there. It's been a long time between wins," Jack says rubbing his eyes, "but that was a little too much partying. So back to business. What can you tell me about bearings?"

"The bearings we need for the new gyros came from back east. They're telling me that European orders are eating up supplies. What I was talking to Mori about was putting in an order that would see us through the next six or eight months. With a larger order we gain preferential treatment and a better discount."

"Okay, thanks Scotty, I think you're right. Put together an all-inclusive eight months order, a one-year order and a two-year order. Mori can help 'cause he's the best at that stuff. Bearings may just decide the outcome of the war that's brewin'. The biggest bearing manufacturer in America is owned by a Swedish company that's in bed with Hitler. I'm gonna be in early tomorrow so I'll look into their other manufacturing plants in Canada and South America.

"We may be able to get better supply and price if we buy from Canada or Brazil." Jack raises his arm to look at his watch with obvious relief. "It's five o'clock so I'm goin' home to a good home-cooked dinner. You guys have a good night I'll see you in the morning."

After having a good dinner with Maddy, Jack goes to bed early and gets up before the sun. The streets on the way to the plant are nearly empty. He passes by a few trucks, their headlights pointing the way to their deliveries in the early morning darkness. Novac turns inland on a deserted Jefferson Boulevard driving just under a mile to the plant.

Entering the plant's parking lot, Jack's headlights pick up a human form lying on the ground. Getting out of the car, he hears raised voices at the back of his building. He crouches down, running to the still body. The plant's guard lies face down, his right arm extended, a pistol a few inches away from his outstretched fingers.

Jack bends down to check the guard's condition, wary of voices that are getting louder. Probing the guard's neck, he finds the pulse is good. A strong beam of light blinds his eyes, a voice calls out, "Hey Novac, this is perfect. Die in hell, you bastard!" A fiery object flies past Jack's head, exploding on the ground behind him.

Jack shades his eyes with his left hand, reaching for the guard's gun. Grabbing the pistol, he looks up: the bright beam of light now lies on the ground. He sees the dark shape of the man illuminated by a small flash of flame. With the illumination of the flame, Jack can see the man struggling to light a rag stuffed into a bottle. The rag blossoms in flame, the man cocks his arm back to throw it. Jack snaps the pistol up and fires it, the flaming bottle jerks back from the man's hand, falling behind him as he collapses to the ground.

Cautiously approaching the downed Molotov cocktail thrower, Jack senses movement, twists around gun up, when he sees another man with a bottle in each hand come around the rear corner of the plant. As soon as Jack levels his pistol, the man drops the bottles and runs away screaming, "Don't shoot me, don't shoot me". After watching the second man run off the property, Jack looks down at the man he shot, who is lying on his back.

He picks up the dropped flashlight to look at the man. A pool of blood from a massive neck wound is all Jack needs to see to know the man is dead. He turns back to the guard who is sitting up holding both hands to his head. In mid-stride Jack stops and turns back to the dead man. Bending over the body, he shines the light on the man's face. "I'll be damn, Mark Drum."

Jack returns to the guard helping to his feet. "You okay?" Jack asks.

"I guess so," the guard replies. "I mutsa tripped comin' around the corner. I saw flashes of light out the back windows and heard voices. Did you get the guy?"

"Yeah, I shot 'im with your gun. He's dead. I better call the cops. Here's his flashlight. Can you go stomp out the fire? Just kick the rag outta the bottle, don't touch the other bottles. I want the cops to get fingerprints off 'em."

"Sure, okay, Mr. Novac. You wanta give me my gun back?"

"I better hold on to it till the cops get here."

Mori found Jack and the guard being questioned by the police soon after he arrived. When Mori pieced together what happened, he called Maddy to tell her what he knew before she heard it from the news. Maddy rushed to the plant. As Maddy enters the office Jack is shaking hands with a police detective.

"Hi Maddy, this is Detective Vance, he's in charge of investigating the shooting."

Vance offers his hand to Maddy. "Nice to meet you, ma'am. I think I got all I need, Mr. Novac. I'd like for you to come down to the station tomorrow and sign a statement. That should wrap it up."

"I'll be there, Detective. Thank you," Jack says.

After the detective exits, Maddy hugs Jack. She looks up into his eyes, holding his head in her hands. "Mori told me all about the shooting. Are you all right, Jack?"

"Yeah, I guess; I didn't mean to kill 'im, Maddy. He threw one firebomb that went over our heads and he was lightin' the next one. I picked up the guard's gun and snapped off a round. I was just tryin' to scare the guy. I didn't know it was Drum till after I shot 'im."

"Let's go home, Jack. You've had enough for the day," Maddy says.

Jack goes back to his desk, his finger poised on the intercom switch. "I came in early to get some work done, Maddy. How 'bout gettin' us some coffee from downstairs? Let me get with Mori for a minute to sign some work orders an' then we'll go get lunch, okay?"

"Okay, I'll be right back," Maddy says.

Mori and Jack are working on the weeks' orders when Maddy returns. "We won't be much longer, Maddy. Mori says the phone's ringin' off the hook with people wantin' to know about the shooting. As soon as the reporters thin out, we'll blast outta here."

Outside the plant they get into Maddy's car. "Where do you wanta go?" Jack asks.

"I know just the place," Maddy answers.

She turns up Centinela heading north. Jack watches out of the side window, his mind wandering. Maddy turns into the Clover airport, heading toward Ross's place.

Jack looks up, then smiles at Maddy. "You're a smart lady. Did I ever tell you that?"

"You didn't need to, Jack. I'll go find a deli and bring back a big lunch for all of us. You go relax with Carl, and Ross, and your airplane."

Maddy, carries a box full of burgers and fries to the front of Ross's office thinking the men would be gathered there talking. A paper on the office door has 'Out on a flight lesson' neatly typed on it. She rolls her eyes, then lugs the box around to the back. Both Jack and Carl are in coveralls; Carl welds a small diameter tube that Jack holds in place. The dark goggles the men wear reflect the bright blue-yellow flame from the gas torch.

Maddy puts down the box, waiting for Carl to finish the weld. With the tube in place, Jack steps back and raises his goggles. Maddy waves to catch his attention, and points to the box.

"I've got beer in the car, I'll go get it."

A loud pop sounds as Carl turns off the gas torch.

Jack takes off his goggles. "I'll go get the beer, honey."

They group around a plywood panel resting on saw horses. Plans for the airplane's frame are rolled up at one end, the wrapping papers of the burgers and fries along with empty beer bottles leave little space. The food quickly disappeared after Ross returned from giving the flight lesson.

Ross hides a small belch behind his clenched fist. "Thanks, Maddy that hit the spot. I've gotta get the paperwork done for the airport. I'll be back in a few minutes."

"Do you have any other coveralls?" Maddy asks.

"You'd have to roll 'em up a bunch," Ross replies.

Maddy comes back from the front, pirouetting her fashion wear. "How can I help?"

Jack puts the bottle down finishing his beer. "Carl's startin' on the frame an' I'm forming the tubes an' holdin' 'em in place while he starts the weld. I'm gonna form some more tubes to the specs on the drawings so Carl can keep goin'. Can you file the welds smooth?"

"Sure, if you'll show me how," Maddy says.

Jack clamps a frame tube in a bench vise. He runs a file over a weld just enough to skim the high spots and clean the surface.

"That's what I'm lookin' for. Wanta try it?"

Maddy takes the file going to another weld joint. She rakes the file over the weld sawing back and forth. Jack stands behind her holding her hand.

"Push the file over the weld then lift it when you pull back. If you drag the file back over steel, it dulls the teeth. If we were doin' aluminum, you'd drag the file back over the material to clean the teeth."

"Okay," Maddy says, "I think I've got it."

Jack circles his arms around her waist, kissing her neck. "This is just the tonic I needed. You're the best baby, I love you."

Carl puts on his goggles. "Get to work you two; I ain't payin' you guys to smooch.

Chapter 24

It is mid-morning by the time Jack returns to the plant from the police station after he signed the Drum shooting statement. In a sour mood, he passes through the building on his way to his office without the usual acknowledgement to employees. Mori enters the office later to find Jack staring out of the window.

"Morning, boss. Did you get a chance this morning to find out anything on the bearing supply?"

Jack swivels his chair around to face Mori. "I called Canada before I went to the police station. I asked about the bearing numbers we need most. They were interested in why I would want bearings from them. They're in short supply too because England needs bearings for their war build-up. I called Brazil and if we get them the quantities, they will help if we have a buyer in Brazil to sell to."

"You seem a little down today, Jack, is something wrong?"

"I'm a little pissed off, Mori. The cops tell me that Drum's brother wrote a statement and says I shot his brother in cold blood. The cops said they have to investigate his allegation and that I was not to leave town. I asked them how Drum's brother could make that story up. He would have to have been there and involved in tryin' to set fire to the plant. The brother says I asked them to meet me there and staged the whole thing.

"The story's so dumb the cops don't believe it either, but this Drum's got some kinda pull with Hollywood types. You know I didn't even know it was Drum; I sure as hell didn't mean to kill the guy."

"Why don't the cops arrest Drum?" Mori asks. "Didn't they find the fire bottles? Where'd they think they came from?"

Jack shakes his head. "They got the bottles and got some finger prints from 'em, they're gonna try matchin' 'em to their files. I told 'em to take my finger prints just to make sure I didn't plant the bottles. Okay, enough of that stuff, I'm tired of stewin' over it."

Jack squares his shoulders and reaches out for the intercom box. "Have Scotty come to my office please." He returns his attention to Mori. "Let's put our heads together and see if we can get the bearings under control. I think maybe Robbins might help us with gettin' a Brazilian buyer."

A few minutes later Scotty enters the office with a notebook. "Good Morning. I worked on the bearing numbers and have a good idea of the quantities we'll need."

Before Scotty can continue Mori asks him if he knows Mark Drum's bother.

"Sure, Victor, only he spells it Viktor because he's a big wig in the L.A. Communist Party. He's like that Nazi guy... can't think of his name, you know Hitler's propagandist."

"You mean Goebbels?" Jack asks.

"Yeah, Goebbels. Victor likes to twist things around. Anything to make him or the Communists look good. He got booted out of college because he tried to get the Dean fired. The Dean warned Victor to stop rabble-rousing the students, so Vic started making up wild stories about him."

"He's trying to frame Jack for murder," Mori says.

Scotty slaps his notebook down. "That little rat, I'll bet he's the one that ran off screaming. That would be just like him. If you caught him in a lie, he'd just deny it. The stories he could come up with were outrageous. I'll testify to that if it will help."

"It's up to the cops now," Jack says, "I couldn't identify the man that ran away, it was too dark. The bottles he had weren't lit, I only saw him by the light of the burning bottle Drum dropped. We need to get busy on the bearings, I want to leave early and help Carl with the plane. I'll be in early tomorrow and make the call to Brazil."

Scotty, anxious to change the subject, asks, "how's the plane coming along?"

Jack's face brightens. "Carl's makin' good progress. If you and Ben can spare a coupla weeknights we can start putting the outer skin on. Ben talked me into lettin' the Douglas men do the wings and landing gear: they've got all the fixtures an' they're a lot faster than we'd be. I've got four of the old Miller boys doin' the complex metal shapes. Those guys work wonders. We could be in the air before the month's out."

"Just let me know when you want me there; I'll be happy to work," Scotty says.

Mori rolls his eyes. "We better get to work before the plane's done. I probably won't see much of you when you start flying."

"The plane's gonna help the business, Mori. I'll be here as much as ever. I wanta go for a speed record that'll make people take notice. If we can beat Howard Hughes's record, we'll be big news. Our instruments will be onboard and we'll play it up for the papers. Scotty's new gyro will be center focus. We can say that the speed and reliability come from the instruments we make."

"That's very good, Jack," Mori says. "I'm impressed. Maybe you should write the copy for the newsreels."

"Sure, sure, Mori. Let's get our heads together on the bearings."

The three men huddle over Scotty's notebook. The meeting ends with Jack reminding them he'll call Bill Robbins, his government contact, and the bearing people in Brazil.

Looking out of the windshield of his car at the field where he shot Drum, Jack huffs out a breath.

He braces his hand behind his neck, then rotates his neck to relieve the day's tension. He backs out of the parking spot, then pulls around to exit the plant. Heading toward Clover Field his body uncoils, he sits up in the seat looking forward to working with his hands again. Maddy greets Jack at the hangar. She has a new pair of coveralls she bought that fit her much better that Ross's hand-me-downs.

Carl welds in metal stringers to the frame's tubes that the aluminum panels will rivet to. Jack puts his arm around Maddy's waist as they take in the skeletal shape of the plane. The frame tubes taper gracefully back to the rear of the plane where the framework outlines the vertical stabilizer and the rear wings.

Maddy looks up at Jack's face. "You look tired. Is everything okay?"

"I feel much better seeing you and being here with the plane. Let's get to work. I'll tell you all about the day when we get home."

Jack waits until Carl finishes a weld. "Whatta you want me to get busy on, Pard?"

Carl lifts his goggles. "Give' me a hand placin' the last two stringers an' we can clamp the first panels on to be drilled for the rivets."

"I'm going to get my camera," Maddy says, "I'll be right back."

When Maddy returns Carl and Jack have a long bare aluminum strip they are carrying to the plane.

"Hold it up by the plane so I can take a picture," she calls out. "Okay, that's good, now look at the camera, one more, good. Carl, can you give me a hand when you finish clamping that in place?"

"Sure, Maddy. Let me show Jack how to place the drillin' template on the aluminum an' I'll be right with you."

Jack attaches the steel template over the aluminum strip and begins to drill the evenly spaced holes that rivets will go through after they clean up the holes and paint the frame.

Jack hears a clatter behind him, he pulls the drill back and turns around. Carl stands behind a beautifully-crafted aluminum seat he set on the floor. Maddy is beside Carl, holding a brand-new parachute.

Jack puts the drill down, going to the seat. "Wow, where did you guys get that? It has my initials on it too."

"Maddy got it for you, Jack; I just carried it in for her."

Jack runs his hand over the top of the seat. "Man, that's nice, Maddy. We'll have to get a cushion for it."

Maddy shoves the parachute into Jack's hands. "That will be the only cushion you will ever need in that plane, Jack Novac."

"Baby, you know I'll be at low altitude, the parachute won't help me," Jack says.

Maddy looks up into Jack's face, her hands on her hips. "If something goes wrong, you pull up, gain altitude, then bail out just like your hero, Jimmy Doolittle, would do. I've read his articles; he has saved himself many times by bailing out. We have lived through rough times together. You will promise to come home to me. You will not die in that airplane."

Jack straightens up giving Maddy a stiff salute. "Yes, ma'am."

"Do not get cute with me, Jack Novac."

"I've been tellin' people if I got killed, you'd murder…"

"Stop right there, Jack; it is not amusing," Maddy commands.

Jack glances over at a bemused Carl. "Don't look at me, Pard," Carl grins. "I know a General when I see one."

Maddy balls her fists on her hips, mouth turned down. "I have heard better cabaret performers in Russia."

Jack puts his hands up in surrender. "Okay, okay baby. General has the word; the parachute's my cushion. If you help Carl put up the next strip, I'll drill."

They get two more strips finished. Carl and Maddy deburr the holes and mark where each panel goes after Jack finishes drilling.

Jack wipes sweat from his forehead. "Let's call it a night, Pard. I've gotta be in the plant early tomorrow. I'll try to be back here after lunch."

"Okay by me," Carl says. "I'm plannin' on paintin' day after tomorrow. The panel beaters can finish the shaped panels and we'll rivet 'em on after I string the rudder an' elevator cables. You guys go on, I'll clean up here. See you tomorrow."

"You go on home, Jack. I'll pick up some dinner for us on my way there."

"Thanks, Maddy. I'll take a shower, then mix us a Martini."

After dinner Jack tells Maddy about the morning at the police station. Afterward they sit together listening to an FDR fireside chat. The radio station returns to big band music after the President's talk. Maddy soon stretches, saying it's time for bed.

Jack is asleep from the instant his head hits the pillow. In an early morning hour, both Maddy and Jack bolt upright in bed at the sound of a loud crash.

"Stay here, Maddy. Nothins' shakin', it isn't an earthquake. I'll go have a look."

Jack leaves the lights off, he picks up a baseball bat by the bedroom door and pads down the hallway barefooted.

Maddy hears Jack swear; she puts on her robe and heads for the living room. In the dim light from outside Maddy sees Jack sitting on the sofa, looking at his foot.

"Don't come in here with bare feet," Jack calls out. "Turn on a light, will you?"

It takes a second for their eyes to adjust to the light. "What happened, Jack? Are you all right?"

"I think someone threw a rock through the front window."

Broken glass litters the living room floor. A cool breeze ruffles the curtains of the large living room window. Most of the glass is on the floor.

"Are you hurt, Jack?"

"Nah, I just got a little cut. It surprised me more than anything. I wonder who I pissed off this time."

"I'll get a cloth and some alcohol and help you clean up the glass," Maddy says.

"Put on some shoes, Maddy. I'm okay."

Maddy returns with a dust pan and broom.

Jack picks up the larger pieces of glass and puts them in a paper bag he got from the kitchen.

"Let me see your foot, Jack."

"It's okay, Maddy. I'll go put my shoes and socks on and take a look outside."

Maddy is running a vacuum cleaner over the floor when Jack returns to the living room. When he puts down the flashlight he used outside, Maddy shuts the vacuum off to show him a handbill she found.

She hands him a torn, crumpled paper. "The People's Party for a Better America sent us a notice, Jack; your picture is on it. I found it under the coffee table tied to a brick."

Jack's face sours as he reads the paper.

Maddy watches Jack read the paper with concern. "What is the People's Party?"

"I'm pretty sure it's Victor Drum's Communist group. Scotty says Drum's big with the Hollywood set. He makes up a good story with half-truths and lies. I wonder how many people are gonna buy into this drivel? I'll call the cops and make a report. They can take the note, but I don't think anything's gonna come from it."

"Don't let it go, Jack. You do not want something like this to go unchallenged. We need

214

to call the newspapers and tell our side of it before this sort of thing gains traction. Calling you an unrepentant murderer protected by the rich and that you are wanted in Germany for murder can not go unanswered by us. This is how the Nazis gained power: with lies and deceit. If we stay silent it will only serve to make Drum bolder."

"I'll go find this Victor Drum bum and have it out. Maybe what he needs in a good thrashing."

"That would be just what he wants, Jack." Maddy takes the paper from Jack waving it at him. "The note calls for the party members to make you pay for Mark Drum's death. If you get rough with him that would just confirm to them you are the bad man he says you are. I hope to God almighty that the terrors of a police state cannot come to this country."

Jack studies her face as she talks. Her eyes give way first to fear, then anger. He sees the way she waves the paper knowing that she's sure evil will come. The sound of glass breaking in the night must have taken her back to bad memories of the Nazi takeover, the deaths of her father and brother at the hands of monsters.

"Okay, Maddy, I guess you're right. Let's pull the curtains across the window opening and go get an early breakfast. I'll get the window replaced today. Are you gonna be home?"

"I planned to write today. This makes me more determined to finish my book. I will be here when the window is replaced."

"I'll go into the plant as soon as we have breakfast. I promise to file a police report an' call that Times reporter to tell 'im our side. I'll be home after lunch. I'd like to go to the hangar an' work on the plane a little. I want you to come with me; I don't want you here alone."

"I'll take care of the window, Jack. You go work on the plane; it will be good for you."

"I'll come for you after work and we'll go to the hangar together." He hugs her to him wanting to wash away her hurt. The emotions he saw run across her face bring pain to him too. He wants her to be happy, to have them both happy together. Jack kisses her forehead, then her lips, holding the kiss.

Maddy smiles, her eyes wet, as he goes to get dressed. "My sweet cowboy," she says to herself.

Chapter 25

"It was an accident, Bill," Jack proclaims on the early morning phone call with Bill Robbins.

"You stood your ground, Jack. I'm telling you that just may have saved the Navy deal. The old hawks on the board love that 'defend against the red peril at any cost' kind of play. I hear they had all but given the whole deal to Sperry. The talk is that they want you to get the instrument panel part of the contract now to see how you handle it. That would be a good start, and if you can deliver the job on time and within budget you'll be on your way."

"I'm grateful, Bill. The reason I called is because I need a buyer in Brazil for a ball bearing order I'd like to place. I probably won't need all the bearings if I don't get the instrument contract but if we go to war some other American defense contractor will. Germany is gettin' a lock on bearings. The Swede's are in bed with the Nazis and I can't get the bearings I need from their factory in Philadelphia."

"So, you're saying that the bearings made here are going to Germany?"

"That's right, Bill, that's exactly what I'm sayin'."

"I need to look into that, Jack."

"That's all to the good, Bill, but I need a bearing supplier now. Can you find me a buyer in Brazil?"

"I'll give you a name, Jack, but you'll have to do the deal on your own. I've been warned to keep my nose out of South American affairs."

"Will do, Bill. Just give me the contact information an' I'll take it from there. I thank you and I'm sure Sonja would send her best too. I know she loved her birthday party."

"I don't know why I put up with you, Novac. If I could remember that night, I'll bet Sonja loved me. I'll have a man bring you a file on the guy I want you to use in Brazil. Take care, buddy."

Mori enters Jack's office with coffee and a box of donuts. "Morning, Jack, I brought coffee and donuts from a new place up the street." He puts the box down on the desk to take a handbill from his pocket.

Mori hands the handbill to Jack. "Have you seen this?"

"Yeah, we got one of these tied to a brick through our front window this morning. Where'd you get this?"

"A guy handed it to me at the donut shop. I wasn't going to takc it until I saw your picture on it. Should I call the police?"

Jack puts the notice down to lift the lid of the donut box. "I don't think there's a law against handin' out that stuff, Mori. I called the local cops this mornin' about our window, but I don't expect anything from 'em. Maddy wants me to call the papers an' give 'em my side of the story, so I'll call that Times reporter."

Both men look up when Scotty knocks on the door frame before entering. He holds up another handbill.

"Oh, I see you already got one of these."

"Where'd to you that one?" Jack asks.

Scotty frowns shaking his head. "They're all over town. You remember we had that talk about Communists? Well I'm quickly changing my mind about the whole group. I know it is freedom of speech, but this is just one lie on another."

Jack nods his head agreeing. "Maddy wants me to call the newspapers an' give 'em our side, so I'll do that this mornin'. That's about all we can do for now. The good news is, it looks like we could get the Navy contract to build the instrument panels, but not the instruments. We need to be ready and deliver on time, on budget. We do that an' we'll be doin' more business with 'em."

Jack nudges the donut box toward Scotty. "You better have a donut before Mori eats 'em all; you're gonna need your strength."

Glancing at Mori, Scotty opens the box to select the biggest chocolate covered donut then takes a bite before Mori protests. Scotty's adams apple jounces as he swallows. "When are we going to get to work on the plane?"

Jack grins as Mori watches Scotty devour the donut.

"I'm gonna leave after lunch," Jack says. "I'll pick up Maddy and we'll help Carl put a primer coat on the frame. We should be ready tomorrow night to start fittin' panels. It would be good for you and Ben to be there, so we could all agree on any access panels we need for maintenance. It'll be a lot simpler to make access panels now than have to cut panels in later."

"Ben and I will be there after work. It's pretty exciting to see the plane coming together. I've got the instrument panel ready to go in. I'll bring it with me for a trial fit."

"Thanks, Scotty, I'm expecting a guy this mornin' to bring me a contact in Brazil for the bearings. I'll keep you up to date and we can decide what we want to stock up on. If we get this Navy deal, the three of us will need to work closely to make sure we get it right."

"Sounds good to me," Scotty says. "Thanks for the donut, Mori."

Mori inspects the donuts. "You should be, you took the best one."

"Sorry," Scotty says.

Mori grins at Jack, then turns back to Scotty. "I'm just kidding, you're welcome anytime. I'm looking forward to the Navy deal if we get it. You guys do the mechanics and I'll make the numbers work. You can count on me for the donuts."

Jack looks at his wristwatch, then chooses a donut. "I've gotta make some phone calls so I'll see you guys later. Thanks for the donuts, Mori. I'll check in with you before I leave."

After talking with the Times reporter Jack walks through the offices and departments in the plant talking with his employees. He keeps the banter light letting the people know the business is doing well and the future is bright. Many in the workforce are happy to have good jobs in the existing economy but are reluctant to ask about the Communist handbills that seem to be everywhere.

Jack briefly explains his side of the shooting to relieve any anxiety and to let them know he hired another night guard and a daytime security guard to keep them safe at the plant.

He returns to his office to find the fidgety little man Robbins sent with a file he has Jack sign for.

"Is it top secret?" Jack jokingly asks the little man.

"I wasn't told." The man, now very serious, answers. "You can't be too careful in this business."

Jack hands the receipt to man who quickly leaves without another word.

Inside the sealed envelope is a photostatic copy with information and a picture of Robbins's man in Brazil.

Jack has no luck in contacting the man in Brazil. He stops by Mori's office on his way out.

221

"I couldn't get our Brazilian contact on the phone. I left a message at his hotel to call here. If he calls while I'm out, you can call me either at Ross's or at home or ask if I can call him tomorrow. I'll be in early in the morning. See you tomorrow."

Chapter 26

As Jack turns into his driveway, a plywood panel that covers the front window opening catches his eye.

"Hi, Maddy, I'm home." he calls as he enters the living room.

Maddy comes to the living room from a spare bedroom Jack made into an office for her.

"Do you want some lunch before we go?" she asks.

"No, I'd like to go to the little taco stand Ross likes and get a big bag of tacos for all of us. Ross and Carl can eat dozens of 'em, but I enjoy watchin' 'em eat. Reminds me of when Carl used to say he loved goin' out after work with the Miller guys. He called it drinkin' beer, ichin' an' scratchin' an' tellin' tall tales. You listen to stories Carl an' Ross tell an' you can't be blue for long, I'll tell ya."

Jack pulls back a curtain to see the plywood panel. "What's up with the window? It's kinda dark in here. Oh, by the way, did I tell you that you're the most beautiful, wonderful woman in world today?"

Maddy smiles rolling her eyes. "Pure blarney I think the Irish call that, Jack, but I love you for it. The window company said they have to order the glass. They said it is not a standard size."

Jack stands facing the window with his hands on his hips, head cocked. "You know let's call' 'em before we go an' have 'em hold up till we think about it. We could put a bay window in an' have little windows on the sides that open to get some air in here. What do you think?"

"I like that," Maddy says. "We could put a window box under it and plant some colorful flowers. I would like that, Jack. I'll go call the window company."

Jack looks at Maddy's smiling face, her dark mood lifted when she returns. "I am ready, Jack. The glass company will come back tomorrow to measure for the bay window. Let's hit the taco stand."

Maddy and Jack are back in the car with bags full of tacos and cold beer. She sits close to Jack, her head resting on his shoulder. "Why do you call Carl, Pard?"

Jack's forehead wrinkles. "Where did that come from?"

Maddy raises her head to study Jack's face. "I just wondered where 'Pard' comes from and why you both address each other that way."

"Well, I guess we got it from the old Saturday matinees. The cowboy stars were all tough guys an' they called people 'Pard', or partner. We just started callin' each other 'Pard', maybe 'cause we thought that made us tough guys. I know it gets some odd looks nowadays but to me it means kinda like brother. Carl's been like a brother for a long time. You know what I mean?"

Maddy rests her head back on Jack's shoulder. "You are a good man, Cowboy."

Jack pulls into Clover Field; the airplane frame sits outside of the hangar in the bright sunshine. Carl, standing on a stool, bends over the frame, tightening bolts on the aluminum seat in the cockpit. Maddy springs out of the car with the bag of tacos, heading for Carl. He steps down, turning to Maddy, putting the wrenches in his back pocket.

"Howdy, Pard," she says, shoving the bag to him.

Carl takes the bag. Lowering his eyebrows, he looks at Jack quizzically who shrugs his shoulders.

Maddy goes into the hangar looking for Ross.

Jack brings the beer, setting the bottles in the shade, then hands one to Carl. "You musta stayed late to get the front of the frame painted. It looks good."

Carl puts the taco bag down and deftly pops the bottle cap with pliers. "Yeah, I wanted the paint dry this mornin' so I could lay out the cockpit controls. What's with Maddy an' the 'Howdy, Pard'?"

"She got a bad scare last night. Some bum threw a brick through our front window with a handbill wrapped around it. She doesn't wanta show it scared her, but I think she's happy to be outta the house an' around friends," Jack explains.

Carl's jaw muscles tighten. "This about that guy you shot? I don't wanta see Maddy scared. Me an' Lu think she's the best thing that ever happened to you."

Jack nods, wrestling with the bottle cap. Carl takes the bottle and pliers, pops the cap and hands it back.

"I'm surprised you didn't see the handbills," Jack says. "People are tellin' me they're all over town. It has my picture on it and the meat of the thing is that I murdered Drum an' outta be punished for it."

Carl takes a pull on the beer before speaking. "I was up early an' Lu made breakfast, so I didn't stop on the way in. I'm glad I didn't see one of 'em. Who's sendin' out that stuff?"

"Drum's brother," Jack says. "Scotty says he's some kinda big shot Communist party guy. He told the cops I set up the whole firebomb thing so I could murder his brother."

"So, whatta we gonna do with this guy?" Carl asks. "Sounds like he needs a lesson in manners to me. Maybe he outta fix your window and apologize to Maddy." Carl looks at Jack, his face hard. "Maybe he outta just eat dirt."

Jack raises his bottle in salute. "I'm with you, Pard, but Maddy wants to let it lie for a while. The crash of glass in the night brings back all that Nazi crap to her. I'm tryin' to make her forget that stuff, so for right now I'm layin' low. Maddy had me call the Times newspaper reporter. I gave him my side of the story and he said he'd print it and look into Drum's past. He wants to know why Drum's story's so wild."

Jack and Carl stop talking as Maddy brings Ross with her in to the hangar.

"You boys ready to eat?" Ross calls out.

Maddy rolls up the airplane's plans to make room on a table to spread the food out.

"Come and get it," she says.

"Don't need to ask me twice." Carl makes for the table.

Ross unwraps a taco, then takes a huge bite, crunching through the fried corn tortilla. "Man, these tacos are the best. You guys are makin' good progress. How long before you try her out, Jack?"

"I'll be able to tell you more after the weekend. We'll have everyone here an' I hope to get a lot done. Carl's flat out as usual…"

"I'll have the engine in before the weekend starts," Carl interjects.

Ross shakes his head. "You guys are fast, I'll give you that. Take your time to make it right. Fallin' outta the sky ain't fun you know."

Maddy looks up at Jack.

"Don't worry," Jack says quickly. "Ben's got a serious test plan, we'll be doin' taxi runs before we put her into the air. I've got good people on the job; all of 'em have been around Indycar racin' or airplanes. Ben and Scotty'll be here later to plan the panel installation."

"Can't be too careful, Jack," Ross says. "I'd be happy to help out Saturday; I've got a lesson Sunday."

Jack grins at Maddy, thinking that she probably wanted Ross to look over the plane. "We'd be glad to have you."

Carl tucks his chin in, pulling his fist to his mouth and giving a soft belch. "That was mighty tasty. I'm gonna get back to it."

"What do you want us to do, Pard?" Jack asks.

Carl turns back to them. "We need to finish paintin'. I've got some tarps to put down on the ground. You guys could do that and get the spray gun and paint ready while I finish the cockpit. I've got paint brushes so we can touch up places I can't get to with the spray gun."

Carl goes back to the plane while Jack and Maddy clean up the table. Ross's phone rings and he goes off to answer it.

They finish painting and let the paint dry in the afternoon sun. After Ben and Scotty join in later, they pour over the plans to agree on any revisions to make before they rivet the aluminum skin. It is after 7 o'clock before they roll the airframe back into the hangar for the night.

When they get home, Jack picks up the newspaper that is by the front door on his way inside.

Maddy heads for the kitchen. "I'll mix some martinis. Why don't you go relax and read the paper?"

"Sounds good to me," Jack says.

Maddy brings two martinis, handing one to Jack. He lifts the glass, taking a sip. "That hits the spot, Maddy. Wait'll you read the Times article. That reporter went to the cops and found out they pulled Drum's finger prints off the Molotov bottles. They've hauled Drum in for questioning again. The article goes on with details of Drum's past that make him look like a total nut case."

Chapter 27

Victor Drum walked out of the police station in a foul mood. The police grilled him mercilessly, called him a liar, but could not charge him. The police interrogation was nothing new to Drum, he'd committed petty crimes from his childhood. Stealing chocolates from candy stores, shoplifting toys his parents would not buy him, then in high school organizing a gang of toughs to steal lunch money from fellow school mates. He always had a story for the police, it was always someone else. The more proof the police had, the greater the story he would concoct.

This behavior served him well until college. He was outraged when the Dean booted him to the curb after refusing to listen to any more of his lies. Of average height and build, his youthful chiseled face and strong voice projection gained him entrance to Hollywood. A lack of talent plus an annoying habit of spreading Communist unrest among cast and crew, soon ended his dream of fame and fortune.

He became an angry man convinced that the world conspired against him. His work with Communism grew with speeches that others wrote for him, and that he delivered with relish. To him Communism meant everyone was equal, there would be no talent greater than his. He shunned any type of manual labor and relied on his younger brother to earn enough money to live on. He did receive a small stipend from the People's Party to spread their dogma.

From the police station Victor hopped on an L.A. Railway Yellow Car to Exposition Park where he disembarked, then walked on to an old wood-framed apartment building on Grand Avenue.

In the back of the building is a door to the storage area. Victor knocks on the door then impatiently taps his fingers on the change in his pocket. A bearded young man opens the door and Victor enters a gloomy room without outside light that smells of printing ink.

"Hey, look who's here," calls a heavy-set man dressed in a busman's uniform lounging on a threadbare old sofa. "It's Vicky."

"Shut up, Bob," Victor yells. "Where's Gustavo?"

An older grey-bearded man enters the room, wiping his hands on an ink-stained rag. "I am here, what is the yelling about?"

"Bob's being stupid again," Victor bleats. "I need to talk to you alone."

Bob bolts upright on the sofa. "Watch who you're calling stupid, Vicky. I don't go running away from somebody that just shot my brother, screaming like a little girl."

Victor snaps around to Bob. "What, what did you say?"

"You heard me, Vicky. Haven't you read the paper today?"

Gustavo holds up his hands. "Stop, both of you. Victor, come with me."

Gustavo leads Victor back to the room he came from and closes the door behind them. The main feature of the room is the manual printing press. Stacks of paper and a type setting table take up most of the space.

"I need some money, Gustavo; I may need to hire a lawyer."

"I do not have funds for a personal attorney to help your case, Victor. The newspaper article is quite embarrassing to our cause. The article contains a long list of your petty crimes and the elaborate fabrications that you made to the police about your brother's shooting. The paper also makes it sound as if you are leading the People's Party in a vendetta against this Novac man."

"He killed my brother. If you won't give me money for a lawyer, I need some to bury my brother."

Gustavo's face hardens, his dark eyes bore into Victor's. "You will have to find work as everyone here does. You come and go here as you please. You used this printing press for your own purpose without my permission. We work to make the party a platform for the working man and you are ruining that work. The newspaper article about you is one of deceit and cowardice."

"It's lies, all lies," Victor screams, "I have worked hard for the party, I am a loyal member. I will refute these allegations and confront Novac man to man."

Gustavo harshness softens. "If you confront this Novac, there must be no doubt you are avenging a terrible wrong. You must do it bravely for all to see."

He takes five dollars from his wallet, holding the bills out to Victor. "This is all I have to give you. Take these pamphlets and pass them out on your way to glorifying the party."

Victor takes the money and a handful of party pamphlets as he turns to leave. He goes through the outer room without a word or acknowledgement to anyone. At the door a voice calls out, "Bye, Vicky." Victor stiffens, then goes out the door.

Outside, his face contorted with anger, Victor lets the pamphlets slip from his fingers as he walks down the street. The papers swirl up behind him from passing traffic, landing crumpled and torn, the party's message spent in the gutter. Hands clasped behind his back, shoulders hunched forward, Victor plods down the street unaware of his surroundings.

Newspapers catch his attention as he passes a newsstand. He grudgingly pays the newly-increased 3-cent price for the Times. In the shade of a building Victor unfolds the paper. On the third page an old mug shot of him jumps out. He quickly pulls the paper shut, his head darts up, suspiciously looking about. The few people on the street take no notice of him.

He unfolds the paper again; his old picture in the paper came as a shock. The article is a long one, his lips move unconsciously as he reads. He looks up from the paper, his eyes watering, he sniffs, running his shirt sleeve under his nose.

Novac, that damned Novac, I've got to kill him. he says to himself. *I must have respect, I've gotta find some way to kill that bastard.*

Chapter 28

Ross is stooping to check a fuel filter under the Staggerwing when he sees Maddy run past. A moment later he sees her coming back on the run. Concerned she may need help, he steps out away from the plane.

"What's up, Maddy? Everything okay?"

"Had to get my camera. Jack is sitting in the cockpit of the plane with his hand on the control stick. Carl has the engine in but there is no fuselage yet, just the frame. I think he may spread his arms like a little boy and make plane noises like he is racing or shooting down the Red Baron. I must have a photograph."

Ross laughs and follows her to the hangar. Jack is still in the cockpit looking out over the top of the long V-12 Allison engine. Maddy quickly snaps photos.

Carl's head emerges from the rear of the plane. "Pull back on the stick, okay, push forward. Looks good here, Jack, how's it feel now?"

"Nice an' slick, Pard. That was a dandy idea usin' those sealed bearings to take up the cable slack; it's smooth as butter. The elevator control on Maharris's plane either had too much slop in it or, if I got the slack out, it felt rough. This is nice. It gives a much better feel; we need to make all the controls like this."

Maddy lowers the camera when Jack notices her.

"I thought you were alone playing racing pilot. You looked so cute I had to get a picture," she says.

"Yeah, Jack, we both thought you looked real cute," Ross hollers.

"That's better than you ever looked, pal," Jack retorts.

"Hey, Ross," Carl calls out. "How 'bout helpin' me an' Jack liftin' the gas an' oil tanks in the frame? It'll be easier with all three of us."

"Sure thing," Ross says, hitching up his pants. "You fellows need a good lookin' man of experience."

"Let me know where we can find one, will ya?" Jack shouts back.

Carl shakes his head. "Let's get to it, okay? We'll have all the guys here tomorrow to rivet the panels on. It'll be a lot easier to fit the tanks and get 'em plumbed now."

After the three men work together to fit the tanks, Ross goes back to his plane, while Maddy leaves for home. Jack and Carl work late into the night, cutting and fitting supply and return lines for the fuel and oil.

Jack wipes his brow as Carl finishes the last line fitting. "Let's knock off, Pard. Ben couldn't get here tonight so I asked if he and Scotty could be here early tomorrow. I need to get with them an' organize the work for the weekend. Why don't you sleep in a little? That way one of us will be focused on gettin' the jobs done right."

"I don't need much sack time," Carl says. "I'll be in early and we can plan the work together. I'm kinda excited to see what she's gonna look like with the panels fitted."

"Okay, Pard, I'll call Scotty and we can all meet at Kathy's breakfast place in the morning."

At 5:30 the next morning Jack, Carl, Ben, and Scotty, their hands cradling steaming mugs of coffee, sit at a table at a Main Street all-night eatery that panders to the gambling ship trade. After a waitress clears their breakfast plates, Ben spreads out a plan of the aircraft.

Ben's finger brushes over the plan. "These are the first panels to rivet. I've numbered them so there shouldn't be any confusion. The shaped panels will be the last to go on; most of those are removable anyway. All of the engine section panels are removable for maintenance, so I think we should concentrate on the main fuselage today and see how much we can finish."

Jack squints through the smoke from his first cigarette of the day. "Looks good, Ben. If we all agree, then I think we should meet again tomorrow morning and see where we are, and if there are any problems we need to solve."

Jack looks around the table as the men nod their agreement.

Carl gets up from the table. "Let's get to it."

Maddy waits for the men to open the hangar to bring in donuts. She asks Jack to help her bring in a coffee urn and set it up on a table. After she arranges the donuts and coffee cups, she returns from her car with two bundles tied with string.

The men watch as she heaves the bundles on the table to untie the strings. She unfolds a white coverall holding it up before her. On the back, Novac Engineering is embroidered in large red letters. On the front over a patch pocket, smaller letters spell out Carl. "I have one for each of you."

Carl takes his, holding it up in front of him. "It's a thing of beauty, Maddy, thank you. Hey, it's got a zipper front, too."

"I had them all made with zippers, so we can wear them over our clothes and just be able to pull them on and off. They're made from heavy cotton and have patches sewn on over the knees, so you can replace them." Maddy finds hers in the pile and holds it up in front of her. "This one is for me. I hope you like yours."

"We will, thank you."

Maddy hands the other coveralls to the men. "I have one for Ross; I'll go find him."

Jack busses Maddy's cheek. "Thanks, these are really nice."

The metal crafters Jack hired, file into the hangar. "Here come the troops," Jack says. "Let's get busy."

Ben and Scotty go over the work to be done with the men. After coffee and small talk, the men start applying the aluminum panels. Carl starts an air compressor, soon the hangar vibrates with the rapid-fire banging sounds of air hammers setting rivets.

All of the new metal crafters are very familiar with the work at hand. Only one had not used flush rivets. It took little time for the men to find a rhythm. Soon panels covered the framework; by the end of the day they completed the main fuselage. The plane's shaped spine, from the cockpit headrest to the rudder, was all that was left for the next day's work for these men.

Jack and Carl break out cold beer for the crew, then stand back to admire the work. Jack bats Carl's shoulder, a broad smile lighting up his face. "She's comin' together, Pard, she looks good. I can't wait to get her in the air."

Maddy joins them, patting dust from the leg of her coveralls.

"Did you enjoy riveting?" Jack asks.

"I did except for the noise, but I was the only one who could fit inside the tail section. Even with cotton in my ears the noise was unbelievable."

Jack hugs her to him. "Carl says you did a fine job."

Maddy taps Carl's shoulder. "Thanks, Pard. By the way, why don't you come over for dinner

239

tonight? Lulu said she was going to San Diego to help open a restaurant. I'm cooking pork chops."

Carl cuffs Maddy's shoulder. "You've got yourself a deal, little lady. You guys go ahead. I'll meet you after I clean up here and send these guys home."

Jack and Maddy hang their coveralls up in the hangar then leave for home. At home Maddy heads for the kitchen while Jack uncaps a beer, then sits down to read the newspaper.

"Jack," Maddy calls. "I'm having trouble with the stove, and I can smell gas."

Jack puts down the paper, heading to the kitchen.

Maddy has her hand on the range's burner dial. "I can light the top burner, but it won't go to full flame. I think we have a gas leak."

Jack comes to the range, turns off the burner and peers behind it. "I smell it, too, but I think it's coming from outside. Maybe the gas meter's leaking. I'll take a look."

Jack finds a wooden box under the gas meter. The coupler to the meter is loose, a pipe wrench lies beside the box. He very carefully lifts the lid on the box. A ticking alarm clock, four sticks of dynamite and a coil of wires, make his eyes go wide. He gingerly picks up the box wondering for a moment what to do with it.

Jack goes around the house with the box, intending to put it in his car and take it to the beach to throw it in the water. He has no idea when it will explode. At the front of the house he meets Carl.

"What ya got there, Jack? Do I smell gas?"

"It's a time bomb, Carl." Jack holds the box in his arm and pats his pocket. "Dammit, I left my keys in the house." He gently puts the box down. "I'll be right back."

Jack goes into the house. Maddy, brows knitted, comes from the kitchen. "What is it, Jack? What did you find?"

Before he can answer he hears Carl's motorcycle fire up and roar off.

"Oh, no, I gotta go after 'im Maddy. Somebody planted a bomb at the gas meter. I think Carl's got it."

Chapter 29

Victor Drum's mood darkened as he made his way home from the People's Party headquarters. Fellow passengers on the Yellow Car edged away from Victor as he first mumbled, then smashed his fist against his knees. Finally at home, he fitfully returns from self-pity to his Jack Novac problem. Entering his brother's room, he searches the closet for a pistol from a collection his brother kept.

Four pistols hang on the rear wall behind hanging clothes. He chooses a 9mm Broomhandle Mauser, knowing that it has the killing power he needs to put Novac down. Victor holds the heavy pistol in both hands, then with his right arm extended he squints over the sights. His hand shakes so uncontrollably he brings his left hand up to steady the pistol. He can't keep the pistol still.

Victor puts the Mauser back and takes out a .22 caliber short barrel Colt Woodsman. A much smaller caliber, lighter gun meant he would have to be close to his man to kill him. But it is a gun that he shot for sport as child. When he brings the pistol up and tries to envision Novac's face on an opposite wall, his hands again shake uncontrollably. He angrily throws the pistol on the bed, tears welling up in his eyes. After a moment he shakes his head, picks up the pistol, looking at his reflection in the dresser mirror.

Staring deeply into his own reflected eyes, he grips the pistol hard. His hand trembles as he slowly raises the gun, his eyes locked into their reflection. The gun suddenly bucks in his hand shattering the mirror; shards of glass sting his face. Shocked, frightened, Victor drops the gun and throws himself on the bed, convulsing in tears.

In the morning, after sleeping fitfully, he wakes on his brother's bed, his clothes damp with sweat. Awash with self-pity, he sits on the edge of the bed cradling his head in his hands. He wipes dry spittle from the corners of his mouth before rising to get water. Turning toward the door, he is horrified to see the grotesquely distorted image of his face in the broken mirror. Frightened, he quickly turns away from the shattered mirror to almost step on the Colt pistol lying, like a deadly snake, on the floor.

For the rest of the day Victor wrestles miserably with what he will do about Novac as well as his own fate. Pacing the floor, mumbling, clenching his fists, nothing comes to mind to solve his dilemma. At the bathroom sink he splashes water on his face, avoiding his reflection.

Entering his brother's room, he ignores the broken mirror, then reluctantly looks down at the Colt pistol. He studies the gun as if it were alive. Squatting down, he touches the pistol tentatively before picking it up to put it back in the closet.

Hanging the Colt on a peg in the back of the closet, his foot touches a wooden box on the floor. He reaches down to grab the box. Backing out of the closet he puts the box down on the bed to pull the top off. "That's it, that's it, I forgot all about this, I'll blow his lousy house up." He looks inside the box: the clock, battery, and wiring are still there. "You and your beautiful talented wife, you think you've got it all."

Jubilant, Victor backs out of the closet to raise both fists in the air. "I've got you now, you can't be rich and famous if you're dead, and I'm gonna kill both of you. You'll both pay for my brother, and I'll be the hero, I'll be the man to bring you to justice. The People's Party can bow at my feet."

After the big flood early in the year, Victor and his brother Mark stole dynamite from a construction site that was clearing debris. Mark planned to bomb homes and offices of anticommunist officials and businesses. Gustavo nixed the plan, knowing that law enforcement would take a dim view of such actions. The People's Party was a small cell that did not have the power or resources to fight law enforcement.

Mark built the working bomb; then, after Gustavo's order, removed the dynamite to store it in a shed behind his house. Victor knew where Mark put the dynamite and was sure he could make the bomb work. Out in the shed Victor finds the sticks of dynamite in a shallow hole dug into the dirt and covered with some wood. The sticks are cool to the touch and show no sign of leakage.

Victor sets the box and dynamite on the kitchen table and starts to assemble his weapon. Pulling on leather work gloves he disconnects the battery, then tries to rewire the dynamite. The heavy gloves make the work very awkward. He pulls off the gloves, thinking the explosion and fire will wipe out any fingerprints anyway. Finished, he carries the box back to the closet. With a broom and dust pan Victor sweeps up the broken mirror glass.

He decides that he must plant the bomb before thinking too much about it—that could destroy his resolve. It is early afternoon when he calls the Novac home on the phone to make sure no one is there. He knows, from previous visits, the home's layout. There is only one neighbor close on the Novac's side of the street and a wood fence in the backyard separates the properties.

Driving his brother's Model A Ford, Victor passes by the Novac house to make sure no one is there and that the neighbor isn't visible. The boarded-up front window makes him smile; he loved the feeling of smashing the brick through it. He parks down the hill where there are no houses, waits to see if there is any traffic, then gets out to get the box out of the back. Hunched over, creeping, with the box cradled in his arms, he makes his way to Novac's backyard.

He and his brother had planned another home bombing where they thought of loosening a gas meter connection to amplify the explosion. He finds the meter near the ground under a kitchen window. Putting the box down, Victor takes a pipe wrench from his pocket and kneels by the meter. He stops and listens for any sounds of the neighbor, wishing he had brought his gloves. His hands are sweating; he puts the wrench down to rub his hands on his pants.

Adjusting the jaws of the wrench to fit the gas connection, Victor tries to unscrew the fitting. The fitting won't budge; he stands up, splaying his legs to have more leverage, and pulls hard on the wrench. The fitting loosens with an unholy loud screech. The neighbor's dog begins to bark, then scratches at the fence. Victor drops the wrench and flattens himself to the ground. He hears the neighbor call to the dog; the dog continues to bark. The neighbor yells at the dog to shut up.

Victor crabs backward to the corner of the house as he sees a man come to the fence to drag the dog away. The man looks over the fence at the Novac's backyard before turning away holding on to the dog's collar. Victor, wiping sweat from his forehead, waits, listening for any movement. Crouched down, breathing hard, his pulse beating hard in his throat, he decides to leave the wrench and get out of there. Crawling on the ground past the patio, he slithers to where the ground slopes away, then runs to his car.

It takes some time for him to breathe normally; he just begins to think of getting home to listen for news on the radio when he hears sirens. He looks up in the rearview mirror to see red lights flashing in the distance. He grips the steering wheel so hard his hands hurt, he looks at passing street signs for any name that is familiar. Victor slows the car as he goes by Pico Boulevard trying to think of where to run.

He almost jumps out of his skin when a loud horn blares right behind his car. His eyes snap to the mirror, huge headlights inches from his rear bumper blind him. Red lights flash, a siren wails. He puts a hand up to shade his eyes, the horn sounds again. Looking at the mirror on the car's door, he sees a fire truck with the driver waving frantically for him to get out of the way. Victor yanks the wheel hard to the right, running up over a sidewalk curb.

When he gets home, Victor goes to a kitchen cabinet for a bottle of bourbon. He takes a long pull, coughs, then takes the bottle with him to his bedroom, the radio forgotten.

Chapter 30

"Jack," Maddy beseeches her husband. "Please do not leave. The gas could blow up our beautiful house."

Jack turns around to see Maddy wringing her hands. "It's okay, Maddy, you're right. I'll go turn off the gas and fix the leak. I don't know where Carl went anyway."

Jack shakes his head as he goes past Maddy to the gas meter. "I just hope we don't see a big fireball in the sky. How 'bout opening some windows?"

Picking up the wrench Victor left, Jack adjusts the jaws down to turn off the gas valve. He looks down at his hand holding the wrench. "Damn it, I shoulda thought a fingerprints." Back in the kitchen Jack picks up a dish towel, then goes back to the meter. He wraps the towel around the wrench handle to tighten the pipe connection.

Jack finds Maddy at the open kitchen window, fanning a dish towel.

"We'll let the place air out a little before I turn the gas back on and relight the pilot lights. Grab a coupla beers and we'll sit out back. That damned Carl, I hate like hell to worry about 'im."

Maddy hands Jack a beer. "I am surprised at you," she says. "He took the bomb away to save us. He is a very brave and good friend."

"That's not how I meant it, Maddy. All I can think of is him bein' blown up by a bomb that was meant for me. I don't want him hurt, or killed, Maddy. I told you he's like my brother."

"I am sorry, Jack. I worry about him, too."

Hearing Carl's motorcycle blasting up the street, Jack jumps up out of his chair. He and Maddy run to the front of the house.

Carl carries the bomb box under his arm, a huge grin on his face.

"Good to see ya in one piece, Pard," Jack says nonchalantly.

"Your bomber ain't the sharpest tool in the shed," Carl says, "the battery's dead."

Jack slowly shakes his head. "You scared the life outta both of us, man. We've been waitin' for the big fireball."

"Hell, Jack, you'd a probably blown yourself up if I'd let you go off with this thing. I smelled gas at the front door an' knew I had to get the bomb away in a hurry. I opened the box an' saw the clock hand tickin', so I got on my bike an' blasted off to the beach. I drove out to the water thinkin' I'd throw it out in the bay. The waves are comin' in too hard, so I took the top off to see if I could just yank the wires out.

"I sat the box down in the sand an' real gentle like, coaxed the clock up." Carl looks up, grinning, to make sure he has their attention.

Jack rolls his eyes. "Go on, go on."

"I see the clock's set for 7:00. I look at my watch an' it's after 7:00. I shoulda been dust in the wind." Carl looks at them again, enjoying himself. "I get the wires outta the clock and bend 'em back so that they can't touch, then I get the battery disconnected. I pulled the rest of the wiring out, so the thing can't blow up. The clock was workin' so I'm wonderin' why, I'm wonderin' why—get it?"

Maddy and Jack both shake their heads.

"Go on," Maddy says.

"Yeah, that's right, spoil a guy's fun, you two," Carl says. "Okay, the battery has a clamp to keep it secure in the box, so I took the dynamite out an' stuck the sticks in the sand. I took two wires, attached one to each battery post and touched them together. Nothin', no spark, nothing: the battery's dead as a door nail. I threw stuff back in the box, put the sticks a dynamite in my saddle bags and hurried back for those pork chops you promised."

Maddy lunges to grab Carl in a fierce hug. She looks up at him with tears in her eyes and kisses his cheek. Carl looks at Jack with wide eyes.

"You men," she says, "you are so frustrating sometimes. Carl, that was just so brave and you pass it off as though it was nothing. Jack won't say it to you, but he was having a fit worrying about you. He said you are like a brother to him."

Both Carl and Jack look uncomfortable, neither man looking at the other.

Jack clears his throat. "Uh, Maddy, I think the gas has cleared. I'll go turn it back on and light the pilots, so you can cook Carl his pork chops."

Maddy, hands on her hips chin out, "Phooey!" she says.

Jack finishes relighting the gas pilots. "You've earned yourself a beer, Pard. Let's go out back."

Seated in the backyard chairs with cold beer, Jack raises his bottle to Carl.

"You're a little too brave at times, Pard, but I salute you. You saved our bacon an' neither me or Maddy will forget it."

"You'da done the same for me, Jack."

Jack nods. "I would, and I will."

"Whata you gonna do with the bomb, Jack."

"I'm gonna take it to that Detective Vance and see if he can get any fingerprints from the damned thing. I'd be willin' to bet the farm, Victor Drum is the culprit. I'm beginnin' to think if the cops can't do anything with Mr. Drum, I'm gonna have to. I'll take the box to Vance in the mornin' and meet you at the hangar as soon as I can. I'm really lookin' forward to seein' our plane finished."

It is almost noon before Jack gets to the hangar. Maddy runs out to meet him.

"Oh, Jack, the plane is so beautiful, you will be so pleased."

She takes his hand, leading him to the plane.

Jack pushes his hat back on his head. The plane supported by sawhorses, gleams in the light. The unpainted aluminum fuselage, now complete, shows off the trim lines of the craft. From the pointed nose to the engine compartment, the fuselage smoothly tapers out to surround the engine before tapering back to the small cockpit. Behind the cockpit, a semi-conical shape extends to the tail wings and rudder. The team used every effort to keep the craft compact and light weight.

Jack hugs Maddy to him. "She's beautiful. It's like a dream come true."

Maddy, her arm around Jack's waist, looks at his face, happy to see his joy. "I can't believe how big the propeller looks compared to the rest of the plane," she says. "It looks so powerful, like it just wants to be unleashed."

Carl comes toward them, wiping his hands on a rag. "Whatta ya think, Pard?"

Jack reaches out to shake Carl's hand. "She looks a winner, man. You guys have out done yourselves. Maddy says the plane looks like it wants to be unleashed. I like that. It does look like a powerful animal, strainin' at the bit."

Carl smiles as the three of them admire the plane. "The crew's gone to lunch. Lu's back an' brought some burgers, so let's eat. I wanta finish some work in the engine compartment, an' Ben's gonna finish the hydraulics for the landing gear. I think this afternoon we can fire it up an' do a systems check. You can sit in the cockpit an' play pilot."

Jack nods enthusiastically. "That's my kinda afternoon, Pard."

It is early evening before Carl is ready to fire up the engine. Jack paid the metal workers earlier, promising them a party to celebrate later.

Carl leans over the cockpit showing Jack the controls he will use to start the engine. Jack has a printed sheet detailing the starting procedure on his knees as he gets ready.

Carl finishes, ready to climb down. "I'm gonna pull the prop through 4 or 5 times, then you take it from there. If we over prime the engine, we'll go through that procedure again, okay? Give me an okay sign when you've got oil pressure. We don't wanta run it too hot, so after it warms a bit, we'll try the landing gear."

Jack nods. "I'm ready when you are."

The engine fires, running unevenly until it generates some temperature. The noise is deafening. Jack, noting the oil pressure reading, throttles back, then uses his thumb and forefinger to give Carl the okay sign.

Ben stands on the wing, wind from the spinning propeller blowing his hair back, his cheeks fluttering. He has to yell for to Jack hear him.

"Okay, Jack, try it."

The landing gear smoothly folds out and with a clunk locks into place. Ben jubilantly pounds Jack's shoulder.

"Okay, retract 'em," he says.

The gear retracts, locking up into the wing.

"It's good," Ben says. "I'm going to climb down and watch. Give it another test when I get down."

Jack works the landing gear down and up, much to Ben's delight. Carl waves to get Jack's attention, then runs the back of his thumb across his neck signaling him to cut the engine off. Before Jack can get out, Scotty is on the wing with a clipboard asking about the instruments.

"I like the locations, Scotty, but I forgot to tell you that I want all the temperature and pressure gauges set so that the needles point straight up when the temps and pressures are normal."

"Uh, okay," Scotty says with a wrinkle on his forehead. "Can I ask why?"

"Oh, sure, of course, Scotty. I always set them like that on my race cars. I can see at a glance that if all the needles point straight up that they are normal and don't need more monitoring. If one of the gauges has a reading to the left or right, I know at the glance I need to pay more attention to it."

Scotty's face brightens. "I like that boss, it makes good sense."

"I'm next." Carl stands on the other wing with a notebook and pencil. "Give me temps and pressures."

Jack gives Carl the gauge readings.

"How's she lookin', Pard?"

"There's a little oil seepage but I think when we stabilize a normal temp, she'll seal up okay."

Jack climbs out of the cockpit. "I'll tell you, she feels good once the engine smooths out. I like the feel of all that power you put into her, Pard. So when can I take her up?"

"Hold your horses, Jack. I wanta do a coupla days of runnin' up an' down the runway before we try flyin'. I can check all the systems, you can get a feel of her, and if somethin's not right, you don't fall outta the sky."

"Okay, Pard, you're the boss. How bout we get cleaned up here an' I'll buy the beer."

Maddy puts her camera away as Jack steps off the plane's wing. "How about some food with that?"

"Sounds good to me," Jack says.

Carl, Scotty, Ben, Jack, and Maddy sit around a restaurant table, each with a mug of beer. "Where is Lulu?" Maddy asks Carl.

"She went home to bed after she made lunch. That place she helped open kept her up 26 hours straight."

"I wish she could be here," Maddy says, "this was such a good day."

Jack raises his mug. "Here, here, as the Brits would say. May all our days be so good. I wanta thank all of you. That plane's gonna be good, I can feel it. Right after we finish testing, we're gonna go after Howard Hughes' record."

All at the table raise their mugs and cheer.

Chapter 31

Victor feels a terrible pounding in his head. He groggily opens his eyes, groaning at the daylight. The pounding starts again: someone is hammering at the front door.

"Police! Open the door, Drum, or I'll break it in."

Victor looks dully around him, wondering if he is a having nightmare. He braces his hands on the table to get up out of the chair. He stands, then bows, holding his splitting head with both hands. The front door crashes in, men pour in through the house. Victor falls to the floor, curling into a ball. Two men lift him to his feet. Victor promptly vomits, splattering their shoes. They immediately drop him; one man kicks him in the back, then wipes his shoes on him.

"That's enough of that," Detective Vance hollers at the two policemen. "Take him outside and hose him off, then get him to the station."

When Victor wakes again he is in a cramped jail cell. He tries to remember what has happened. A uniformed officer peers into the cell. "Go get Vance," the officer says, "His boy is back in the land of living."

An officer takes Victor to an interrogation room. "Man, you stink to high heaven." The officer says as he leaves the room. Victor hears the door being locked. As Victor waits, he remembers making the bomb and taking it to Novac's. He begins to feel a little better, hoping that Novac and his wife are dead from the explosion. The police must want him for questioning. *Ah, he thinks, they can't pin anything on me.*

The big detective that questioned him about the firebomb at Novac's plant comes into the room. He grimaces as he pulls out handcuffs, placing them on Victor's wrist and a table leg.

"What's that for?" Victor complains.

The detective pulls a chair back away from the table to sit down. "I'm leaving the door open 'cause you stink. You're here because I'm arresting you for the attempted murder of the Novac's. You wanta help yourself out and tell me all about it?"

Victor tries to defiantly fold his arms across his chest only to jerk at the handcuff.

"I don't know what you're talking about."

Vance leans back in his chair to yell over his shoulder. "Hey, Donnie, bring in that box, will you?"

A uniformed officer brings in the box Jack Novac brought in. He puts it down on the table. Vance moves it out of Victor's reach.

"That's all, Donnie," Vance says. The officer exits the room.

The room grows quiet as Vance watches Victor trying to ignore the box. Victor remains motionless, staring down at his lap. Slowly his head cocks, looking up at Vance. "Is that thing ticking?"

Vance smiles back at Victor. "Sure is, and the clock that's got your fingerprints all over it is wired to dynamite sticks that's got your prints on 'em too. We aren't sure why it hasn't gone off yet."

Victor's eyes go big. "You, you mean it's a bomb?"

Vance grins at Victor's discomfort. "Yeah, Victor, it's a bomb. But you already knew that since you made it. We were kinda hoping you could tell us how to turn it off."

Victor begins squirm in his chair. "I don't know anything about making bombs; you better get that thing outta here."

"How'd it get your fingerprints all over it if you didn't make it?"

Victor tries to move his chair away. "Novac must have broken into my house again and planted that thing. He hates me. You know he murdered my brother and you did nothing about that. You let him go."

Vance sits up in his seat. "How'd you know the bomb was for Novac if you didn't make it to blow up his house?"

Victor looks away chewing his lip.

"Well, come on, Victor, you gonna let this thing blow us up?"

Victor is silent. He hesitates, trying to think of a way out then his eyes narrow and he looks at the detective with a smirk.

"You're not going to blow us up with that bomb I know nothing about, and you told me it was Novac. Now I want my lawyer."

Vance stares at Victor, fire in his eyes. He gets out of his chair without a word and leaves, slamming the door behind him.

Chapter 32

Jack waits impatiently for Carl to finish his preparations. Ben and Scotty use their lunch break to watch the first test of the plane. Maddy readies her camera as Carl buttons up the engine cover and motions for Jack to get in the plane. He climbs up on the wing with a printed sheet of a preflight checklist on a clipboard that he hands to Jack.

After they run through the list, Carl leans in the cockpit.

"We're okay to use the taxiway, just watch the temps and pressures. Taxi down to the end, then turn around and come back to the hangar. Oh, and keep the wheels on the ground, will ya?"

Jack looks up at Carl, who is frowning back at him. "Yes sir, you're the boss."

The sun has warmed the day considerably, the engine's coolant temperature rises quickly, Jack adds throttle and starts down the taxiway. The plane's nose-up attitude on the ground makes it hard for Jack to see where he's going. When he sticks his head out to sight alongside the nose the engines exhaust blasts in his face. He quickly learns to use the edge of the pavement to guide him.

It takes a while to get the feel of this beast; turning around to come back is a slow process. With no obstacles in his way, Jack opens the throttle more for the return. Turning around at the hangar takes less time now as Jack learns to use the engine's torque to help swing the plane. As he goes down the taxiway the engine note rise; Jack is feeding in more power.

On the return he is tempted to open it up even more when he glances down at the gauges. The coolant temperature needle is already past the 2 o'clock position. He throttles back but the needle continues to climb. Jack shuts the engine down well before reaching the hangar.

Carl is already on the way to the plane carrying a fire extinguisher. Ben and Scotty run behind him.

Jack stands up in the cockpit as Carl nears. "It's okay, Pard, the temp just kept climbing; I shut it off at 210 degrees."

Carl touches his hand to the engine cowling, then pulls his hand back, shaking it.

"She's good'n hot alright; let's get her back to the hangar."

Jack jumps off the wing and they all push the plane back to the hangar.

"What do you think?" Scotty asks.

Jack shakes his head, grinning. "I think it's got a ton a torque---feels like it's gonna twist the plane into a pretzel. I can't wait to get her in the air."

Carl and Ben are busy removing the engine cowling. Carl calls Jack over to him.

"How 'bout goin' to the grocery store an' gettin' a few big bags of ice. I'll shovel some in the cooling duct and we can finish this phase of testing today."

Ben and Scotty go back to their jobs after lunch and Jack brings back ice to keep the plane's engine cool. He and Carl continue with the tedious running of the plane on the ground. After each run, they bring it back to the hangar to do a systems check.

After they push the plane into the hangar at the end of the day, Carl wipes the sweat from his forehead.

"Okay, tomorrow she flies, Jack. No stunts. Just twice around the field with the landing gear down an' bring her down. If we take our time now, we won't have to pay for something we overlooked later."

"I got it, Pard," Jack barks. "You'd take it personal if I busted up your baby. I won't do anything dumb, you tell me how you want it an' that's what I'll do. I gotta go into the plant tomorrow mornin' so I'll see you here about lunch time."

"Don't get your feathers ruffled, Jack; it's more like I don't want you fallin' outta the sky."

"I know, Pard. I guess I'm just anxious. See you mañana."

Driving home Maddy sits quietly with her arms crossed. Jack glances over at her several times. "I know what you're thinkin': I'm a heel."

"These people love and respect you, Jack. They do not want to see you hurt," she says.

"Like I told Carl, I'm just anxious. That, an' everyone seems to think I'm gonna do somethin' dumb."

"All of us want you safe, and I think everyone is anxious about the plane flying for the first time. I'll fix you a good dinner and we'll make it an early night, so you will be well-rested."

Jack is up before daybreak and goes directly to the plant. Keeping his mind on the business has the desired effect of passing time. Mori comes in before Jack leaves for the airfield to wish him luck.

Jack taps Mori's shoulder on the way out. "If we get it goin' real good, maybe I'll do a fly by before you go home tonight."

Carl has the plane outside of the hangar when Jack gets there.

"She's ready, Pard. Lu an' Maddy have lunch. Let's get some before the rest of the guys eat it all."

"You go ahead," Jack says, "I'm not hungry. I'll get started on the preflight list."

Jack is in the cockpit showing Maddy the instruments when Carl finishes lunch. The rest of the men follow chattering, all now anxious to get their bird in the air.

Maddy hands Jack his cloth helmet and goggles, then helps with his shoulder harness.

"Have fun, Jack." Maddy squeezes his shoulder before climbing down off the wing.

Carl is up on the other side of the cockpit. "I know you wanta get goin'. Just give me a coupla touch an' goes, get a little feel for her, an' bring it back."

"Will do," Jack says. He is in his element now, doing what he believes he was born to do. "Let's wind her up."

The plane looks small going by the DC 3's, heading to the runaway. Jack turns into the wind and lifts off to gain altitude. He circles the field and brings the plane in to touch down on the runway. He lifts off again to repeat the touch and go, then taxis to the hangar.

Jack unlatches the seat belts and climbs out of the cockpit smiling. The crew gathers around him.

Jack gives the okay sign. "She's good, the controls are really slick. Touch the rudder or the stick and she's right there. It doesn't take a bunch a throttle to get her off the ground either."

"How's the temps and pressures?" Carl asks.

"All good, Pard," Jack reports. "Coolant temp goes to 210 taxiing but goes back to 190 once she's in the air. Oil temp 190, pressure 70."

"How's the landing gear feel?" Ben asks.

"It is stiff," Jack replies. "But maybe it'll loosen up. We're not runnin' much fuel so it's pretty light. If we were landin' on a dirt runway it'd probably rattle my teeth."

"I can lighten it up if we need to," Ben says. "It looks good though; you brought it down real smooth."

"Whatta ya wanta do, Carl?" Jack asks.

"I'll check the engine, Ben'll check the landing gear and hydraulics, Scotty'll check the cockpit and instruments. If we're good, you go back up with the gear down and circle the field at, say, 500 feet. I'll put enough fuel in so you can get a feel for it. If it looks good after we check it out, you can go again and open her up some."

They make the next test run and Jack returns the plane to the hangar. Carl's program of test and check is becoming routine. Scotty has gone back to the plant, Ben back to Douglas.

"Okay, Jack, it all looks good. I put plenty of fuel in so go have some fun. If anything feels odd, get her back here pronto."

Jack gathers his helmet and goggles looking at his watch. "I'd like to go buzz the plant; it's about time for them to go home. If you see me dip down, it'll only be for a second."

"I ain't scared, Jack, the plane's good an' it's not like there's a bunch a traffic."

"Yeah, that's the ticket, Pard. Let's light her up."

Jack hauls back on the stick---the plane seems to leap into the air. He makes a steep climb, then a hard turn to zoom back over the field. He turns sharp again; the bright aluminum on the wings flashing in the sun. The plant, a scant three miles as the crow flies, comes up fast. Jack dives down, the engine roaring. He sees his employees stop by their cars to look up. He pulls up hard, does a snap roll, then heads back to the airfield.

Wearing a big grin, Jack jumps down off the wing to pound Carl's back.

"She's good, Pard, really good. I wanta try moving the fuel tank to under the cockpit seat, she's a bit nose heavy. Then we're ready for the record run. I'll drain the fuel and get busy."

Carl massages the back of his neck, rotating his head. "We haven't tested the landing gear yet, and it's best to do that here. The people and parts are right here if we need to fix something."

"Right, right, okay, let's pull the fuel tank and get started."

"Can't the fuel tank wait?" Maddy asks. "Carl's been up since daybreak working on the plane."

Jack snaps around frowning, then softens. "Yeah, yeah, okay, we'll just get the tank out now and do the install tomorrow."

Maddy rolls her eyes. "I'll see you at home. Goodnight, Carl."

"Goodnight, Maddy," Carl says. "It won't take long to get the tank out. I'll get the 'I just can't wait boy' home in two shakes."

They drain the tank and wrestle it out of the fuselage.

"Go on home, Jack. I'll get the tools cleaned up, say goodnight to Ross, and see you in the morning."

Chapter 33

Victor Drum sits at his kitchen table counting and stacking various denominations of money. Licking his thumb and forefinger to separate the bills, he is totally immersed in his newfound wealth. He jumps when there is a loud knocking on the front door. His eyes blink owlishly as if awakening from a dream. His head jerks back, eyes flicking about, thinking someone must be after his money. He scoops the bills into a grocery bag and stuffs it under the sink before tentatively going to the front door.

"Who's there?" Victor asks, standing back away from the door.

"It's me, Bob, open the door, Victor."

"Bob?"

"Yeah, Bob, from the People's Party."

"What do you want, Bob?"

"I wanta talk to you, Vic. I gotta plan to help you with your Novac problem. You want me to yell it through the door?"

Victor opens the door and steps back to allow Bob to enter. Taller than Victor, Bob has shaggy black hair matched by a bushy beard. His barrel chest and ape-like arms rightly give him the look of a low-class tough.

"What kind of plan do you have, Bob?"

"Ask me to have a seat, offer me a drink, can't you? I'm here to help, Victor. You don't want to make me mad, do you?"

"Come on, Bob." Victor poses with his hands on his hips. "What do you want?"

Bob makes himself comfortable in an upholstered chair. He looks up at Victor with a smile showing yellow uneven teeth.

"I'll take care of Novac for five hundred bucks. He can be dead tonight."

"How do you think you could do it, and where do you think I'd get five hundred dollars?"

"Look, Vic, I been studying Novac. I know he's working on a plane at Clover Field. I know he goes to work at his plant early every morning. If I can't get him at night working on his plane, I'll waylay him on his way to work. You know you can't get him cause you're the first guy the cops'll want to look at. You take a trip somewhere for coupla days, make sure people see you and come back when you read about his murder in the papers."

"Do you really think you can do it?"

268

Bob takes a Luger pistol from his pocket. "He won't be the first guy I've dusted. You give me the dough and Novac's a dead man."

"I don't have that kind of money."

"Sure you do, Vic. You just got your brother's life insurance money."

"What! Why would you think that?"

"Come on, Vic. The paper had your attorney saying that he was just at the cop station to help with an insurance claim. He said he wasn't a criminal attorney. You called him 'cause you didn't know anyone else. Your brother told me you guys had life insurance policies. You must be rollin' in dough. You know I could just go to the cops and tell 'em what I know. I'm tryin' to help you here, Vic."

Victor goes into the kitchen returning with a bottle of whiskey and two glasses. He splashes some in a glass and hands it to Bob.

"The insurance policy wasn't worth much and I have to pay the attorney and my brother's debts. I'll give you two hundred dollars, a hundred now and a hundred when the job's done."

Bob downs the whiskey and holds out the glass for more. "Okay, Vic, you drive a hard bargain. You better go get yourself an alibi right after you give me the cash."

Victor counts out nine ten-dollar bills and two fives, then he hands the money to Bob. "That's all I have here. I'll have the rest when Novac's dead."

Bob puts his glass down to count the money. "You've got yourself a deal, Vic. See you soon."

After Bob leaves, Victor knocks back his whiskey. "If you actually kill Novac, I just may have to go to the cops and tell them what I know."

Bob stops by a pool hall to while away the day. After a few hours he drives to a good restaurant on Wilshire to have a steak dinner, congratulating himself on his scheme to bleed Victor of all his money once he kills Novac. After dinner he drives to Clover Field to wait for dark. It is a moonless night, the place is still, with only a few cars in the lot as Bob soundlessly squeezes the door shut on his car and heads to the hangar he reconnoitered earlier.

Creeping past a row of hangars, there are still lights on in some of the hangars and a few men about. When he reconnoitered, the place was deserted at night. Bob begins to lose his resolve. Bringing a pint bottle of whiskey out of his pocket he takes a deep pull. He can see the door on the hangar where Novac keeps his plane is still open. Bob stays out of the light, his breath coming faster as he checks his gun again, cocking the toggle. As he gets closer, he sees a man in white coveralls with Novac Engineering embroidered on the back standing on a ladder working on a plane,

Bob nervously looks around; he is out of sight from the men he saw. He uncorks the pint but hesitates, then rams the cork back in, and shoves the bottle back in his pocket. Sweat beads on his forehead. It's now or never. He checks to see if anyone can see him. Crouching down, he runs to the hangar; now only a few yards away, he begins shooting. The Luger fires 7.65mm rounds as fast as Bob pulls the trigger. He sees the man on the ladder start to turn, then fall to the ground. A dog begins to bark, lights snap on in the next hangar. Bob flattens to the ground, waits a moment, then runs back into the shadows and doesn't stop until he gets to his car.

Carl Sander's body hits ground with dull thump, a pool of blood swells out beneath him.

Chapter 34

Maddy is busy cataloguing her photographs when she hears the phone ring. Jack is in the backyard writing down his thoughts and ideas for the plane in his journal when Maddy rushes out of the house, tears streaming down her face. Jack, looking up from the journal, stands up immediately concerned.

"What's wrong, Maddy?"

"Ross is on the phone: Carl's been shot."

Jack rushes inside to grab the phone.

"Ross, what the hell's going on?"

Ross explains that he thought he heard popping noises in the hangar and went out to check. He found Carl lying on the ground in a pool of blood. He called the hospital for an ambulance, then called the police. The medics showed up right away and took Carl to the hospital. The police wanted Ross to stay with them at the hangar.

Jack grips the phone hard, rapidly firing questions. "Will Carl be okay? What did the medics say? How do you know he was shot? Did you see who did it? Did you call Lulu?"

"Hold on Jack, give me a chance to answer. The medics said Carl lost a lot of blood, and that could be the deciding factor if he going to survive. They need to find his blood type and then a donor."

"Did they take him to UCLA?" Jack asks.

"Yes…"

"I'll call you later. Carl and I have the same blood type."

Jack turns to Maddy. "I'm gonna go to the hospital and give blood for Carl. I don't know if Lulu has been contacted."

"I'm going with you, Jack. I'll call Lulu when we get there."

Jack races to the hospital, slams on the brakes in the parking lot and vaults from the car. He rushes through the door to the front desk.

"I'm here to give blood for Carl Sanders."

The nurse on duty casually looks up at Jack from her desk.

"Did the hospital call you?" she asks.

"No, a friend called me from the location where Carl was shot. I understand he may not survive without blood. I'm here to give all he can use, where do I go?"

"Do you know his blood type?"

"Yeah A+, we're both A+."

"Are you related to Mr. Sanders?"

"Yes, yes! That's right. I'm his brother. Now where do I go to get him the blood he needs?"

"I'll have a nurse come and get you."

"Yeah, fine, hurry up, will you?"

Maddy comes into the hospital room where Jack gave his blood. She sits down in a chair by his bed and reaches out to squeeze his hand.

Jack's face is pasty white, his eye lids flutter, then open. He looks up, slowly taking in the room. Maddy stands up to bend over him.

"How do you feel, Jack? They took a lot of blood from you."

"I feel okay. Have you heard anything about Carl? These people wouldn't tell me a damn thing."

"The doctor says Carl's going to be okay. A bullet struck him under his arm and nicked an artery. They said he lost a lot of blood and would have died without your blood."

"Can we go see him?"

"Your doctor says you need to rest, they had to keep getting more blood from you. They want you to stay for observation."

"Aw, hell, Maddy, I'm fine. A coke and a burger and I'll be strong as King Kong."

Jack throws back the bed cover and swings his legs out. He stands up, sways a moment and collapses back on the bed.

Maddy lifts his legs back on the bed. "Okay, Kong, you rest a minute and I will find out if we can see Carl. I haven't been able to call Lulu; she doesn't answer their home phone. I have called every place I can think of to find her. Maybe Carl will know where she is."

Maddy comes back to the room as a nurse comes in with a food service.

"The doctor says we can see Carl after lunch. He wants a nurse to take you in a wheelchair."

"I can walk," Jack says.

"Not if you want to see Carl today," Maddy says. "Doctors orders. I'm going to see if I can find Lulu. I'll be back soon."

When she returns, Maddy tells Jack that she gave Ross Lulu's phone number and asked that he keep calling.

A nurse lets Maddy wheel Jack into Carl's room. Carl stirs, looking over at Jack being wheeled in.

"This must be some kinda nightmare," Carl says. "You look worse than I feel Jack. What's ailin' you, boy?"

"I'm glad to see you so chipper, Pard. Course you know if I hadn't given you my good Novac blood you'd be on your way to Hades about now. We're real blood brothers now."

"Novac blood!" Carl cries. "God almighty, I must be in hell. All the years I been steerin' clear of Novac madness an' now I got it. I guess I gotta start struttin' around, my chin stuck out, my face all wrinkled up with that silly look of determination…or maybe that's just constipation, I never have figured which."

Jack and Maddy both wipe the tears from their eyes. "Jeez Pard, you make me laugh any harder an' you're gonna have to give me some a that blood back."

Lulu bursts into the room almost diving on the bed with Carl to hug him. She kisses him, then pulls back to caress his face with her hands.

"I'm so sorry, Carl; Ross called and said you'd been shot. Oh, my God, when I got home I knew you hadn't slept there. I was going to ball you out for workin' on that damned plane all night."

Carl kisses Lulu's hand. "Well, I guess I can't be in hell if you're here. You may not want me anymore though; I got Novac blood in me."

Lulu looks over at Jack. "What, what does that mean?" She looks back to Carl.

"I leaked all mine out an' they filled me up with Jack's. I may never be the same."

"Please don't act silly, Carl; I don't know what happened to you," Lulu says tearfully, wringing her hanky. "No one told me."

"I think somebody was shooting at the plane and I got in the way. I was on a ladder when I heard gunfire, then saw a hole punched in the plane just above my head. When I turned to see where the shooter was, I lost my balance and fell. I musta hit my head 'cause I got a big goose egg on the back of my head. I don't remember gettin' shot; it didn't hurt then and still doesn't."

Lulu's eyes widen as real alarm spreads across her face. "Who would shoot at you? Why would someone shoot at you?"

"I don't know, Lu. The local cops don't know—and I don't think they're all that interested—but I was kinda groggy when they were here. I'm kinda runnin' outta steam now."

Maddy standing behind Jack's wheelchair taps his shoulder. "I think we should get you back to your room and let Carl and Lulu have some time by themselves."

"Hey, Jack," Carl says. "Why don't you get the plane painted while we're both laid up? That way you won't be bustin' a gut when you're ready to fly."

"Hey, yeah, that's good thinkin', Pard," Jack exclaims. "That's thinkin' like a real Novac."

Carl's head sinks back into the pillow. "Oh, my God, I've got it bad, Lu. Get on outta here, Jack."

Chapter 35

Maddy stands on a ladder snapping the shutter of her camera. The plane's new gloss white paint job requires unique camera angles to filter out the sun's glare. Jack and Carl have been moving the plane around since morning to give her different lighting. Carl suggested that they jazz up the plain white paint job with a broad blue stripe on top of the fuselage that goes from the propeller tapering back to meet the rudder. Two red stripes follow on each side of the blue paint.

The red stripes go all the way to the rear edge of the rudder giving the plane a sense of motion when viewed from the sides. They decided to paint a lucky number seven on each side in red below the stripes. Carl was back working on installing the fuel tank behind the seat in less than a week after he was shot.

Jack explained to Carl that he went to the police with his suspicions. The police questioned

Victor Drum but found that he traveled by bus to Yosemite on the day of the shooting. At the time of the attack he was having dinner at the Ahwahnee Hotel.

"I think Drum had somebody else do the shooting and they thought you were me. Now I gotta find who did it or beat it outta Drum myself."

Ross Elmore comes from his office at the front of the hangar to tell Jack he has a phone call. "It's a Detective Vance and he doesn't sound happy."

Jack picks up the phone. "Hi ya, Vance, what's up?"

"What's up is that I got a call from somebody named Robbins who I find out is a big shot government type. He says you're some big deal, and that it's my job to find out who's trying to kill you. I'm gonna make this short: I'll bring Drum in but I'm not a rubber hose kinda cop, see? You be here after lunch and I'll cut Drum loose. You can put the fear of God into him and see if you can get any answers.

"You can question him when he gets out of the station, but you don't kidnap him, and you don't beat him up. You can threaten all you want, but no rough stuff. If you get anything outta him, I'll go to bat for you. You can do me and yourself a big favor: don't ever have your bad ass government guy call me again, got it?"

"I had no idea Robbins would call you. He likes to meddle. I owe him, and he knows it. I will ask him not to interfere, but I can't promise he'll listen. I'll be at the station and keep it cool. Thanks, Vance."

Jack returns to the hangar. "I gotta go see Detective Vance. It won't take long, I'll be right back."

Jack waits by the concrete steps at the police station. He steps out, grabbing Drum by the arm pulling him back to the side of the building. Bob, who was crossing the street to meet Drum, walks away to the corner where he can watch them.

Jack stands nose to nose with Victor, gripping him on both arms to hold him still. "I wanta know who you sent to kill me, Drum. You better talk or I'm gonna make it my business to make your life miserable."

Drum frantically looks around for someone to help him.

"I don't know what you're talking about. I told the cops I was in Yosemite. I don't have anything to do with your problems."

"You're my problem, Victor. You're lucky I can't wring the truth outta you here. You can save yourself a lotta grief if you tell me which of your commie buddies you sent to kill me."

Victor's head snaps back, wide-eyed.

"Buddies, what buddies? I, I don't know what you mean."

"Thanks, Vic, you just confirmed what I thought. I'm gonna find your People's Party pal and make him talk. Then I'll go to the papers and tell them all about how you and the People's Party use murder and mayhem try and force your ideals. I'll make sure, when the cops put you in prison, to find some bad guys there that can make your life a living hell."

Jack bears down on Drum's arms. "You or your commie buddies come after me or my wife or my friends again, you won't live to see prison."

Jack lets go of Victor to slap him hard with an open hand.

"Think about it, the only way to save yourself is to tell me what you know. I'll give you some time to get smart. After that, I'll keep after you until you tell me everything I want to know. I'll get it outta you, one way or another."

Jack returns to the hangar not knowing whether he feels better or worse bracing Drum. His mood soon lifts.

Carl and Maddy are standing by the plane. "I got her warmed up, Jack. Let's go see how the landing gear works."

"You bet, Pard, let me get my coveralls on."

Jack sits in the cockpit as Carl points out landing gear functions.

"I know you know this is the main gear lever," Carl says pointing to a lever by the seat. "This is a gauge Scotty put in to show hydraulic pressure." Carl points to a gauge on the instrument panel. "He put four lights on the top of the panel to show if each gear is locked down or not. Green is locked, red is not locked.

"Let's try it a few times in the air. Bring the gear down then cycle it back up. Do a couple easy rolls and try the gear again. Come in for a landing, then take off and do it again. Can you think of anything else?"

"Nope, sounds good to me," Jack says.

Maddy snaps pictures as Jack gets in the cockpit.

"Have fun, Cowboy; I'll take some pictures of the plane in the air."

Belted in his new racing airplane he revels in the sensations of the sleek, powerful racer. The roar of the engine, the acceleration taking off. The blades of the huge propeller blur, chewing into the air to bolt him into the sky.

Hard back on the stick, kicking the rudder, he snap rolls the plane. Visuals flash by, earth, sky, earth, sky. Blood rushes to his head as the safety belts bite into his shoulders. The force of gravity loads on his body are greater than anything he felt in a race car. After putting the landing gear to the test, he reluctantly brings the plane back to the hangar.

Carl jumps up on the wing with his notebook as soon as the plane stops.

"Temps and pressures are good; the landing gear is slow to extend and slow to retract. One side of the gear is slower than the other. I think it's the left side but it's hard to say for certain."

"I'll have Ben check it out," Carl says. "We wanted it to be lightweight, so it's got a small pump. We just wanta make sure it works when it's supposed to."

"She's fast, Pard. I wanta go for the speed record."

"I know, Jack, so do I, but we gotta make sure everything works and that she'll stay in the sky first."

***

Bob Block, Victor's gunman, watched Jack brace Victor. He waited after Jack left to be sure Novac wasn't coming back before he went to Victor. "What did he say?" Bob has Victor by the arm walking him back to the corner.

"He wants to know who shot his friend. He says he's going to expose the People's Party as murderers if I don't tell him what he wants to know."

Block pulls Victor close to him. "You're not gonna tell him nothin'. I'm sticking to you till we get rid of the Novacs for good. You got yourself a house guest…buddy boy."

Chapter 36

Block calls Gustavo at the People's Party to say that he has to stay close to Victor in order to protect both the Party and Victor from Jack Novac's attacks. Block is a minor criminal that found a room and board job at the Party's apartment house keeping the members in line. Gustavo also uses him to intimidate uncooperative employers. Bob actually has no Communist convictions: he just lives off the Party so he can occasionally extort money from people he intimidates.

He holds Victor a virtual prisoner at a run-down hotel, telling him that it is for his own protection from Novac. When he does allow Victor briefly out of his grasp to get groceries and liquor, he searches Victor's house for the hidden money.

Victor, unhappy with Block's hold over him goes to Gustavo to complain. Gustavo is uncharacteristically on edge, telling Victor that the police barged in and ransacked the place looking for Block. They found shell casings at Clover Field with his fingerprints.

Gustavo pulls at his chin whiskers nervously. "You tell Bob to either go to the police and turn himself in or get out of town. I will not have your bungling attempts to murder this man, Novac, bring down all the work I have done for the party here. Neither of you were working for the party when you tried to kill Novac and that is what I told the police. You and Bob are no longer welcome here. After the police left, I had all of Bob's belongings burned."

"But you knew we were avenging my brother," Victor pleads.

"I knew nothing of the kind. Get out of here Victor; I don't want the police to find you here."

Victor rushes back to his house to tell Block. Victor scowls angrily. "That lousy bastard, Gustavo, gave me a couple hundred bucks to get us outta town."

"But I say no," Victor says defiantly. "You screwed up the Novac shooting, Bob. So, you help me kill the Novacs and I'll make it worth it for you."

Bob grabs Victor with both of his big hairy hands tightening around Victor's neck. "Give me the money or I'll beat you to death."

Victor squirms, trying to pull Bob's hands away.

"That's all you guys think of. You all want to beat me up; well go ahead, you won't get any money. Novac will never let me alone if we don't kill him. You told me you could do it. I trusted you. You want money? I'll give you a thousand dollars after both of the Novac's are dead. Novac killed my brother and he won't stop until I'm dead, too. You shot his friend; he'll kill you too."

Block, taking his hands away, eyes Victor wickedly. *'Thousand bucks, how much money has he got?' he wonders.* An evil smirk crosses his face. *'I'm gonna squeeze every penny outta this little jerk.'*

***

Jack glances up at the clock in his office; it is past 9 pm. The Navy contract requires his attention and he is adamant that his company's performance is exemplary. He has been spending a great deal of time with his airplane trying to iron out the bugs in the landing gear. He stacks the paperwork he has been working on, getting ready to go home. Jack is about to switch the office lights off when turns back to his desk to unlock the drawer where he keeps his pistol.

Earlier Detective Vance called to tell him they matched the fingerprints from the shell cases found at the scene of Carl's shooting. The prints belong to Robert Block, a minor criminal that Vance believes works for the People's Party. He sent a wanted poster with Block's mug shot and told Jack to be on the lookout for him. The police think that Block is with Victor Drum but have not been able to locate either of the men.

Jack drives up the hill toward his house, it has been a long day and he is anxious to be home. He passes a car parked off the road in an empty lot just below his house. He wants to be home but decides to stop and back his car down across the street from the other car to check the registration. The hood of the car is still warm to the touch. Jack opens the car's door to see the registration attached to the steering column. Mark Drum's name and address are on the card.

Jack returns to his car to get his pistol and a flashlight out of the glove box. He locks his car before going to Drum's car to lift the hood and yank out the distributer cap and wires. He throws the cap and wires down the hill.

Cupping the flashlight, Jack follows a trail of trampled brush to his backyard. Lights are on in the house and Jack can see into the kitchen through the screen door. He switches the flashlight off but is too far away to make out what is happening in the kitchen. Dropping the flashlight, Jack crouches down to make his way closer to the house, staying away from the light spilling out through the kitchen door.

He silently approaches on the soft grass to where he can hear raised voices inside. Pressing against the house, then moving slowly, he peeks through the screen door into the kitchen. He can see Maddy in a chair with her arms behind her. Victor Drum has a handful of her hair, pulling her head back. Bob Block stands in front of her with a Luger pistol pointed at her head.

Block swipes the air past her face with the pistol. "Call him or I'll mess your face up so bad no one will ever wanta look at you again."

Maddy is quick to reply. "If you are going to kill me anyway why should I care what I look like?"

"Oh, you're a real smart little bitch, aren't you?" Block yells. "Well, I like makin' the smart ones scream, but we don't wanta wake the neighbors. Vic, get something to gag her with."

Boiling with anger, Jack steps through the screen door. "Stop right there, Victor. You with the gun, drop it!"

Block's shoulders jump but he doesn't turn to face Jack, he keeps his Luger trained on Maddy.

"It's Novac," Victor yelps. "Shoot him, Bob."

Block keeps his back to Jack, covering Maddy. "Drop your gun, Novac, or I'll blow your wife to kingdom come," Block growls.

Jack hesitates. Victor glares at him with an ugly hatred. The gunman blocks Jack's view of Maddy.

"That the kinda yellow bastard you are? You can't face me? Big man with my wife tied down, huh? Well that's probably a good thing for you, 'cause she'd kick your fat yellow ass."

"Shoot him, shoot him, Bob," Victor screams. Block extends his arm out with the gun as if he is going to surrender, then spins around to snap a shot off at Jack. The round narrowly misses, thudding behind Jack into the door frame. Block jerks the gun back, centering on Jack.

Jack's pistol booms twice, punching huge holes through Block's chest. He is dead before he hits the floor. Victor rushes for the dropped Luger. As Victor bends down for the Luger, Jack kicks it away, then kicks out at Victor's head. Victor screeches like a child, then scrambles up to Jack, clawing at his face.

Jack smashes Victor with his pistol; Victor falls to the floor. Jack shoves his pistol away to straddle him. A blood lust adds to his fury as he clamps his hands around Victor's throat to choke the life out of him.

"Jack!" Maddy snaps. "Don't kill him; you don't have to kill him. You are not a murderer, Jack. Please come untie me and let the police take care of him."

Jack looks over at Maddy, focusing on her bruised face. He slowly releases his grip, then backhands Victor before getting up and grabbing the coughing red-faced man by the collar to drag him over to her chair. "He can trade places with you. Is he the one that put that bruise your face?"

"No, the other one did that, but I think he is beyond any punishment for it."

Chapter 37

The big day has come. Jack suits up to take his plane up for a speed record attempt. For the record to be official under the auspices of the FAI, the speed trials measure the best speed out of four timed passes over a three-kilometer course that has to be no higher than 200 feet above sea level. The pilot is allowed to dive from no more than one thousand feet on each pass. The plane must also land safely after the runs are completed.

Ross Elmore will fly his Staggerwing with Maddy as copilot at one thousand feet to mark the level. Jack lines up alongside the Staggerwing for his first attempt. He dives, building speed, pulling up in a smooth arc to keep from scrubbing off any speed.

Carl and Jack removed all the weight out of the plane they could. He has no radio in the plane and just enough fuel for the four runs. He can adjust fuel mixture with a cockpit lever while watching the temperatures and boost levels. He brings the plane back up to the Staggerwing, Maddy holds up a chalk board with 351.8 written on it. Jack puts his thumb and forefinger together forming an okay sign and dives again.

He holds the dive a little longer before smoothly leveling out, runs the course, then comes back up to the Staggerwing. Maddy holds up 356.6. They have the record. Jack holds up both hands with okay signs, Maddy blows kisses.

Jack dives again, this time adding more fuel. At the bottom of the dive he sees the temperature climb, but the boost and rpm's are up also. When he joins the Staggerwing, it takes him some time to read the board that Maddy is enthusiastically bouncing. 362.9! Jack nods. This is the run that will put the record out of reach for a while he thinks.

He dives, shoving the throttle full open. This time he will skim the ground getting every ounce of speed and boost he can. At the bottom of the arc just as he pulls back on the stick, the left-side landing gear suddenly pops down. The plane rolls left, the wing now perilously close to the ground. Jack gently manages the controls trying not to overcorrect and crash. As he brings the plane back to level flight the landing gear is locked down.

Climbing to gain altitude, Jack works the landing gear lever. The panel light indicates the right-side gear will not deploy. Jack immediately pulls the fuel lever to full lean knowing there cannot be much fuel left. He has one wheel stuck down and the other up. He puts the plane into a hard dive, then abruptly pulls up hoping to dislodge the right-side gear. The right-side red light glares back at him!

Jack uses the speed of the dive to gain more altitude. This time he uses the rudder and ailerons to violently shake the plane. Last chance, he thinks, to get the plane safely on the ground.

He dives, pulls up hard, red light. Jack curses, then dives again, the ground coming up fast. He shakes the plane hard, angrily yanking back at the stick. He feels the right-side gear bump down even before the light goes green.

The engine coughs and dies before he hits the runway. People rush to plane before he gets it stopped. Carl and Maddy climb up on the wings. Carl bats Jack's head.

"Nice job, Pard. I thought you were gonna go back up that last time to bail out. We got the record an' I'll bet we didn't spend a tenth of what Hughes did."

Maddy smiles though her tears and leans into the cockpit to kiss Jack. "You looked like a real cowboy on a bucking bronco."

"Shucks, ma'am, weren't nothin'," Jack says.

Maddy smiles, rolling her eyes. "You should take a look at the landing gear, Cowboy: it has grass growing on it."

Jack unbuckles the seat belts to stand up in the cockpit, turning to Carl. "She's got more speed in her, Pard. I've got some ideas we should try for the next run. Man, she was gainin' boost every time."

"We'll do it, Jack. I'm just happy it's all in one piece. First thing we gotta do is get that damned landin' gear fixed. You need to get your plant's geniuses to make a lightweight radio, too. I like-to-died wonderin' what was goin' on."

When they get back to Clover Field there is a huge celebration. A banner on the Douglas hangar has *Welcome Home Winner* written on it.

Monday morning Jack turns into the plant's driveway. A sign on the front of the building proudly displays, *Home of the New Airspeed Record Holder.*

Jack holds court with all the employees, telling them all about the adventure and what they, at Novac Engineering, had contributed to make it successful.

Detective Vance calls after lunch to congratulate Jack.

"I just read the paper; that was some show, Novac. It's nice to see a local boy do good. I usually only get to see the ugly stuff."

"Thanks, Vance," Jack says, "I don't know how the Drum thing would have worked out without your help. I know the local cops weren't interested."

"I'm sorry it ended up in a shootout, Novac. We're going to keep a close eye on the People's Party. I thought you should know Victor Drum hung himself in his cell last night."

"I can't say I'm sorry. I am glad Maddy kept me from murdering him."

"I am too, Novac. I would hate to have to put you behind bars. Take care and stay out of trouble, will you?"

"Will do, Vance. Don't let the bad guys get you down, buddy. Be seein' you."

Epilogue

Jack hangs up on the phone call from Vance to answer to the next call.

"Hello Jack, congratulations. I just saw a newsreel. You sure know how to put on a show."

"Thanks, Robbins. You made it possible gettin' that Allison engine."

"You earned it, Jack, and I've got another good deal for you."

"I'm almost afraid to find out what that might be, Bill."

"I've got you set up with some big money races in Australia. This is an all-expense-paid trip by your old Uncle Sam. You can take anyone you want with you, too. How's that sound?"

"Ah, I'm waitin' for the other shoe to drop, Bill."

"Well, we'd like you to see what the Japs are up to while you're there and maybe see if you can find Amelia Earhart. Some bigwigs here think the Japs may have grabbed her."

"I'd like to pass on this one, Bill. The Navy contract will take most of my time here anyway."

"Mori can take care of that, Jack. Come on, man, you get to see exotic people and places. I know Maddy will want to do it, take Carl and Lulu too. You guys will have the time of your lives."

"I wish you hadn't called, Bill, I was having a good day."

"I know you're going to do it, Jack. I'll be out there next week, and we'll plan the whole thing out. See you then, pal."

###

Acknowledgements

The cover art and editing are done by Kathy Downs. Without her excellent work there would be no Mike Downs novels.

Thanks to Kas Kastner and Jan Torbet, the best, most supportive friends and beta readers an author could have.

About Mike Downs

Passion is a sustaining element in Mike's life. After a forty-year career of professionally racing factory sports cars, writing became that passion. As an avid follower of American history and early auto racing Mike combined the two in novels.

He finds bringing to life fictional characters in historical events and locations fulfills his passion. Making the stories and characters exciting is a grand challenge. The many hours in crafting a novel are enjoyable ones spent trying to become a better storyteller. Finding new ways that can illuminate a scene to bring the reader into the moment is a lovely satisfaction.

His stories take place in the fascinating era of the 1920's to the 1940's. Auto racing then was truly death defying, an adventure in itself. To that he adds characters living their fast-paced lives on the go. Sometimes their adventures are caught up with Nazi intrigues where they must raise their game in order to survive. Love and passion are essential ingredients for these characters also. For them living life on the edge is sometimes more than they bargained for.

The Mare Island World War Two novels are about the adventures of the men and women working on America's largest West Coast Naval Yard. 45,000 workers daily filed into the yard during the war: they worked in three shifts, 8 hours a day; 24 hours 7 days a week. Ships of all types had their battle damage repaired on the yard. Our finest generation lived, loved, and dedicated their lives to the war effort. One of the novel's Mare Island characters devotes his life to submarines, another to protecting the yard from saboteurs. A hunger for action and justice drives the characters here.

Living in Northern California, Downs is able to indulge in another passion, research. The San Francisco area is rich in libraries, museums, old naval bases, and parks. He and his wife make frequent trips to Mare Island, going to the museum and hiking the grounds. He also writes articles for Victory Lane Magazine. His wife, Kathy, creates the cover art for the novels and does the editing. Both he and his wife have businesses in an area of auto racing: she in graphic arts, promotional products, and embroidery; his in building racing engines and classic race car restoration. Together reading, (Kathy is voracious) and writing consumes our sunfilled days.

Connect with me online

Want to know when the next book is coming out? Have a question about what the future holds for Jack and Maddy, or Barry and Mary? There are several ways to contact me.

The Mike Downs Mysteries website: https://www.mikedownsmysteries.com is full of information about the books and other things going on in my world. You can sign up for my email list to be notified when new books are in the works. I don't use the list for endless messages but will let you know as a new book is coming to life, and I like feedback from readers about what interests you so I can make my books more interesting to you.

I post research articles and other comments on Facebook: Mike Downs

I also post snippets to Twitter: #Mike Downs Author

We have an author page on Goodreads: Mike Downs. I'm happy to answer questions about the characters in my books, the writing process, or anything else that comes to mind.

And, if you want Amazon to notify you when a new book has been released, please follow me on my Amazon Author Page: Mike Downs Author Page.